Would You Share Your Secret?

Jo Hook

Would You Share Your Secret © Jo Hook 2016

First published in Great Britain in 2016

For my folks and their unconditional love.

Contents

Prologue   6

Part 1   11

Chapter 1 - Mia   12

Chapter 2 - Ben   39

Chapter 3 - Lucy   53

Chapter 4 - Jessie   64

Chapter 5 - Mia   78

Chapter 6 - Ben   94

Chapter 7 - Lucy   106

Chapter 8 - Jessie   118

Chapter 9 - Mia   132

Chapter 10 - Ben   145

Chapter 11 - Lucy   151

Chapter 12 - Jessie   168

Chapter 13 - Mia   177

Chapter 14 - Ben   187

Chapter 15 - Lucy   191

Chapter 16 - Jessie   205

Part 2   213

Chapter 17 - Mia   214

Chapter 18 - Ben   225

Chapter 19 - Lucy   230

Chapter 20 - Jessie   241

Chapter 21 - Mia   252

Chapter 22 - Ben   267

Chapter 23 - Lucy   281

Chapter 24 - Jessie   294

Chapter 25 - Mia   311

Chapter 26 - Ben   324

Chapter 27 - Lucy   332

Chapter 28 - Jessie   342

Chapter 29 - Mia   350

Chapter 30 - Ben   360

Chapter 31 - Lucy   367

Chapter 32 - Jessie   382

Chapter 33 - Alex   393

Acknowledgements   405

About the Author   406

Prologue

Touchdown. Mia exhaled deeply. She couldn't quite believe they had finally landed and in one piece. She usually quite enjoyed flying, especially at night when it was fairly peaceful. Getting out a good book and having a cheeky little miniature en route to her destination was her usual ritual. However, the return journey home had not been the three hours of the smooth sailing she had hoped for. In fact, it had been a total disaster. When the air steward had finally told the passengers to put on their seatbelts to begin their descent, she felt a great sense of relief. Mia had known that this was not going to be her normal carefree flight home because she was travelling with her older sister Lucy and Lucy's two children. Unfortunately, due to their later than anticipated arrival at the airport, their seats were allocated at opposite ends of the plane. Mia had agreed to have Oliver, her 6-month-old nephew, for the first half of the journey. She had waved Lucy and her four-year-old niece, Evie, off to the rear end of the plane. Mia and Oliver got settled and strapped in pretty quickly, he was smiling at her and she was feeling quite smug with her 'parenting' skills. She was soon to learn that when you travel with a baby, nothing should be taken for granted. Mia had not anticipated that the nappy-wearing little tyke would let her down quite so spectacularly. Within minutes of take-off, Oliver decided to take a huge, stinking dump. Before Mia looked up at the seatbelt light that was still firmly on, she said a little prayer that everyone else had no sense of smell. The seatbelt sign continued to glow stubbornly, meaning that there was no escaping that eye-watering stench. The ten minutes that followed until the light finally went out, felt like hours. Mia thought that smell was just going to circulate around the plane. It wasn't like they could open a window. Understandably, her neighbour, Lorraine, looked at Oliver with disgust. Mia herself did throw him a *'How could you Ollie?'* look through gritted teeth. Although, she felt that Lorraine had a bloody cheek being so judgemental. Mia had to admit that Oliver's pong was outrageous but, to be fair, her halitosis could rival her nephew's bottom any day of the week. After a trip to the loo, the offensive smell finally seemed to dissipate, Mia felt calmer and Ollie seemed to be too.

For half an hour he had been happily watching some pre-downloaded programme on her tablet. Then it hit like a thunderbolt. Turbulence. Mia knew that Oliver could be an epic screamer, as her sister had informed her many times before, but she thought Lucy had been exaggerating. Oliver proved his mother right. Mia's embarrassment was intensified, as Ollie had continued to howl even after the turbulence had stopped and people were loudly tutting at him. Mia had a good mind to stand up and say 'This is not even my child!' Feeling like Judas at the thought, instead she pulled him in close and attempted to rock him quiet. The turbulence had been pretty bad, so much so, she was convinced that they were going to plunge into the sea. Although, tackling one of those inflatable slides with a wailing banshee on her hip seemed like a step too far for even her, the doting aunt. Eventually, after all of the chaos, Lucy appeared and offered to take Oliver. Mia looked at her messy hair and sleepy eyes and thought that she must have had a wonderful sleep, 90 minutes of pure bliss by the look of it. 'Did you not hear Ollie screaming?' Mia asked.

'What? Sorry? Evie and I have been out for the count. We even slept through the turbulence apparently.' Lucy said, pulling the earplugs from her ears.

'It doesn't matter.' Mia said, as she passed Oliver to her sister. Lorraine looked like she was going to burst into tears of sheer relief. Of course Oliver was the perfect baby for the remainder of the flight, she didn't smell or hear him, not even once.

Mia decided she would also 'sleep' so that Lorraine would keep her breath and her stories to herself. She closed her eyes and thought about how glad she was that they had been on this family holiday, it had been just what the doctor ordered. The last few weeks had been the worst of her life. Mia had been in turmoil about keeping her secret from her friends and family, but she had made a promise. She was not the type to break promises and anyway, she had known that it had been the right thing to do. If she shared her secret, too many people would have an opinion and she did not want people to look at her differently. Her secret had eaten away at her for too long but she refused to let it define her. She would not let it destroy her life and she knew that if she told anyone, it would completely destroy his life too. Sometimes, she believed that it was best to keep secrets. Perhaps this is what her sister thought too, as she had no doubt that Lucy was also hiding something. Regardless of how close they were, Mia realised that her sister would only confide in her when she was good and ready. Mia knew, that sometimes the truth could actually cause more harm than good and right now that was her justification for keeping tight lipped. She just hoped she was doing the right thing.

Part 1

Chapter 1

Mia

Everyone obsesses. People obsess about their weight, their looks or truly random things like, the television volume having to be on an even number. Obsessions are strange but people accept that people obsess. Mia Richards was currently obsessing over Dusty, her beautiful Springer spaniel. This was a habit of hers. Two weeks ago, just before she moved house, she had been obsessed by the way her immaculately kept Springer hankered after Rex, the next-door neighbour's mongrel. With Rex a distant memory, she felt relieved, however Dusty had greeted her new surroundings with trepidation and her anxiety was evident in her peeing all over her new living room floor.

'I love you Dusty, but seriously!' she said as she mopped up the huge yellow puddle that had been left for her underneath the breakfast bar. Wringing the mop out for the fourth time she looked over at the dog again, thinking how grateful she now was for her wooden floors. 'Dust, stop giving me those puppy dog eyes,' she said smiling.

Mia lifted the bucket and hunted for her keys. In the search she knocked over a huge pile of magazines and one fell open on a picture of a very sexy man wearing only boxers, without her glasses though she could barely make out his face. Unfortunately, the smell of dog urine broke her squinting at, what she could only assume was a 'Hollywood' good-looking man. Weaving in and out of the boxes that still adorned her living room, she stood with her back to the door and scanned the open plan living room and looked into the kitchen. If only keys could talk, she thought. She scanned the room again, but more slowly this time. Then she spotted her red lanyard dangling down the leg of a stool, a pile of books concealed the actual keys. She smiled to herself and stepped over a sleeping bag and pile of cushions that lay on the floor. Grabbing the keys and placing the large bunch around her neck, she turned and opened the front door with one hand, whilst the bucket swung in the other. Out in the corridor, she watched as Dusty danced around her legs as she tried to unlock the back door that led out onto the street. Mia then gently placed the bucket by the wall and unlocked the boot of her car. She fished out the three bottles of bleach that she had bought that day in anticipation of Dusty relieving herself on the floor yet again. She then put the bottles on the top of the wall, picked up the bucket and walked over to the nearest grid she could find. She stepped back to ensure that she wouldn't get any splash back on her feet and aimed for the grid. It was at that moment that Dusty came charging through her legs and knocked her off balance. She ended up swivelling around and throwing the water towards the pavement. The majority of the water bounced off the curb and landed on a pair of legs. Mia looked up to see that the person at the end of the legs was Ben, the owner of the top floor apartment in her building.

'Oh God. I am so sorry,' Mia said as she scrambled to pick up the bucket that lay at his feet.

'That's okay,' he said smiling while wiping the wet from his legs with the towel that had been slung around his neck. 'It's just water, right?'

'Yeah,' she lied. He was clearly in his gym gear and was more than likely about to get into the shower anyway. There was no point in telling him that he had dirty dog water all over his legs, certainly not as this was only their second meeting.

'You working hard?' he nodded towards the bucket. 'Busy cleaning I take it?'

'Yep. That and unpacking still,' she said as she wiped her itchy forehead with her wet hands. Realising what the wet patch on her head meant, she decided that as soon as she stepped in her flat she must shower.

'Best let you get back to it then,' he said as he gently stroked Dusty. She loved it and rubbed up against his leg. The damn dog was such a good flirt, thought Mia. If she didn't love Dusty so much she would have happily said to her neighbour, 'Gorgeous isn't she? But bloody incontinent of late!'

*

'Mia, will you take table five's order for me please?' asked Jessie as she grabbed her phone and waved it in Mia's face. 'It's the electrician, I have to get it!' she said hurriedly as she scurried out, letting the staff door swing back and forth as if she were in a western saloon. Mia was a soft touch and her best friend knew it. So, she walked over to table five and, smiling politely, took their order and let the baby pull on her apron strings. She hated it when people brought their kids to the restaurant. *Imagination* wasn't the type of restaurant that children should be taken to. It was every inch a 'grown up' restaurant. Plus, the parents who dined there usually assumed that as well as being their waitress for the evening, you should be their baby-sitter too.

It had started calmly for a Saturday night, but soon picked up and by 9.30pm Mia felt like she was rushing around like a headless chicken. The baby had been taking up lots of her time, running back and forth warming bottles and blending food, she was quite relieved when they decided to call it a night. Then she had a very raucous foursome on table eleven – two men and their wives. One of the husbands hadn't taken his eyes off her arse all night and it was starting to annoy her as he was old enough to be her grandfather, never mind her father. Then there was the miserable looking couple sitting on table fifteen, the girlfriend had done nothing but nag him since they arrived. She had ice blonde hair to match her ice-cold demeanour and he had short dark hair and amazing teeth. Those perfect sparkly type of teeth that celebs pay thousands of pounds for. They were one of those handsome couples you just knew that one day would have beautiful children, she thought to herself as she scraped vegetables from the plates she had just cleared.

'Mia!' She turned to see Jessie standing next to her pointing into the bin, 'you've just dropped a fork in there! Here let me get it,' she said as she leant in to fish it out.

'Thanks Jess, I'm not quite with it. I'm done in from the move,' she said as she rinsed her hands under the tap and dried them on the tea towel that was hanging over the back of her apron.

'It's almost three weeks ago now!' said Jessie, smirking.

'I know, but I still have stuff everywhere. I didn't realise I had collected so much over the years!'

'Do you want me to come round tomorrow and help out?'

'Awww thanks Jess, but you helped tons when I first moved in. I'll manage the rest on my own.'

'Jessie, table ten, now thank yooooou,' bellowed Robert, the owner, as he popped his head into the clearing area. He only turned up sporadically and when he did everyone was on their toes. As Mia was manager and the restaurant's longest serving employee, Robert had a soft spot for her. He also knew that she was too good at her job and completely over qualified.

'Hey Robert, how's Harvey?' Mia asked after Robert's Alsatian, who had hurt his leg pretty badly on some broken glass in the park.

'He's okay Mia, thanks for asking. He had to have stitches, but he's been bouncing around like a lunatic for the last two days!'

'Bless him. I'll have to bring Dusty round for a visit,' Mia said as she picked up her pad and pen from the side and pushed her glasses back up her nose.

'Definitely, although he'll only go all gooey-eyed around her. He's still absolutely infatuated with her!'

'So, have you made any decisions on desserts then?' Mia said as she smiled at the miserable couple.

'None for me,' said the ice queen. Then she rudely slid her menu towards Mia, instead of passing it to Mia's

18

outstretched hand. As the customer was always right she ignored the rudeness, picked up the menu from the table and turned to the striking yet sad looking partner. By this point, Mia had observed them long enough to see the lady in this partnership appeared to be the driving force behind the misery. He just looked like he was being taken along for the ride. More fool him Mia thought.

'And you sir?' She said, catching his eye, and he smiled in acknowledgement.

'I'm torn between the crème brûlée and the cheesecake, which would you recommend?'

'Well, I love both. But that's because I have a sweet tooth!' Mia said rather too eagerly as she thought of both desserts.

He smiled up at Mia. He really did have lovely teeth she thought, as she returned his smile, and then attempted to do the same to his girlfriend - but she was too busy staring into her glass of red wine, which she picked up and swirled around and around.

'I can't have both!' he said smiling again.

She felt like telling him that it took more muscles to frown than it did to smile, and he suited it much more.

'Izzy, are you sure I can't tempt you?' he said touching her hand tenderly. She pulled away quickly and gave him a stern look.

'I told you. I can't. I have that shoot next week,' she said as she tilted back her head and drank the remainder of her wine. Well that explains the figure - she must be a model, thought Mia. Although wine had heaps of calories in it, but that didn't seem to bother her.

'I'd go with the cheesecake. It's homemade and this week it's toffee and chocolate, it's delicious,' Mia said, feeling awkward but needing to say something to try and shake off the terrible atmosphere around the table.

'Sounds great, thank you,' he said as he attempted to pass Mia the menu, although it never made it to her hand and it dropped to the floor. 'Oh sorry,' he said as he lent down to get it, as did Mia. It was the first time that she had seen the other side of his face, which had been hidden as he was sat against the wall. There, catching the light, was a huge scar that ran from the corner of his mouth, almost to the corner of his eye. He saw Mia look at the scar, caught her eye and looked away in embarrassment. She could see his face blush.

'Right sir, I'll go and order that dessert for you!' she said smiling so falsely that it hurt, 'and I'll bring a second set of cutlery just in case.' She looked at him again, but now, all of a sudden, he seemed different. He did not return her smile as she had expected. He clearly felt as awkward as she had. However, before she had a chance to give it another thought, the sleazy man on table eleven had called her over to order yet another bottle of champagne.

'Oh my God. How much is that woman on table fifteen just a complete bitch?' Karl, the head barman was almost spitting the words out. 'She has just clicked her fingers at me, the cheeky cow!' Karl was furious. His cage wasn't often rattled, but rude people grated on his last nerve.

Oh dear, thought Mia. Clicking your fingers at a waitress was *the* cardinal sin. They had discussed it at length, but couldn't understand why people clicked their fingers as opposed to making some sort of eye contact or shouting a simple yet polite, 'excuse me'. It was something that riled the pair of them so much that they found it difficult to actually show well-mannered service to any 'clickers'.

'She didn't!' exclaimed Mia in shock. 'Well, she is a bit of an ice queen,' she added in agreement.

'A bit… a bit?! If she does that again I'm gonna tell her to talk to the hand girlfriend!' Mia let out a little giggle. Karl was one of the reasons most staff loved working at Imagination. You were guaranteed to be smiling all through your shift if his name was on the rota with yours. Jessie appeared from around the corner.

'Let me guess what you two are talking about… the bitch on table fifteen?'

'Hell yeah!' Karl said, as he high-fived Jessie.

'And what I want to know is what the hell is that hottie doing with her? Although that scar is pretty horrific isn't it?'

'Jess!'

'Well, it is. I'm only saying what everyone else is thinking!' And she usually was. Jessie's philosophy when it came to the truth was, in the famous words of Roy Walker from Catchphrase, 'Say what you see,' and in Jessie's case she always did.

*

Mia had spent the majority of her Sunday morning lying in bed after a very late night in the restaurant. Robert had insisted everyone stay for 'one' drink, which led to a lot more than one. You could always tell when his wife was away, it was like the ball and chain had been severed. He always made the most of it. He was the epitome of a free spirit. Mia stretched and brushed her hair out of her eyes, as she did this she smelt the lemon on her fingers and shivered. She had hated tequila for a very long time. After an extremely bad experience when she was fourteen she had sworn never to drink it again, but when your boss was practically pouring it down your neck for free, what could you say but, 'Yes please?' She looked around for her clock. In the process, she knocked her work clothes onto the floor from the boxes that had become her bedside cabinet. Finding it, she saw it read 11.30am. She felt super lazy wasting her day, so despite her pounding head; she sat up, put on her glasses and swung her legs onto the floor. Coffee, she thought, that's what she needed and she knew where that was. She couldn't face a day without at least two cups of coffee within the first hour of rising, whenever that might be. Flicking on the kettle she reached over to the pile of magazines on the floor, grabbed a handful and jumped up onto the worktop. Dusty sat eyeing her crossly from her basket. 'You want out lovely?' She walked over and let Dusty out of the patio door for her morning pit stop. She must have been busting. She spent the next hour just sitting, putting off any sort of tidying or unpacking. Ah, now she knew why she had brought the magazines with her, to procrastinate. Something that she was very good at. Her intense reading of all the latest gossip – even though the magazine was three months old, Mia didn't seem to care – was broken by her phone ringing. As she pulled it out of her bag, which was conveniently in arm's reach, she saw 'Lucy' flashing on the screen.

'Hey Luce,' Mia said swigging the last bit of her coffee and licking her lips.

'Oliver NO!' Mia quickly pulled the phone away from her ear, so that the noise of her sister shouting at her nephew was not about to burst her eardrum.

'So how was your birthday party last night?' Mia asked as she jumped down from the worktop and began moving all the boxes she still had left to unpack into the middle of the floor. She needed to get organised as it was driving her mad that she couldn't find anything.

'Good, but I wish you'd been there, I can't believe that Robert wouldn't let you have the night off. The tight arse, you're always doing *him* favours.'

'I know,' Mia lied, she just couldn't be bothered with her sister's in-laws; they were so dull and pretentious. 'Not to worry Luce, we can celebrate next week on our own, no hubby or kids. Just me, you and loads of booze!'

'Sounds like a plan Mia, I can't bloody wait!'

'So, what did you get from Ed and the kids?'

'A watch,' she said sounding about as enthused as you could over a watch. Unless it was encrusted with diamonds and designed by Gucci of course, but as it was from Ed, that was doubtful. He probably bought it at the last minute.

'Nice,' I said echoing her tone, 'anything else?'

'A naked birthday serenade,' she said.

'Really?' Good God, now Mia had images of a naked Ed in her head which she wasn't too happy about. 'Ed was naked? Was it his way of seducing you on your birthday?' Mia gave a similar shudder to the one that the tequila had induced earlier.

'Ed naked?' she laughed. 'No I was the naked one! Ed and Evie were waiting for me as I walked out of the bathroom... starkers! I then had to stand there and wait for them to sing happy birthday to me.'

'That's so funny!' Mia said as she continued to giggle.

'You think that's funny; it was then followed by Evie asking me why I had hair on my front bum. Which then meant that the three of us just stood staring at my fanny!'

'I love Evie... she's hilarious!'

'Oh it gets better... Ed then proceeded to mouth to me "You could do with a trim love!" the cheeky bugger!'

'I'm coming!' Mia shouted as she heard someone knock on her front door. She was a little confused as to who it might be. Having an intercom system meant that usually people would have to call through before they knocked on the door. Catching herself in the mirror she pulled the band from her hair that had been keeping it in a topknot and gave it a ruffle. The 'cleaning' look was not a good one on her.

'Hey Mia,' said a smiling Ben at the door.

'Hey,' she replied, relieved that she had taken her hair down. There was an awkward silence for a moment as he stood there and she forgot her manners, finally saying, 'sorry, come in.'

'Thanks,' he said as he stepped inside.

'Can I get you a drink? Tea? Coffee?' Mia said while waving the mug she had just picked up from the coffee table at him.

'Yes please. Coffee, black, one sugar,' he said. Dusty was now brushing up against his leg and he ruffled the top of her head.

'Take a seat,' she said pointing to the high stools that had been left by the previous owner.

'Thanks. So you're getting yourself sorted then?'

'Yeah, I finally finished sorting out the last few boxes this morning. I'm so glad; they were getting on my nerves!'

'I bet. It's always such a big job moving. Did you have far to move?'

'No, my folks only live a few miles away. Well they did, before they upped and left to move to Spain.'

'Did they make the move permanently?' he asked looking a little surprised, just as most people did upon hearing the news.

'Yeah, hence all of my mismatched furniture – although I'm not complaining as it's free. Plus they didn't want to ship all of it. They've bought all new stuff over there.'

'So in what part of Spain do they live?'

'Murcia, it's lovely. They've had a house out there for a few years and then they both took early retirement and just decided to give it all up. I'm really pleased for them, but I do miss them.'

'It's only a few hours away on a plane though, isn't it?'

'Yeah it is,' Mia said as the kettle boiled. She turned away from Ben to make the coffee.

'So, you're probably wondering why I dropped by?' She smiled at him, but had been wondering that since she opened the door to him. 'Well, Alex and I are having a few people round for my birthday on the twenty-third. We were just wondering if you could make it? Lots of the neighbours are coming and it would be a great way for you to get to know them.'

'That sounds great, that's a Saturday right?' she asked him.

'It is yeah.'

'I'll have to try and get the night off work though.'

'Oh right, what do you do?'

'I'm a waitress, well the manager of Imagination in town.'

'I know the place. It's really swanky isn't it?'

'Yeah, but some people might say pretentious!' Ben laughed and she continued, 'I'll let you know.' Ben looked at her puzzled. 'About the party.' He nodded and smiled to acknowledge his understanding. 'Can I bring someone?'

'Yeah, sure,' he said as Mia handed him his coffee.

'So, how long have you lived here for then?'

'Since they were built six years ago, Alex and I bought it then.'

'Alex, I haven't met her yet, have I?' Ben laughed

'What's so funny?'

'Alex is a guy.'

'Oh right,' she felt her face blush. She was confused, as Ben looked every inch your alpha male. He was tall, broad and looked like the typical rugby sort. He seemed like such a nice guy. There was something attractive about him even though he wasn't overly good looking. His eyes had a real sparkle to them, it's like they smiled. 'I'm sorry, I didn't realise that you were...'

He laughed again, louder and harder this time. 'No, no we're not. He's my best mate and has been for years.'

'Sorry, I'm always getting hold of the wrong end of the stick!'

'Not to worry, you're not the first to make that mistake.'

'Well, that's a relief!' she smiled. 'So do you like living here?'

'I do yeah. It's a good area. Safe, and you've got everything you need on your doorstep.'

'Good good,' Mia said drinking the last of her steaming hot coffee. One day, she thought her throat would eventually give up the ghost. It would admit defeat no longer able to take any more boiling hot drinks that she guzzled down.

'Right, I should make a move. I'm off to the gym,' he said pushing himself away from the breakfast bar. Mia stood up to see him out.

'Thanks for popping in and you're welcome anytime,' she said.

'You too, you know we're on the top floor, right?' She nodded. 'Oh by the way... the party is fancy dress.'

'Cool, what are you going as?'

'Ahhh now that would be telling. But it's a movie star theme.'

'How will I recognise you then?'

'Ha, I like your style – trying to find out. Let's just say that you'll know who I am. But here's a clue: I'll be the one in the skirt!'

*

As Mia pulled on her running shoes, she exhaled deeply. It had been months since she had last ran anywhere. She was anxious, but believed that her new place was the beginning of new start, so what better time to start running again? She did all the right stretches before she left the house and tied up her long curly hair. Mia grabbed her dog's aqua coloured lead. Dusty looked up upon spotting this and began jumping around like she was on a trampoline.

'Calm down Dust,' she tried to attach the lead to her collar but she was just too excited to sit still. 'DUSTY, SIT.' Mia said in her very stern voice, the only tone that Dusty would pay any attention to. She clipped the lead onto her dog's collar, put her iPhone in her armband, slipped the headphones into her ears, closed the door behind her and started jogging. Her ankle felt like it was going to snap, but there was no pain, it was clearly psychological. She knew that she was being ridiculous, that just because she was running again did not mean that she was going to break her ankle again. It had been eight months and the Doctor had said that it would be fine to start running again. Mia was determined to complete the half marathon, the one she had started and never finished. She had tripped mid-race, falling very awkwardly and breaking her ankle in the process. She had been in a cast for three months, which had been awful, but it wasn't just the pain that had stopped her from running, but the embarrassment too. What if she fell again? But as all these thoughts dashed through her head, she took out her phone to change the song and saw that she had already run a mile and a half, so she pulled on Dusty's lead to slow her down. She smiled to herself and realised that her demons had been lifted. She was running and it felt so damn good. Why had she waited this long to try it again? That didn't matter she thought, she was just so happy to be running at all. She breathed in the freshness of spring, her favourite season to run in. As she ran around her local park, the flowers were just starting to pop up, dozens and dozens of sunshine-yellow daffodils. It was perfect running weather, hence the herds of runners in the park. She smiled when she passed them, and they smiled back. Mia was half way around the park when the heavens opened. Gosh she had forgotten how much she loved to run in the rain. She could see most runners starting to speed up to get home, whereas she just carried on smiling as the rain bounced off her cheeks. One girl ran past her with mascara running down her face, it baffled Mia why people ran with make-up on. She saw a handsome man approaching; as he passed her they locked eyes and smiled. Mia couldn't help herself, she knew that she recognised him, but just couldn't place him. Probably because the rain was blurring her vision and her lack of glasses – she seriously needed contacts. She turned to look again, as did he. Then she caught sight of his scar, even without her glasses on she knew it was the guy from the restaurant. Wow, she thought, he looked good in his running gear. They locked eyes again and smiled at each other. He didn't look sad today, maybe because he was without his miserable girlfriend. She turned and looked at him one last time and watched as he sprinted away into nothing but a dot. She did the same in the other direction until her chest hurt from the speed of her sprinting. She walked the rest of the way home, as her stamina was not as good as it had been eight months ago. Dusty had loved running for the first time in months, and if she had had her way she would have dragged Mia all the way home.

*

'Can you believe that Robert gave us both the night off?' Jessie said as she opened the patio doors and lit a cigarette. Dusty was quietly laid out on the cold patio flags.

'Well, I am dog-sitting Harvey in a few weeks. I suppose he owed me a favour.' Mia said as she finished braiding her hair and brushed her fringe over.

'You look hot Mia, your legs look amazing in those tiny shorts,' Jessie said pointing in Mia's direction.

'You are looking very sexy yourself in that get up of yours Miss Hepburn, that *Breakfast at Tiffany's* look really suits you.' Mia said as Jessie took a long pull on her cigarette, which was in a long black cigarette holder.

'Thank you darling! Who doesn't love a blonde Audrey?' Jessie replied in her poshest voice. 'Shall we have another glass of wine before we leave?' Then slipping back into Jessie speak, she added 'we have time, right?'

'Yep, let's.' Mia said looking at the clock in the kitchen. 'Why not?'

An hour and a bottle of wine later, Mia and Jessie started making their way up the stairs. They were both a little more light-headed than Mia had anticipated them being, but she knew that it would make it a little easier to meet all of her new neighbours.

Mia knocked on the door, pulled out one of her guns and stood posing at the front door – yep; she definitely was a little drunker than she originally thought. She turned to Jessie to see her posing too, she had put her sunglasses on and fixed her tiara, and then finally she placed her cigarette holder in her hand.

'Mia, I'm glad you made it!'

'Ben?' asked Mia as she stood staring at the half dressed man before her. He was painted half blue and half white showing his incredibly toned chest. His hair was covered with a longhaired, straggly wig and he had a big sword in his hand.

'Yeah, it's me. See...' he pointed towards his attire, 'I told you I'd be wearing a skirt!'

'Indeed you are. Although, I did have images of you being dressed as a woman!'

'Ha! So you must be Lara Croft,' Ben said gesturing to Mia, 'and you must be Audrey?'

'Hello Braveheart, yes I am Audrey, also known in my dressed down time as Jessie.'

'Well, Jessie it's good to meet you. I'm Ben, Mia's neighbour. Come in. Let's get you guys a drink.'

'We brought these,' Mia handed Ben two bottles of wine, 'a glass of that is great thanks, for both of us. Right Jess?'

'You know me Mia, I'll drink anything!'

As Jessie and Ben chatted and he sorted out the drinks, Mia surveyed the room. There were tons of people already there and they were wearing some brilliant costumes. She could see a very realistic Mr T; he'd even shaved in the Mohawk, Dorothy from *The Wizard of Oz* wearing very eye-catching sparkly red shoes and a man-sized Dalmatian that was standing next to a wicked-looking Cruella De Ville.

'Here we go,' Ben said as he passed Mia a glass.

'Thanks and I forgot to say earlier... happy birthday!' she leant towards him and kissed him on the cheek.

'Yep, happy birthday Ben!' said Jessie as she clinked her glass with his sword.

'Cheers girls. Oi Alex!' Ben shouted towards the corner of the room where it looked like half the cast of *Fame* were hanging out. 'Come and meet our new neighbour.' Walking towards the three of them was Maverick from *Top Gun* wearing a jumpsuit, with his collar up and ray bans. What a great outfit, Mia thought to herself.

'Alex, this is Mia our new neighbour and her friend Jessie,' Mia stuck out her hand to shake his.

'Hey Mia, it's nice to meet you,' Maverick said as he met her outstretched hand.

Although they had never formally been introduced until now, it was as though they had met before. Maverick slipped off his shades and underneath them she met the sad man at the restaurant, the running man in the park, the man with the scar and the amazing teeth. That same man was now standing before her and that man apparently was Alex, her new neighbour.

Chapter 2

Ben

'You too,' Mia said smiling at Alex.

Ben thought she looked awkward somehow, and wondered if Mia was another one of Alex's conquests from many moons ago. 'Have you two met before?' Ben asked, as he did he flipped his eyebrow up to Alex as if to say "you know what I mean".

'Well...' Alex started to say, but before he could finish a drunken Julia Roberts jumped in.

'Yes, we have met her darling, she was our waitress a few weeks ago in that restaurant, what was it called?'

'Imagination,' replied Alex.

'Mia, this is Izzy. Alex's girlfriend,' Ben said hoping that Mia was not upset by Izzy's sheer rudeness. Izzy stuck out her long elegant fingers towards Mia, who politely shook her hand, and Ben hoped this meant that Mia was not offended.

'I remember you from the restaurant too,' Izzy continued and put out her hand towards Jessie.

'Hang on a minute,' Jessie stood clicking her fingers – ignoring Izzy's outstretched hand - and then pointed at Izzy, 'Ahh I remember you now, you looked like you were having a shit time.' Ben saw Mia kick Jessie. For a brief moment Ben felt like he was watching a pre-recorded show where everyone else around him knew what was going on in the script, but him.

'Anyway, let's get you a drink birthday boy. Look at you standing there with nothing but a sword.' Mia said, clearly trying to steer the conversation away from the uncomfortable moment that had just occurred, but Ben winced at her question and of course Izzy was there first.

'Oh, he doesn't drink... he's an alcoholic!' said the inebriated Izzy. God he thought, what are Mia and Jessie going to make of him now? He saw Mia's face flush the colour of crimson.

'Recovering alcoholic.' Alex said in his defence. His loyal friend then quietly excused himself and Izzy as he guided her away into an empty corner of the room.

'I'm soooo sorry!' Mia said as she touched his arm. Her hands were so small and soft he thought, 'See I told you, foot in mouth syndrome!'

'Don't be daft! It's fine, I've been sober for eighteen months now,' Ben said smiling at her.

'Why the hell would you put yourself through this torture if you can't drink?' exclaimed Jessie in disbelief.

'Well, I have to live a normal life and this is what all my friends do.'

'Aww bless you,' said Jessie, 'I couldn't do it though! But good on ya,' Jessie said as she patted his back in a patronising, "well done" sort of manner. 'Oh shit, look.' She said showing Ben and Mia her hand, 'blue paint everywhere, I'm gonna go and wash it off and have a smoke... where's good for that?'

'Well, bathroom for hand washing and balcony for smoke. Just past Mr T!'

'Thanks.' Jessie said, not before putting on her huge sunglasses and straightening herself up into her best Audrey strut, and away she went.

'You look like you need topping up Mia; here let me take your glass.' She followed him to the kitchen area.

'I *really* am sorry Ben...'

'Stop apologising, you weren't to know. I'm sorry for Izzy being a bitch. You were right about pretentious people going to your restaurant though; Izzy is so showy. Anyway what was with the clicking?' Ben said confused, imitating Jessie's actions.

'Well, don't say anything, because Alex seems like a good guy. But when they came into the restaurant they were so miserable and then Izzy clicked her fingers at Jess, it's a BIG no-no to waitresses.'

'I bet,' Ben shook his head in amazement, 'It's a rough time of year for them, I mean I'm not defending her actions and you're right Alex is a good guy, but it's a tough time.' Ben turned and passed Mia her now full glass.

'Oh right. You got any ice?' Ben liked the way Mia did not pry into his or Alex's business as most girls would have at least attempted to do. He popped three cubes of ice into her glass. 'Thank you.'

'No problem, hey come here, you have blue paint on your face.' He grabbed a tea towel and wet a corner. She openly gave him her face and he gently rubbed it clean. He noticed how blue her eyes were as she looked into his and smiled.

'Thank you... again!'

'Ben!' shouted Buzz Lightyear from the balcony, 'come and see this.'

'Will you be alright?' he felt bad leaving Mia on her own.

'Of course, I'm a big girl!' she replied.

As he walked onto the balcony he saw his friend standing on the ground floor in a Spiderman costume. Suddenly he began scaling the wall to get onto his balcony. He laughed to himself, knowing that it was Andy, who was a base jumper and wouldn't be fazed by scaling the Empire State Building never mind two measly floors. He waited until he got to the top and congratulated him.

An hour later Ben scanned the whole room looking at the party in full swing. He was looking for Mia, but couldn't see her. It was only when Captain Jack Sparrow took a step back that he could see her tiny frame. God she was gorgeous. He had thought that the day he had set eyes on her even in her scruffy jeans and T-shirt. She had the most amazing hair; it was as black as the night sky and tumbled down her back so effortlessly. She caught him looking at her and they smiled at one another. He was so glad when she had turned up with Jessie, he was sure that she was going to bring a boyfriend. Although, he reasoned that just because she didn't have one with her didn't mean to say that she didn't have one at all. Only time would tell, he thought. He continued to scan the room and saw Alex and Izzy, she had kept him hustled up in that corner all night, like he was a naughty school boy not allowed to play out with his friends. Ben still remained puzzled by their relationship, Alex was so unhappy with her, but at the same time understood why he stayed with her. She was absolutely beautiful and only she could pull off Julia Roberts as *Pretty Woman*, she had legs up to her armpits and a figure that he knew most women would kill for.

By 2.00am the party was still fairly raucous and people were dancing and having a great time. Ben was delighted. He still found it hard putting himself in these situations, but as his sponsor had told him that if he wanted certain people in his life, then he had to have some very strong will power. He also had Alex around all the time to keep him on the straight and narrow, just as he always had since they were kids. Izzy had been put to bed an hour before, after she had been sick on the balcony. Alex had been embarrassed but naturally had whisked her off, cleaned up the mess and made no fuss about it whatsoever.

'Thank God Cruella's gone.' Ben overheard Jessie say to Mia as he poured himself another orange juice.

'She hasn't gone; she's just outside having a smoke.' Mia replied sounding confused.

'I mean Julia 'bloody up my own arse' Roberts. She should have come as Cruella, the bitch.' Ben smiled to himself. He knew that Izzy would have gotten on everyone's nerves - she was a terrible drunk.

'Stop it Jess!' He smiled again as Mia told her off. He decided to stop eavesdropping. Although it was funny, he also knew that it was very rude.

'More wine ladies?' Ben turned around and topped them both up, only a little though. Seeing through sober eyes rather than very hazy drunk ones, it was pretty obvious when people had drunk enough. It was fair to say that everyone in the room was much more than merry, except for himself, obviously, and the nun across the room, who ironically was concealing a baby bump.

'Hey,' Alex came over from the sofa. He'd been slumped there for the last hour just laughing with the boys like the good old times.

'Hey Maverick,' said Mia, 'how's your night been?'

'Good, thanks,' Alex replied, 'and yours?'

'So much fun! Thanks for the invite boys,' Mia smiled as she eyed them both, 'it's been great getting to know everyone.'

'Did you meet Jimmy?' Mia looked at Alex confused, 'He was Worzel Gummidge.'

'Ah, yes I did,' Mia replied. 'He's very funny.'

'He's brilliant.' Ben interjected, 'He's like the granddad of the building. Anything you need to know, he's your man.'

'Who else did you meet?' Alex asked.

'Erm...' Ben could almost see the cogs in Mia's brain ticking over; it looked like it was hurting her to think. 'Simon, Clarissa... Peter... Nicky, Bernadette and John,' she eventually said smiling, clearly pleased with herself for remembering their names.

'Bernie and John mean well,' said Alex as he caught Mia's look of uncertainty.

'They're a little bit nerdy. But Alex is right,' Ben said, agreeing with him.

'What happened to the ever pleasant Julia?' Jessie piped up and all three of them turned to her to actually check that the voice had come from her. Up until this point she had not uttered a sound. Ben flicked his eyes towards Alex and saw his eyes dart to the floor with embarrassment.

'Audrey shall we dance?' Ben said, pulling Jessie by the hand. He was a bit remiss at leaving Mia with Alex, but he knew that Alex would have diffused the situation in the same manner for him. He watched the pair of them as he swung Jessie around. Alex was like a different person when Izzy wasn't with him; it was like he let his shoulders relax. He then saw the pair of them join them on the 'dance floor' and halfway through the dance Alex swapped partners with Ben. Alex caught his eye and winked at him. Alex could always read him like a book; he could obviously tell that he fancied Mia. He smiled in thanks and swung her round, but pulled her in more closely than he had with Jessie, as close as he could without covering her with blue and white paint. All in all it had been a great night. Even though Izzy had spilt his secret to Mia, she hadn't seemed to bat an eyelid for which he was very grateful. And it made him like her even more.

*

Ben was so glad that Monday was over. He'd had a tough mid-morning meeting that he'd spent all Sunday preparing for. Although he'd had to clean up the flat, doing it without a hangover meant that it was taken care of pretty rapidly, leaving more time to prepare for the meeting, but also more time to worry about it. As he left his office on the far side of town and headed for the train station he felt his mobile vibrate in his pocket.

'Ben Webster speaking.'

'Hi Ben, its Luke Madden.'

'Hi Luke,' Ben said, feeling like he had just shot the 180 foot drop on the Alton Towers ride Oblivion. His stomach did a huge flip. Luke had said that he would get back to him tomorrow, and he was unsure whether the calling him now was a good thing or not.

'Ben, your presentation was by far the best and we would like to hire you to design our website.'

'Brilliant.' Ben wanted to punch the air in delight but knew that he would look like an idiot, so instead began grinning like a Cheshire cat.

'I'll call you tomorrow and we can organise a meeting to run though some ideas.'

'Great, I'll look forward to it!' Ben dropped his phone into the inside pocket of his suit jacket. Without thinking, he walked towards The Rose to raise a celebratory glass in honour of bagging himself a huge contract. As he placed his hand onto the door handle, the chill of the metal broke his thoughts. Good God, what am I doing? He turned and left and as he walked away from the pub, the memories of one of the last times he got a big contract flashed through his head. He had celebrated so hard that he had not only lost that contract but it had also very nearly cost him the business. He knew what he would do to celebrate. Get the train home, collect his car from the station and hit the gym, the only thing that had kept him sane in the last eighteen months.

'NO!' Ben heard Izzy scream at Alex as he put his key in the door. He could turn and run he thought, but where would he go. So, instead he inhaled deeply and stepped into the flat. Alex was sitting on sofa with his feet on the footstool staring at the TV with an almost vacant look in his eyes.

'Hey Alex, how's your day been?'

'Good thanks, and yours? How did the meeting go?'

'I got the contract!' Ben said, sounding delighted.

'Well done mate, that's brilliant,' Alex said sincerely and stood up to shake his hand in the obligatory manner, but then pulled him in for a hug.

'You been to the gym to celebrate?'

'Where else?'

'What about getting a take-away tonight, my treat to say well done?'

'I'd defo be up for that, cheers mate. Will Izzy be joining us?'

'I doubt that very much.'

'Where is she?' knowing full well that the only place that she could be was in Alex's bedroom, or perhaps the bathroom.

'In my room. Sulking over something.'

'Over what?'

'Who knows Ben?'

Suddenly Alex's bedroom door swung open and out stormed Izzy with her suitcase in tow. She had obviously packed it in a rush and there were clothes hanging out of the sides and were dragging on the floor. She also had what looked like her make up bag in the other hand and a pile of coats over her arm. She had clearly been crying, again.

'You off somewhere?' Ben asked, hoping she would say back to her own house and not the corner of the street where she normally got to and then came back.

'Home,' she yelled at Ben. Yeah, yeah, he thought, you little liar. There was a terrible silence that was bouncing off every nook and cranny in the whole of the flat. Izzy stood, waiting for Alex to say something. But unusually he kept quiet.

'You need a hand?' Ben asked Izzy feeling the need to say something.

'Alex.' she said firmly, ignoring Ben. He finally looked away from the TV and towards Izzy.

'What?' he asked, looking disinterested.

'What?' she snapped. 'Is that it? What?' she shrieked as a solitary tear rolled down her cheek and again there was that eerie silence, only broken by Izzy's ice-cold voice. 'Fuck you Alex!' And with that she marched out of the flat throwing her keys on the breakfast bar as she went.

He could hear Izzy's sobs as she nosily banged her case down the stairs.

'What's going on Alex?' Ben said, sounding genuinely concerned.

'Like I said, who knows? Anyway, you up for that curry now?'

Chapter 3

Lucy

'Luce, do you need me to do anything?' Mia asked as she grabbed the dishcloth from the draining board and began wiping the surfaces in the kitchen.

'No thanks Mia, you've done enough,' Lucy said as she turned around from the sink full of dishes and dried her hands on a tea towel.

'If you're sure,' Mia said shrugging her shoulders and throwing the dishcloth back over to the sink area. 'It's been a lovely day and it's safe to say that everyone has been more than appropriate.'

'Oh Mia, there's always time...' Lucy said smiling and wagging her finger in Mia's direction, '...there's always time.'

'Leave them love! We'll do them later,' Ed said as he walked into the kitchen.

'We will, will we?' She knew full well that it would be her that sorted out the mess in the kitchen, not her and her husband. Plus since the dishwasher had packed up she had despised doing the dishes more than ever, and if she had a pound for every time she'd heard Ed say, "I'll sort it at the weekend love," she would be able to buy an electrical store, never mind a new bloody dishwasher. 'Mum and Dad suggested that we open Ollie's christening presents now while everyone is still here, they think it'll be nice.'

'Do we have to?' Lucy said frowning at Ed.

'Come on darling, I agree with them. I really think that it would be nice,' Ed said grabbing hold of Lucy's hands.

'Fine,' Lucy said forcing a smile as Ed grabbed her and embraced her in a hug. She caught Mia's eye as she took a swig from her wine glass and raised it in her direction with a wink.

Walking into the garden, she smiled at everyone who were now staring in her direction. Feeling slightly mortified, she locked eyes with Emma for reassurance, her school friend would know this would be torture for her. Emma gave her a hopeful thumbs up and gulped a huge mouthful of fizz. Lucy hated the attention being on her but Ed loved it, she thought it was something to do with him being an only child.

'Edmund darling, we have put chairs for you both here,' smiled Ed's mother Cynthia, as she directed them both to where they were sitting. Ollie was asleep in the Moses basket next to the chairs. Lucy had tried to hide the fact that she cringed every time that her husband was called by his christened name; it was so embarrassing. Her in-laws really were pompous. Lucy knew that when she had married into the family. She loved Ed because he always tried his best to be down to earth, like her and her family. Unfortunately, Cynthia Brown had disliked the fact that Lucy had only been a nurse, as opposed to a doctor. They had hoped their only child would marry better. She knew however, that Ed's parents had grown fond of her, but unfortunately she couldn't say the same of them. Not since she had once overheard them saying, "Lucy is just not right for you Edmund. She's... well... just not good enough for you." She had stood behind the kitchen door in Ed's parents' house ten years ago and fought back tears, determined not to let them see her upset. Then, to Lucy's astonishment, Ed defended her. He told his parents that he loved her more than anything else in the world and that she was a very intelligent woman. Her tears soon dried up and she strode into the kitchen feeling proud and confident. As the years had passed and she'd had two children, Lucy knew that she had softened, but her relationship with the in-laws had still been less than a smooth ride. They'd had their squabbles in the past but she would not allow Oliver's day to be ruined. Lucy turned to see Evie had found Aunty Mimi and already looked like she was settled on her knee for the night.

'Right, I think you should open our gift for Oliver first,' said Cynthia forcefully passing the envelope to Lucy, who smiled then turned to Ed, closed her eyes and inhaled deeply. He touched her hand and gave it a tight squeeze, acknowledging her irritation. She passed the envelope to Ed and let him do the honours.

'Mum... Dad... this is too much!' Ed exclaimed, as he showed Lucy the cheque.

'Well, nothing is too much for our first grandchild.'

'Evie, Cynthia... Evie is your first grandchild!' Lucy said stunned, she looked over at Mia and rolled her eyes so hard, she swore she actually saw her brain. Mia returned her annoyance with a sympathetic smile.

'Oh, I mean our first grandson! £1,000 for our first grandson is not too much at all! 'And there it was... the inappropriateness had begun. Why Cynthia felt it necessary to tell everyone how much she had given Oliver was beyond Lucy. Although she knew deep down, it was because she was a snob who liked to let people know she was from money.

'Did your parents send a gift over? It's a shame they couldn't make it, isn't it dear?' asked Cynthia. The vindictive little bitch, thought Lucy, she knew why they weren't there. Thankfully however, it was as though Mia had read her mind, as just as those words rattled round her head and she was about to say them, Evie thrust herself into her arms.

'Mummmmy! Can I open one?' Evie looked up at her and smiled. She had chocolate flakes all around her mouth. She mirrored her beautiful daughters smile, picked her up and placed her on her knee.

'Thank you,' she mouthed to Mia. 'Of course you can darling, let's see what we've got here.' Lucy looked around to find the biggest one she could, 'What about this one?'

The remainder of the present opening was slow and painful as Cynthia and Phil whispered to each other during the whole saga. Thank God most of their friends knew what the Browns were like. Lucy was more than relieved when the excruciating half hour was over.

'You know I said no drunk Godmother at the christening Aunty Mia? Well sod that! After that performance, there is now going to be a very drunk mother at her son's christening!'

*

The next morning Lucy woke to what felt like a marching band on her head. She had been so glad when Mia had offered to get up with the kids. Ed had gone off to work early. He was a GP in their local surgery and Monday mornings were always so busy. She looked at the clock and saw that it said ten o'clock; she knew that it was more than a lie in for her, but still didn't win the battle she fought with her eyelids.

'Mummy! Mummy! Look what we made you!' Evie was now bouncing on the bed next to Lucy's head.

'Evie, get down, right now!' she heard Mia say in her sternest voice. Evie was always so well behaved for Mia and stopped immediately, then plonked herself down on a cushion. Lucy sat up and saw Mia holding a tray in front of her with a bacon sandwich on, a pot of tea and a glass of fresh orange juice. Sisters were the best, she thought, or maybe she was just lucky to have Mia as hers.

'Hey, how's the head?' Mia said to her big sister.

'Okay actually. It wasn't two hours ago. I can't believe you let me sleep this long. You're the best.'

'I know I am!' Mia smiled and pulled Evie onto her knee after Lucy had just given her some of her toast.

'Has Ollie been okay for his Aunty Mimi?' Lucy said as she took a huge mouthful from the sandwich.

'He's been fine. He's sleeping now, and Evie and I have been making dens in the dining room.'

'Aunty Mimi is so much fun isn't she darling?' Lucy said, rubbing the top of her daughter's head and she replied with a smiling nod as she stuffed the last bit of toast into her mouth. 'Not like miserable old mummy!'

'Mummy, you're fun!' Evie said, 'and so is Mimi! Can we play den again?'

'Come on then you... let's leave Mummy in peace to eat her breakfast!'

'Thanks Mia,' Lucy said smiling appreciatively at her sister, 'I owe you.'

An hour later and Lucy finally made an appearance, feeling fresh after her fifteen-minute shower. Her longest since Ollie had been born and she'd even managed to blow-dry her hair — now that was some achievement. She descended the stairs and realised something strange, that the house was completely silent. It felt totally bizarre. She realised why when she pushed the living room door open and found Mia and Evie, asleep on the couch together and Oliver was still sleeping in his Moses basket. Although, she was getting a whiff from him that indicated that he would be awake pretty soon. So instead of doing what she always did when she had a moment to herself, which was to tidy the house, she just sat in the huge armchair that was in the corner of the living room and read the paper until somebody decided to wake. She wasn't surprised that it was Ollie who broke the beautiful silence with his wailing; his cries would wake the dead they were so ear-splitting. This ensured that Mia and Evie were awake soon after. After changing Ollie's nappy on the living room floor she saw Princess Evie and Pirate Mia sit up on the couch. Evie had clearly twisted Mia's arm to play dress up. See, she thought, Mummy definitely wasn't as much fun.

'Looking good!' Lucy said winking at her sister.

'Huh?' Mia had evidently forgotten that she was wearing a bandana that was about six sizes too small for her head. She looked down to see the neckerchief that clearly wouldn't have fitted around her neck wrapped around her wrist, and remembered.

'You want coffee?'

'You read my mind,' Mia said as Lucy watched her do a huge stretch.

Lucy lifted Ollie onto her hip and walked to the kitchen. She placed him in his high chair, went to the cupboard and picked out the box of rusks and handed him one. He whipped it from her hand and began to suck on it. That would keep him quiet for a while, she thought, his lack of teeth meant it took him about an hour to work his way through one. Mia walked into the kitchen and sat down at their large kitchen table. She had taken off her bandana and neckerchief and looked like Mia again.

'Sugar... no sugar?' Lucy knew that it depended on the circumstances.

'One please,' she said as she raised her bare legs and feet onto the chair beside her, 'think I need the sugar rush. I was up with the kids at seven.'

'Welcome to my world!' Lucy said feeling her eyebrows rise and sounding like one of those mothers she detested.

'Oh I meant to tell you before Luce, that guy from next door... what's his name... the one whose wife died...'

'Sebastian,' Lucy answered almost too quickly.

'Yep, that's him. He came round before with a parcel for you and said that it had been delivered to his because nobody was in when the postman came here. Which I thought was strange because as you know I was up at seven with the kids!' Mia laughed and Lucy mirrored her laugh but it was completely forced and she was sure that Mia would have noticed. 'You okay sis?'

'Yep, fine. Where is it?' Lucy asked placing Mia's coffee onto the table in front of her.

'Thanks. Where's what?' Mia looked confused.

'The parcel that Sebastian left.'

Mia pointed towards the table in the hall as her mouth was full of coffee. She moved swiftly into the hall, closing the kitchen door behind her and hoped that Mia had not seen the shame that had spread across her face. She knew that Mia would never understand, she wasn't married with kids, she was single, carefree and happy. Lucy however was a bored housewife who wasn't even doing anything wrong. Was she?

Chapter 4

Jessie

'*Walk this waaaaaaaaaaayyyy, talk this waaaaaaaaayyyy! Walk this waaaaaaaay, talk this waaaaaaaaayyy!*' Jessie proceeded to prance around the kitchen strumming her air guitar after she had just thrown her mop, aka her microphone, to the ground. She only stopped when she realised that the radio had been switched off. 'What the fu... oh hi Robert!'

'Hello Jess. Enjoying yourself were you?' he smiled at her. She knew that she wasn't the apple of his eye like Mia, but that extremely drunken cheeky snog under the mistletoe that they'd had last Christmas kept her pretty high up on his "not to sack list."

'I was enjoying myself actually,' most people would flush with embarrassment at being caught mid performance, instead she just smiled at him and he returned it. He wasn't bad looking for an older man, she thought. 'Anyway, what are you doing here?' she said whilst picking up the mop from the floor and placing it back into the bucket.

'I've come to give Mia my key. She's having Harvey next week as Annie and I are away.'

'Oh, yeah of course. She did mention it. Where are you off to?'

'Just Portugal,' he replied. "Just Portugal" she thought, Jesus, she couldn't even remember the last time she'd been abroad. Just bloody anywhere with a bit of sun would be nice.

'Very nice,' Jessie said as she began to polish the cutlery.

'Is Mia about?' he said looking at his watch.

'Not yet, she's due in about...' she turned around to look at the clock '... ten minutes. If you've got somewhere to be, you can leave it with me and I'll pass it onto her.'

'Ah thanks Jess, that would be great. Annie is waiting outside in the car. She wants to do some last minute clothes shopping. I mean, as if she hasn't got enough things to take already!'

'Yeah!' Jessie forced a fake smile and wished them a lovely holiday. More clothes she thought, that was a joke. Buying clothes was all that woman ever did. She could probably open her own M&S store!

Once he was gone, she made herself a coffee and ate the pastry she had bought on the way to work.

'Hey Mia. You okay? You look a bit flustered,' Jessie asked as Mia arrived fifteen minutes late for her shift. Mia was always on time, so she knew something must be wrong.

'The tap in the kitchen started spurting water everywhere and I didn't know what to do,' Mia said franticly. 'Luckily Ben appeared at the door with a package he had taken from the postman.'

'Oooh a knight in shining armour!'

'To be fair he pretty much was. I think I'd still be there trying to sort it now. It was great timing. Although, can you imagine Dust. She thought it was brilliant!'

'Oh, that reminds me...' she paused while she stood up and fished for the key to Robert's house in her pocket, she handed it over. 'Robert dropped by and asked me to give you this.'

'Oh yeah, I'd forgotten all about that for a minute.'

Mia took the key from Jessie. 'Thanks.'

'You want a coffee Mia?'

'Oh yes please, I'd love one. I only managed one this morning, what with all the drama, I think I'm getting the shakes!'

Five hours later and the lunch rush was over. Mia and Jessie took a well-earned rest as they sat and drank a big mug of coffee each before they started setting up for dinner.

'So, are you up for that?' asked Mia.

'A pub quiz….' Mia knew that Jessie wasn't a great one for games or quizzes, but the fact that it was in the pub might swing it for her.

'Come on Jess, there's booze! It'll be fun.'

'Who suggested it?'

'Ben, he came down yesterday and asked if we fancied going.'

'Sounds like Ben has a little crush on Mia.' Jessie tried to sound excited for her but couldn't help feeling a little envious as she'd instantly taken a liking to him, ex-drunk or not. She'd dealt with worse. At the minute she was dealing with David, who was turning out to be a right royal twat. But she was just using him; as she did with most men, and his sell by date was very nearly due to expire. In fact she decided, right there and then, she would call him later and tell him it was all over.

'No he does not.'

'An invite to the party...'

'Which everyone in the building got!'

'Dropping off packages...'

'He just happened to be walking in as the postman was!'

'Inviting you to pub quizzes...'

'With you and Alex!'

'... and if I'm not mistaken he came and borrowed some sugar sometime last week. I mean that is a little clichéd, but God loves a trier.'

'He just ran out of sugar Jess, nothing clichéd about that!'

'Yeah, yeah, we'll see!'

'Anyway, even if that's what it is. I'm not interested; I like him... yes, but only as a friend.'

'Whatever you say Mia, whatever you say. That's you all over; you only like them as friends... come on Mia, give him a chance!'

'Right, Jessica Cole enough chitter chatter. Let's get ourselves up and into gear. I want to get home this side of Christmas.'

*

'You owe me BIG time for this Mia Richards and on my day off too,' Jessie said as she opened the huge front door to her boss' house. 'You know I only stand Dusty coz I love ya. Harvey is an absolute stinker.'

'Ssshh, don't be mean!' Mia cried down the other end of the phone.

'He's a friggin' dog, he doesn't understand me!'

'Well, just be nice to him when you see him. He's been in that house on his own all morning.'

'I will I will! Right I'll call you if there are any problems. Good luck with finding your house keys and getting to work on time!' Jessie opened the kitchen door and Harvey began bounding around. Although she wasn't a dog lover, she liked the way Harvey never barked; he was a quiet dog, like all dogs should be. Just like kids should be, according to some people, seen and not heard. She found the dog food, filled up the bowl, refilled his water bowl and opened the back door for him to have a run around. She then went into the living room and turned on the TV. Mia had asked her to hang around a bit this morning so that the dog didn't feel neglected. So, she kicked off her shoes, flicked on the kettle and went rummaging through the cupboards to see what she could find to eat. As she was looking she felt something poke her in the bum, it was Harvey with a ball. See, she thought, seen and not heard or played with. But he was giving her his "poor me" look, so she caved and walked out of the conservatory and into the back garden. Robert and Annie had acres of land. She moved her arm back ready to launch the ball as far as she could, it was a pitiful effort really as Harvey retrieved the ball and came darting towards her in quick succession, his tail wagging with excitement. She gave it another go, but took a run up along the conservatory, which made the ball travel a little further. She smiled to herself. Harvey retrieved the ball and she did it one last time. This time she did a little jig as she got it even further.

'You've still got it Coley!' she said, as she kissed her throwing arm.

'I'd say you have… yep!' said a strange voice coming from behind a bush and Jessie nearly jumped out of her skin.

'Jesus! You scared the shite out of me!'

'Sorry Coley,' he said winking at her. 'I'm Jake Derby. The Pickford's gardener.' He said showing her the trowel he was holding as though it was some kind of proof.

'I'm Jessie… Cole. Well… Derby you shouldn't be sneaking up on people like that!'

'I know but it was so funny just watching you throwing the ball to Harvey, I saw you kissing the guns!' Oh good God thought Jessie, how embarrassing, not that she'd let him know that she was ashamed.

'Well, when you've got it!' she said, realising that she had just winked at the gardener.

'Yeah and you certainly have,' he said, smiling. Was he flirting with her?

'Well, I'm making a drink, would you like one?'

'A glass of juice or something would be lovely. It's thirsty work this landscaping business,' he said as he pulled off his hoodie. As he did, his T-shirt almost went with it and she caught a glimpse of his ever so toned abs. Mmmm she thought, very nice indeed.

'I'll see what I can find,' she said almost too casually as if she hadn't noticed the flash of abs. She turned on her heels and went inside, poured him a juice and made herself a cuppa. Before she took it out she stood and watched him for a while. He must be at least twenty-eight she thought to herself. Four years younger than her. That's not too bad, she could cope with that. Anyway, she chided herself, why was she even bothering to think that. All the nice ones were taken or gay, or had had enough of being nice and had begun to cheat on their partners already. Plus her tolerance levels for men were non- existent.

'Derby, I got your drink here,' she said as she held it up for him to see. He began to walk over to her. He must have been at least 6"3' and had a very commanding walk. As she handed him his drink, he placed his hand on top of hers, dwarfing it. His hands were very rough, true workman's hands. He definitely was flirting. She wasn't imagining it.

'Cheers.' He took a huge gulp, 'I best get back to it then,' he walked off and placed the glass on the low wall right by where he had been working.

Well this had turned out to be a much better afternoon than she had anticipated. Plus Harvey didn't even do his business while she was there —meaning that she didn't even need to get her hands dirty!

*

'Really? A gardener. Robert didn't mention anything,' said Mia as she took a sip from her glass.

'Yeah, well he was weeding and digging and stuff,' said Jessie, she knew that she sounded like she was trying to convince herself that she knew what she was talking about.

'Wow he sounds like a real Alan Titchmarsh!' said Ben sarcastically.

'Oh God, imagine if he isn't Robert's gardener and he's robbing the place blind as we speak!' exclaimed Jessie.

'Who's robbing what?' said Alex as he appeared behind the three of them, 'Hi everyone.'

'Hey Alex. Jessie is getting herself all worried about nothing,' Mia said in reply.

'What was the hold up? Something at work?' Ben asked Alex.

'Yeah.' Alex looked uneasy and it was clear he didn't want to talk about it.

'No Izzy tonight then?' Jessie asked changing the subject, but clearly not for the better.

'Nope,' he said and took a big swig of his now warm beer that Ben had bought for him twenty minutes ago. 'Excuse me while I just nip to the gents.'

'Did I hit a nerve?' Jessie asked Ben.

'You could say that. I'd steer clear of the subject to be on the safe side.' Before he could continue he was interrupted by the quiz-master.

'Good evening folks, just the three of you tonight?'

'No, four please,' Mia replied.

He passed Ben the blank answer sheet and a pen. 'That's a tenner that pal.'

'Here mate,' Alex said just before he sat down at the table. Jessie watched as Ben looked at Alex with concern in his eyes. She'd never seen two guys so close. Their friendship really astounded her.

'Cheers,' the quiz-master replied taking the twenty from Alex and returning his change. 'Now complete the famous faces sheet first, I'll be back round to collect it in twenty minutes and then we'll begin.'

An hour later and it was going well. There were only two questions that they were unable to answer.

'... and the final question of the night is for you readers... which of the Brontë sisters wrote *Wuthering Heights*?'

'Emily,' Mia said without missing a beat.

'Are you sure it wasn't Charlotte?' questioned Alex.

'Nope definitely Emily,' Mia reiterated.

'She should know, she studied bloody English Literature at university!' exclaimed Jessie.

'Did you?' said Alex completely shocked.

'Why are you so surprised?' Mia asked, confused. Jessie saw his face flush, he realised that he sounded rude. Mia was the most modest person she knew and never boasted about anything. They both knew that she could be so much more than the manager of Imagination, but she seemed happy, so why should she stop doing what she loved? Plus Jessie adored having her there, so why would she encourage her to do anything else but be her boss.

'Erm… to be honest Mia, I don't know… sorry.' Oh dear Alex was in a hole and someone needed to help him.

'I know what the answer is to that question! That tricky one about Finland.' Jessie said changing the subject.

'Really?' said Ben sounding excited.

'… it's erm… erm… no, it's gone. Sorrrrry!' Jessie said smiling, 'my round, who wants a drink?'

Jessie arrived home to her flat, after her long day of dog sitting, man watching and pub quizzing. She had lived by herself for as long as she could remember and she liked it that way. At the front door she kicked off her shoes and walked barefoot towards the sofa and lay there in the darkness. She loved the stillness of the night when she could almost hear her own heart beating. Being alone had been something she treasured and she had pretty much been on her own since she left home at fifteen, the day before she had turned sixteen. She would have done anything to get away from her stepfather. He was never abusive towards her physically, but verbally he tore her to ribbons. She wondered how she ever had any confidence left. She knew, among other things, this is why she over compensated in many situations, drank too much on other occasions and chose men so badly. She was a therapist's dream patient and she knew it. She knew that she should go and see someone, talk about what happened. The thing that haunted her so regularly; the thing that threatened to destroy her unless she could find some closure to the situation. Instead of thinking about it any longer, she stood up and did what she always did when she allowed her mind to wander into the past – got herself a glass and poured herself a large whiskey and another, until she felt numb inside. Just the way she liked it.

Chapter 5

Mia

'Let's head over to Sally for the weather...' Mia heard the local news reporter say as she walked into her bedroom to pull on a cardigan. She thought that Sally might say that the temperatures were dropping to an all-time low for this time of year, as it had been unusually cold this last week. It was surprising too as it was heading into summer. Mia would never know what Sally said as her voice was drowned out by the blasting hair dryer. Once finished, she plaited her long dark hair that was still just wet enough to be wavy when she took the elastic band out later. She pulled on her UGG boots – not before switching on the hairdryer again and giving her feet a quick warm – made herself a cup of coffee and headed into her second bedroom, which had become her study. Well, it had the dual purpose of being her study and a storage room for everything she wasn't quite sure what to do with. Her laptop was sitting on the huge desk she had inherited from her parents, well from her granddad really, as he had given it to them. She flipped open the lid and waited for the computer to load. As she did this she cupped the coffee in her hand and ran her other hand along the edge of desk. It was a huge old-fashioned, walnut desk with tiny little drawers that had individual keys to lock each one. Upon finding out that her parents were moving and getting rid of all of their furniture; it was the only thing that she had actually asked for. She had adored her granddad and been devastated when he had passed away five years ago. He had really given her the passion, the confidence and the ambition to attempt to make something of herself, and to follow her dreams. Finally, the computer was ready, so she began typing in her password.

'*Buuuuuzzzzzzz. Buuuuuuuzzzzz,*' Mia jumped. She did this every time her intercom sounded; she wondered if she would ever get used to it. She picked up the intercom phone and held it to her ear.

'Hello.'

'Hey Mia, its Alex.'

'Oh hi,' she said, sounding pleased to hear his voice.

'I left my key in the flat and Ben's at the gym, can you buzz me in?'

'Yeah sure. You coming here?'

'Erm...'

'Well, if you've got no keys then how are you going to get in?' Mia laughed as she asked Alex the question.

'Oh yeah, that would be great thanks.'

Mia placed the phone back onto the wall and put the door on the latch for Alex to let himself in. She flicked the kettle on and attempted to pull out a mug for Alex from the cupboard. She loved having a dishwasher but was fully aware that she needed to invest in more crockery as it took a while to fill up enough for a load. Instead, she was always trying to find a stray mug around the flat to use. She was standing on her tiptoes when there was a knock at the door.

'It's open,' she said turning her head towards the door so that her voice projected in that direction.

'Hi Mia.'

'Hi Alex, I take it you want tea?' she said, still straining to get the other mug from the back of the cupboard. He was a tea tank and she knew that the answer would categorically be "yes".

'Here, let me get that,' he said as his large frame stood next to her tiny one. He placed his hand on her shoulder and easily retrieved the mug that was sitting snugly in the far corner of the cupboard. 'Why would you put it all the way up there when there is no way you could ever reach it Pippy?' he said laughing.

'Pippy?' Mia said repeating his words but sounding completely bewildered. He indicated towards her two plaits either side of her head. She felt herself blush, forgetting that she probably looked like a seven year old especially with her geeky glasses on, but attempted to continue as normal. 'I didn't put it up there! I think it was probably Ben. Anyway, I'm not the idiot who locked themselves out am I?' she said retaliating to his mockery. Over the last few months, Mia and Jessie had built up a growing friendship, with the boys. There was always lots of laughter when they were together, it was simple yet fun, but she knew that she could rely on them if she needed them and hoped that they felt the same way. 'I know. Can you believe it?' he said rolling his eyes towards the sky.

'Can't you just pick the lock?'

'I'm a policeman not a bloody locksmith! You've been watching one too many American shows!' she smiled knowing he was probably right. All cops in America seemed to know exactly how to get into any locked door whether it was with a hair clip, credit card or coat hanger.

'Watch it Detective Jones, you want this tea or not?'

An hour and a half later and neither of them had even noticed the time; as they had both been so busy chatting about their days. Ben had text Alex saying that he had been caught up in a traffic jam coming home from the gym and that he would be home as soon as he could, so Mia had decided to make Alex some dinner on her evening off.

'That carbonara was delicious, thanks Mia,' Alex said appreciatively. 'From scratch as well, I am very impressed!'

'Well Alex, when you have worked in a restaurant for as long as I have you pick up *some* tips from the chefs. Plus, I am a woman of many talents... just think even little Mia Richards managed to get herself an English degree.' She looked at Alex as though she was about twelve, with a 'pity me' look on her face. See, she thought, the pigtails are coming in handy right about now.

'Stop it!' Alex said and actually blushed. 'You know I didn't mean it to come out like that, that night in the pub.'

'I know, I know. I just like to wind you up,' she said smiling at him.

'Well for a woman with a degree, you're not going to be a waitress forever are you?'

'Oh Alex, there you go again...'

'No, well I didn't quite mean it like that...'

'I'm kiddin', I'm kiddin'!' she raised her hand in his direction in an effort to stop him talking. 'Stop digging!'

'But...'

'No, you are absolutely right Alex, I don't want to be a waitress for the rest of my life – not that there is anything wrong with that might I add. But, like I said, I am a woman of many talents and in time I'm sure you'll find out what they are...'

As Mia climbed into bed that night she reached for the latest gruesome thriller she was reading, but she hesitated before she opened the book to chapter nineteen and thought of Alex. About the great, unexpected night that they'd had together. He really was a good-looking guy. She thought that every time she saw him and then was so thankful for Izzy in the next breath. Having a girlfriend, one she liked or not, meant that she could totally be herself around him. She wasn't giggly and silly when she was with him like she could be with other men that she liked; she was natural, herself. Every time she saw him, she always wondered how he'd gotten that scar. It wasn't a childhood accident scar like everyone has — like her friend Dawn had from cracking her head on the coffee table or the scar just above her hip bone she got from flying over her handlebars at just six-years-old. There was unquestionably more to his scar and she was convinced that there was a shocking story that came with it. Alex Jones was like a closed book, he was definitely hiding something, and yet there were so many questions that she wanted to ask him, like why he was so forlorn the night that he and Izzy visited the restaurant. She had never seen him like that since. How did he have that huge scar on his face? Why was he still putting up with Izzy? She had seen a sobbing Izzy leaving the apartment a few weeks ago with a bag in tow, assuming that there had been a heated row between her and Alex. Mia was hopeful that she was out of Alex's life for good, but sadly she had seen her happily bouncing up the stairs days after their exchange. The list of questions she wanted to ask was endless. However, her mum had always told her that it was rude to pry into other people's business, so she never did. She just hoped in time that as their friendship grew even more, that one day he might eventually open the book and let her read a little of what was inside.

*

Robert and Annie had been away for just over two weeks and this was only the third time that she had been to the house to check on Harvey. Her mum and dad had been really easy going when she lived at home and they had let her bring Harvey to their house, but her flat was just too small to have a big dog like Harvey staying. Jessie seemed to have become a dog lover practically overnight. It was totally bizarre, but Mia wasn't complaining as she had been very busy at work because one of the full time waitresses had called in sick for a whole week. The worst thing was that Mia knew that she wasn't really ill. Talk about taking liberties while the boss was away, Robert would be furious upon his return. Mia opened Robert's huge wooden front door and picked up the mail that lay on the floor and placed it on the side unit with the pile that had already been created. By this time Harvey had come hurtling towards her and was bouncing around her legs with excitement. She knelt down on the floor and showed him lots of attention. He loved it and rolled onto his back to have his stomach stroked. Mia happily obliged. He then leaped to his feet and started circling her; she knew that he was looking for Dusty.

'Sorry lovely, after last time's near catastrophe Dusty was not allowed to come,' Harvey's ears pricked up at the sound of her name, but dropped again in quick succession. There was no way that she could bring Dusty to Robert's house again, they went wild together and it had only been her quick footedness that had saved a very expensive vase from falling from the shelf. The pair of them got a severe telling off and they spent the rest of the afternoon lying together in the shade. 'Let's get you fed and watered,' Mia said as she picked up her bag from the floor and rose to her feet. 'Come on boy let's go,' she said as she patted her thigh trying to encourage him out of his sulk.

After refilling Harvey's bowls she had a rummage through Annie's collection of teas, she was always a coffee drinker but whenever she dog sat Harvey, she always tried Annie's exotic flavoured teas. This time she gave nettle tea a go but after a few sips she wished she hadn't and hastily poured it down the sink. That's not one she'd be trying again she thought, and instead picked up the strawberry teabag and made herself a cup of sweet smelling fruit tea. She knew that she definitely liked that one. As it was such a nice day she grabbed a handful of Annie's magazines, they ranged from *Homes and Furnishings* to *Gardening Glory*. To her surprise, she did not frown at the sight of them, but revelled in what she might find in there for her new flat. She opened the patio doors, slipped on her prescription sunglasses, sat down on their very large garden furniture and rested her feet on one of the many empty chairs around the table. She gave Harvey the treat from her bag that she had bought especially for him. She knew Robert hated him having any sort of treats, but then if he was having a great time sunning himself then why couldn't Harvey be allowed a little indulgence.

A couple of hours had passed and she had made herself a cold drink as it was starting to get warm. That cold spell had only lasted a few days, thank goodness. Harvey had amused himself by running around the garden either chasing his tail or a couple of birds, just like every other man she thought. Suddenly, she heard the back gate slam and she felt her heart miss a beat.

'Hello?' she finally heard her mouth say, although she wasn't sure that she was totally in control of the noises that were leaving her lips.

'Hey, I didn't know that you were coming today. I would have bought that DVD,' said the stranger's voice, who seemed to know who she was. He had a huge smile on his face when he emerged from around the conservatory. It soon disappeared when he set eyes on Mia, perhaps he now realised that he didn't know her after all. 'Oh, you're not Jessie.'

'No, I'm not.'

'You must be Mia then?' said the stranger putting out his hand for her to shake it, as the smile reappeared on his face.

'Err… yep I am.' Still confused, she shook it.

'I'm Jake Derby, the Pickford's gardener.'

'Ohhhhh right!' It was like not just the penny had dropped, but the whole money box. She realised that she had been holding her breath, and breathed a heavy sigh of relief. So, this is why Jessie was so keen to come and look after Harvey, because Jake was here. Now the confusion and initial fear had passed she could see how ruggedly handsome he was. He had that, 'I don't give a damn' kind of stubble all over his face. Of course Jess had not become a dog lover overnight, how stupid of her to think that. She didn't come over for Harvey, but to gawp at Jake. Plus he had clearly been expecting Jessie and seemed more than disappointed when he was met with Mia instead.

'What does that mean?' Jake asked inquisitively.

'What does what mean?' Mia asked more than a little perplexed. She'd had a whole conversation with herself in her head and couldn't even remember what she had said.

'Ohhhh right,' he said, repeating her words.

'Oh that,' Mia said a little too casually and then spun only a little white lie, 'I was a little anxious when I heard the door going and thought that you may have been an intruder so when you explained who you were I was like, 'ohhhh right.' He smiled knowing that it was a lie but humoured her anyway. 'So I was like phew!' she said as though she was wiping the sweat from her brow. She'd never make it as a spy she thought. She was a crap liar.

'Anyway would you like a drink? I was just making one.' She lied again as she stood hiding the drink she had just made herself.

'Yeah, that would be great thanks Mia.' She looked at her watch; Dusty would probably need to be let out to go the toilet. But what the hell, she still had a few bottles of bleach left over from Dusty's initial incontinence problem when they first moved in. She would make Dusty wait, she had a gardener to interrogate, and then when she saw Jessie she would do the same to her. Mmmm, she thought to herself, maybe she wouldn't make a bad spy after all!

'So what was so God damn urgent that couldn't wait till I saw you tomorrow in work? Is your mum okay?' Jessie said as she stood at Mia's open front door.

'Nooo she's fine,' Mia winced a little at the thought of her mum, she wasn't on the best of form if she was honest, but she was almost sure Jessie didn't really want to hear about all of that now.

'What is it then? You sounded like you killed Harvey or something, the sheer panic in your voice!'

'Well...'

'Jesus, he's not dead is he? Can you imagine... Robert would throttle the fuckin' pair of us. Actually he would probably just throttle me, as he loves you. I mean I only fed him what you told me to, except I suppose the last time I was there I gave him a bit of my biscuit, would that hurt him? Oh Mia...'

'Shut up Jess!' Mia finally cut in, 'Harvey is alive and well and still bouncing around like he has ADHD.'

'Oh thank God for that,' Jess said sounding more than relieved. She pulled a pack of cigarettes out of her back pocket and moved towards the patio doors, turned the key, and pulled them open. She placed a cigarette between her lips and fished the lighter from the packet, lit it and inhaled deeply. 'So what the frig is so important? And there best be wine in that fridge

Richards, you can't drag me all the way here and then tell me that there is no wine!'

'It's chilling in the freezer, just the way you like it.'

'Good. Okay, so what's the big crisis?'

'There is no crisis. Chill out Jess. Why do you always think the worst thing has happened? That someone is on bloody death's door?' Mia could see Jessie go tense; she knew this was a sign that she was embarrassed. No one else would know this, but as her best friend she knew that Jessie didn't react to situations the way most people did. She hadn't meant to make her feel uncomfortable. She felt bad, but while she was on a roll she thought she should just spit it out. 'I met Jake today.'

'Ohhhh right.' Now Mia knew exactly how Jake had felt when she had uttered those words earlier.

'Well...' Mia said hoping that Jessie would finish her sentence.

'Well what?' Jessie said trying to sound nonchalant.

'He seems nice.' Mia continued even though Jess sounded disinterested.

'Yeah, I haven't really spoken to him.'

'Well, for someone who you haven't really spoken to he seemed to know a fair bit about you and seemed very interested in learning more.'

'Really?' Jessie perked up a little.

'Oh, I thought you weren't bothered.'

'I'm not.' Mia knew she was lying but didn't push it.

'Oh well I'm glad I didn't give him…. Oh it doesn't matter.'

'Give him what?' Jessie asked sounding intrigued as to what Mia was going to say.

'Give him your number, he asked me for it… twice.'

'Yeah, it's probably for the best. He'll probably end up being a dick anyway, just like the rest of them.' Mia observed her friend as she inhaled the last of her cigarette, threw it to the ground and stubbed it out. Then she watched and saw her shoulders visibly drop, the tension in them had all but disappeared. Plus if she didn't know any better, even though she couldn't see her face, she would swear that Jessica Cole was grinning from ear to ear.

Chapter 6

Ben

'That's all for tonight folks, if you'd like to get yourselves a tea or coffee, it's all at the back of the room,' said Jeff as he pointed to the tables sitting just in front of the stage. Shirley was standing there, as always, with a huge smile across her rosy Scottish cheeks as people approached her.

'Hello Ben, how's work going?' said Shirley as she passed Ben a coffee, black with one sugar. Ben knew that she could tell you everyone's preference of hot drink; she had been doing it for that long.

'Yeah great thanks Shirl, got a big contract a few weeks ago.'

'Oh congratulations, that's brilliant news,' she said sounding genuinely pleased. Shirley was one of the few people he actually liked at the AA meetings he attended every month. She wasn't even an alcoholic; she was just a lovely Christian woman who helped with refreshments. Although she had confided in Ben that her brother had been a raging alcoholic and it had killed him at the age of just thirty-two. This shocking news had certainly given Ben food for thought.

'Thanks. How are the grandkids?' Ben enquired.

'Oh they're wee treasures. Henry has just started walking. You want to see a picture?'

'Yeah.' Ben wasn't the baby type at all, but he didn't mind humouring Shirley as she had been so good to him over the last eighteen months and she wasn't even his sponsor.

Twenty minutes had passed and Ben felt that he had stayed the required amount of time. So, after saying goodbye to his sponsor, Alan, and finding Shirley to thank her and give her a kiss on the cheek, he was off.

The nights were starting to get lighter and it was a pretty warm night so he had decided to walk there and back. He walked out of the church hall and turned left towards home. He'd gotten about 100 metres when he heard someone shout his name. He turned to see Jessie waving at him. He waited until she had caught up to him, assuming that she was going to Mia's anyway.

'Hey... you been a bad boy?' she said as she linked arms with Ben and they continued walking.

'What?' Ben was utterly confused by her question.

'I saw you sneaking out of church. You been confessing all have you?'

'Oh that, no, I've just been to a meeting.'

'I never had you down for an organiser of the summer fair.'

'No it was an... AA meeting,' Ben said awkwardly expecting the usual blushed face and embarrassment, but oh no - not Jessie.

'Oh right, you still have to go to those? You said it's been eighteen months.'

'It has, I just still choose to go. It helps, talking about it.'

'Really? I've never been a talker.'

'Now that does shock me, all you do is talk!'

'Oi!' she said as she gave Ben an elbow to the ribs and he feigned injury. 'Nope, I'm definitely a bottler... no pun intended there Ben. Put it in a bottle and chuck it out to sea, in the hope that you never really have to think about it again.'

'I did that for a while you know Jess. Pretended it wasn't happening and then I would carry on drinking and just feel like shite afterwards. But as soon as I started AA and began talking about it, it was like my

96

demons began to float away... sorry this probably sounds like complete and utter bullshit to you.'

'No...' Jessie hesitated.

Ben realised that he had in all likelihood just babbled on far too much. He usually just saved all his talking for the meetings. It was the only time that he ever did talk about his past, but to the right person - anyone who wasn't part of his life. It was like he had been caught on the hop though, like it was all still really fresh in his mind. Right, he thought, I must change the subject before she is bored to death.

'Anyway, how's work?'

'Yeah... good thanks.'

'You okay Jessie?' She had begun acting really strangely he thought, 'Jess...'

'You know what Ben, I've just realised that I've forgotten something, I've got to go.'

'What is it? We're nearly at Mia's now anyway. I'll get my car and give you a lift if you like?'

'No Ben, its fine. Honest, but thanks. See you soon.' Before he could object she ran over the road, flagged down the bus, jumped on it and in a matter of seconds was gone.

*

Ben watched as Mia threw the Frisbee to Alex, he jumped, then grabbed it quickly and flung it back in Mia's direction. He had lost the toss up as to who would have to walk back to the flat and get the rug to sit on. He and Alex both said that it was the other one who had forgotten it. But his call of heads had let him down. As he approached them, Dusty came hurtling towards him wagging her tail. He let her jump up towards him and he ruffled her ears, then she ran back towards Mia, who he continued to stare at. She had a little summer dress on that swayed every time she threw the Frisbee. As she stretched to grab it, her sunglasses fell from the top of her head and she laughed. He had spoken to Alan, his sponsor, about starting a relationship. Silly really, as he didn't even know if Mia reciprocated his feelings. But it was the first time in a long time that he'd actually liked someone and she didn't seem to be bothered that he was an ex-drunk.

'Yeaaaah, you got it! I need a sit down.' Mia said, putting her sunglasses on her face.

'Really? You're only saying that because you can't catch!' Alex mocked her and sat down on the rug.

'It's not that I can't catch it, it's that you can't bloody throw! I think you think I'm about 6ft and I'm a long way off that!' she laughed as she sat down and Dusty joined her at her feet.

'Excuses, excuses!'

'Whatever,' Mia said as she half ignored Alex and pulled out a can of coke from the cool bag, 'Ben you want one?'

'Yeah, thanks,' he said as he took the can from her hand.

'You... wind up merchant. Do you want a drink?' Mia asked Alex.

'Yes please... loser.' He coughed the loser part under his breath.

Mia opened a bottle of cider with the bottle opener and as she passed the drink to him she started shaking it all over him. Alex grabbed the bottle from her and started shaking it all over her. They both burst out laughing.

'Are you two having fun?' Ben heard Izzy's frosty voice and turned around to see her in the tiniest shorts that made her legs look longer than ever, standing right behind him.

'Oh hi Izzy,' Mia said politely, it was obvious that Mia was courteous because she was such a nice girl.

'Hello Mia, you look a little wet.'

'Well as you saw, *that* was your foolish boyfriend!' Mia said smiling in her direction, Izzy returned it, but it was outrageously false.

'Anyway, I bought your favourite darling, plus some nibbles and a little champagne to celebrate this glorious day. How lucky are we with this weather for a bank holiday?'

'Cool, thanks Izzy,' Alex said smiling up at her and patting the space on the blanket next to himself.

Ben was totally confused by the fact that Alex and Izzy were still together after the huge row that they had, but somehow the pair of them were still clinging on to their clinically dead relationship. He thought that Alex would finally call it a day, but when Izzy had called him and cried solidly for an hour he knew Alex would cave. He had told her to come round and, as always, they had ended up in bed together and things had all but returned to normal.

The next few hours were spent laughing, eating and drinking. Ben had questioned Mia about why Jessie hadn't showed. Mia had just informed them that Jessie was busy. He felt a little guilty that it was to do with something he had said during the previous week, but Mia didn't raise the issue so neither did he. Izzy had been on surprisingly good form and the girls seemed to be getting on well, that was until Izzy had openly insulted Mia.

'Do you know James has given up his degree, Alex?'

'No way, I bet your Aunty Jean is furious.'

'To say the least. He's given it up and is working in a restaurant... a restaurant, I mean how ludicrous. All because he wants to follow his dream and become an actor.' Izzy followed this statement with a little patronising burst of laughter.

'What's wrong with following your dream?' Mia said. All of a sudden Ben felt the mood change and knew things were going to become awkward. Izzy was an out and out snob and he knew where this was headed.

'What's wrong?' Izzy replied almost spitting her words out. 'Well for a start acting doesn't really pay the bills does it?'

'Surely his restaurant job does that?'

'Barely I suppose, I mean it must be minimum wage. How do you cope Mia?'

'Oh, don't you worry yourself, I get by,' Mia said with such raw emotion in her voice not that Izzy even noticed,

'But seriously, he won't make it as an actor. It's ridiculous.'

'You don't know that, you have no idea whether he'll make it or not,' replied Mia.

'No I don't, but darling, let me tell you that being an actor isn't all it's cracked up to be,' she said, as she took a slug of the champagne she had brought. 'I should know having to deal with them, smiling and laughing while they talk nonsense. Then expecting them to do as I ask while directing them on that bloody chat show. All they do is moan and some of the B-listers are real divas! A real talent is writing, or having a skill in sports.'

She was so God damn arrogant, thought Ben, he couldn't bear it any longer and tried to direct the conversation away from Izzy.

'Talking about writing talent... how good is that crime thriller I passed over to you to read Alex?' Ben took a swig of his coke and continued. 'It's by that new writer, Richard somebody or other. It was brilliant, so cleverly written.'

'Ah yeah, Aims...' Alex interjected. Ben looked at him confused. 'That's his surname. It was pretty gruesome, but real. I loved it. I'm only half way through, but I didn't see that twist coming with his brother. Did you?'

'No, I definitely thought it was going to be that weird old uncle. In the reviews they're saying he may be the next Ian Rankin. I'd agree. Rankin is a genius. Totally superb.' Ben said.

'Any talk of another book from his website?' Alex asked.

'It says that he's currently writing... and to watch this space,' Ben replied.

'One to watch out for then. Do you fancy taking a look Mia? I know you like the crime thrillers,' Alex said smiling at Mia and Ben could almost see him searching her eyes to apologise for Izzy's behaviour.

'You know what Alex, I'm fine thanks,' Mia said angrily as she stood, slipped on her flip-flops and picked up her bag.

'Where are you going?' Alex asked, sounding distressed.

'Home,' she said pausing for a second, Ben hoped in anticipation for someone to say something to diffuse the situation. However, neither Ben nor Alex intervened. Ben felt that it wasn't his place and looked over at Alex but instead he just stared at his cider. God, he thought, Izzy has him as good as brain washed.

'Come on Dust, let's go.' Mia leant down and fixed Dusty's lead onto her collar. Watching as she walked away, Ben couldn't help but feel he should follow her and apologise for what just happened. He stood up and ran after Mia. As he managed to catch up with her, he grabbed her arm.

'Mia…wait!'

'Leave it Ben!' she said, furiously shaking her arm from his grasp. He did as he was told, as he saw a tear roll from under her sunglasses, showing how upset and angry she was. He watched as she walked hurriedly away and instead of going back to Alex and Izzy, for fear of saying something that he would later regret, he stood and watched her as she turned the corner and was no longer in sight. Thinking she probably had enough of a head start, he slowly began the walk home too.

Chapter 7

Lucy

'One two three, one two three, one two three... well done Lucy you have lovely footwork,' said her dance teacher, Deborah, as she twirled around to the mellow music of the waltz. She smiled over at her and then at her partner.

'Yes you do have lovely footwork, I'm sorry the same can't be said about me!' her partner said as she smiled at him.

'Don't be daft, I think that you are far better than me,' Lucy said, she knew this wasn't true as he had stood on her foot twice already tonight, but she thought it was kinder to humour him.

'Hey don't talk rubbish now,' he said she laughed a silly little giggle that she was a little embarrassed about.

'Sebastian, try to count the beat in your head, or out loud if it'll give poor Lucy's toes a rest,' said Deborah, with a hint of humour in her voice as she had obviously just seen him stand on her toe for the third time. She loved the friendship she had built up with her dance partner – her recently widowed next-door neighbour.

'See, you're definitely better than me!' he winked at her and she felt her face blush at the flirtation, she lowered her head so he could not see her face.

'Right folks, let's call it a night. We're going to have a go at the tango next week, the dance of passion!'

'Sounds like fun,' said Sebastian enthusiastically and Lucy smiled at him. 'You fancy going for a coffee, or do you have to get back?'

'No… that'd be… erm lovely, thanks.'

They continued chatting as they crossed the road to the pub that they often visited after dancing. Ever the gentleman, he pushed open the door for Lucy to enter first, and naturally she did.

'Cappuccino for you Lucy?'

'Yes please Sebastian. I'll find us a seat,' she said smiling. She headed to the room with the fire in, she knew that it wouldn't be on, but it was home to the comfiest chairs. Their usual spaces were taken so she headed to the bench and shimmied her way down it. Sebastian followed five minutes later with their drinks.

They sat and talked for half an hour and it was nice, she couldn't deny it.

'You've been amazing since Cathy, Lucy,' he said as he placed his hand on hers. She looked down at it, his olive skin against her pale, freckly complexion. His hands were so big and manly. God, she thought she couldn't believe she was thinking about his hands when he was talking about his dead wife. She looked up and gave his voice her attention. She realised that he'd been talking and she hadn't really been listening. Shit she thought, 'So, what do you think?' Right, she thought, do I ask what he was saying or do I just take a wild guess and say "yes, okay?" But before she had chance to make a decision her thoughts were interrupted.

'Ohhhh helllloooo!' said a very enthusiastic grey haired woman standing at the front of the table.

'Hi there,' replied Lucy to the stranger. Wracking her brain for some divine intervention she still couldn't place her, but this person obviously recognised her. A previous patient she thought. She wasn't sure if it was still possible to have 'baby brain' or if it was even real, but she was now blaming poor little Ollie for her memory lapse. Maternity leave was definitely scrambling her brain.

'You're Dr Brown's wife,' the stranger said, still smiling, and then she spotted Sebastian's hand on Lucy's and her smile turned to what Lucy could only describe as surprise. She visibly saw her eyebrows do a skip. Lucy in turn thrust her hand away from Sebastian's.

'Yes I am,' Lucy forced a smile out even though she felt close to tears, 'and you are...'

'Margaret,' she replied and then looked directly to the floor.

'Margaret Walsh,' a voice appeared from nowhere, 'and I'm her husband Frank. Good to meet you,' he said, stretching out his hand to Lucy for her to shake and she politely did. 'Your husband has been wonderful with Margaret.'

'I'm glad to hear it.' Lucy said, she wondered whether someone had come in and lit the fire, as she was actually starting to sweat.

'Well, we'll leave you in peace,' Frank took Margaret by the arm and began to lead her away, not before saying, 'Good night, Mrs Brown.'

'Goodnight,' Lucy replied, she waited until they were out of sight. Sebastian placed his hand on hers again. Lucy looked at him with absolute amazement. 'Were you not just witness to that?' Lucy said angrily.

'What?' he asked looking confused.

'Christ Sebastian, just please take me home.'

Lucy walked the distance from Sebastian's house to her own. As they lived in a large detached house in the country it wasn't your usual 10 yards. But she had insisted she got out at his. She didn't want him driving her to her door. Thoughts raced through her head. Ed is going to find out. Should she just tell him before someone else did? She owed him that surely? Thoughts swirled around her head like she was drunk, they were a complete blur. She put her key in the lock and turned it, fearing what the next ten minutes might entail. She walked into the living room, which was in darkness besides the muted television. She switched the main light on and saw Ed asleep with Ollie on his chest. The light woke Ed, but thankfully not Ollie.

'Hey darling, you're home. You have fun?' Ed asked in a whisper, rubbing his eyes.

'Yeah, I did,' she replied, also in a whisper. Knowing that neither of them would want Ollie disturbed from his sleep as he was a complete screamer at the best of times.

'Good, good... glad to hear it.'

'Here let me take him, you look shattered. Long day?'

'Thanks love,' he said as he passed Oliver up to her, 'Yeah, really busy.'

Now, she thought. I am going to say it *now*. She wondered if she had picked her son up and held him as some sort of protection and she felt guilty about that. 'I met Margaret and Frank Walsh tonight.'

'Really?' Ed seemed really puzzled, her heart was racing. 'How did that happen?'

'I was in the pub after cooking,' She winced as she lied, 'and she recognised me.' Lucy thought her heart was going to burst out of her chest, 'and well... I was with...'

'Recognised you?' he said even more confused than before.

God! She thought. She wished he'd just let her finish her sentence.

'Why is that so bizarre that she recognised me?'

'Well she has advanced Alzheimer's and is not often lucid.'

'Really?' Now she thought about it, her behaviour had been a bit strange but Lucy was so caught up with her own emotions that it hadn't even crossed her mind.

'Lovely couple, they've been my patients for many years now. It's very sad.' Ed continued to talk about Alzheimer's for the next five minutes as she stood holding Oliver in her arms. He was talking but she was not listening. How could she possibly be pleased that someone had Alzheimer's? It was official – she was becoming a bitch and it had to stop. Right now, she thought.

'Darling, did you hear what I said?'

'Huh?'

'I said is Ollie not getting heavy, do you want me to put him to bed?'

'No… no… it's okay I'll do it, you've had him all night.'

Once Ollie was in his cot, she checked on Evie, heard Ed snoring like a runaway train and picked up her phone and did the only decent thing. It was time to put a stop to it right now. So she text:

Need to see you tomorrow. Our place at 1pm. Need to talk. Luce, x

*

'Hey, I was so glad when you text as I needed to speak to you too.'

'Really, what's the matter?'

'It's Mum.'

'What's happened now? It's June and scorching hot in Spain!' said Lucy to Mia. Whenever their mum's name was mentioned she knew that the hairs on the back of both their necks stood up in fear.

For years when they were children their mum had hated the winter with a passion. She remembered the first time it became a real worry for everyone. Lucy was eight and was doing a presentation in school; she had planned it over the weekend with her dad and was so excited to show the class her work. She hated getting up in front of people normally, but having been allowed to pick any subject they'd liked she had picked safari animals. She had always loved them, ever since she watched that programme late one night with her mum.

She saw how they protected their young and roamed so freely in their packs until a predator pounced on them and a war ensued. Their life cycle had amazed her, even now, as an adult; she loved to watch wildlife programmes. That morning Lucy had gathered everything together, even the scrapbook of animals that she had laboriously spent hours cutting out and labelling. Little did she know that Dad leaving early for work that morning would be so detrimental to her day.

'Lucy, you're not going to school today. It's too cold and dark outside.'

'What?' she remembered that feeling to this day, one of confusion and panic. 'It's just like any other day Mum. Plus it's my presentation day today and Mrs Cooper said that she's really excited to see all my hard work about the wild animals.'

'Well, it won't be today love; I've told you we are staying in all day. Anyway just think of it as a day at home. I'll put the fire on and we can sit and watch the Discovery Channel with Mia, it's your favourite.'

Lucy didn't argue with her mum, she never had. So instead she went up to her bedroom and cried so hard that she thought she was going to be sick. At eight-years-old, it was the worst possible thing that could have happened. Mrs Cooper, being the lovely, kind hearted woman that she was, let Lucy do her presentation the following day when her dad had brought her into school and apologised for her being off explaining that she had a stomach bug. But looking back, Lucy knew that was the day it had all started.

'No, she's not had another episode or anything,' and just like that the hairs on her neck settled themselves back into place.

'Thank Christ for that. So what is it?' Lucy knew she had snapped, but still felt pretty on edge this morning and really wanted to speak to Mia, but as usual their mum was getting in the way.

'Calm down Luce! Dad said that it would be nice if we could go over to Spain and visit this summer, bring the kids.'

'Really... I don't know, I'll have to speak to Ed and see if he can get any time away from the surgery.'

'Oh.... Right.... It's just that I think dad meant you, me and the kids,' Mia said as her cheeks started to flush. Lucy felt Mia's embarrassment and knew that it wasn't even her doing, it was her mum's, and Mia was just the messenger. All her life Lucy had tried hard to protect Mia from their Mum's illness. With the five-year age gap, she thought that she had done a pretty good job. Mia didn't know the half of things and neither did she really, until Ed came into their lives. Lucy met Ed in May and had introduced him to their parents in July. He had seen her mum in the highest of spirits. Then, as the months passed and she started to set into her yearly decline, Ed tentatively asked one night as they lay in bed together, 'Is your mum like this every winter Lucy? Or is this just a one off?' Lucy had felt an emptiness as she thought back to all the winters that she had wiped from her mind. But then she had realised that she never made the connection that Ed had picked up on so quickly. She was a trainee nurse and *she* never made the connection, see she really hadn't been clever enough to be a vet.

'Yeah now you mention it, I suppose it is in the winter.'

'I think she has SAD syndrome, you know Seasonal Affective Disorder.'

'Yeah I know what it is, I just can't believe I never made the link... what are the symptoms?'

'It comes in many forms, I think your mum has it quite severely though as she clearly gets very depressed.'

So when it started to get too much for their dad the year before last, her parents decided that they would up sticks and live in their Spanish home permanently. It had been Ed's suggestion and it seemed to be going well, although she never admitted it, she missed her parents terribly. But it was what was best for her mum, so she never said anything.

'Right like I said I'll have to speak to Ed,' Lucy reiterated.

'You okay Luce? You don't seem to be yourself.'

'Well Mia, I have something I need to tell you and you're not going to like it.'

Chapter 8

Jessie

It had been nearly four days since Jessie had seen Mia, she was running out of holidays and sick days and, at this rate, Robert would be running out of good will. Her lovely friend had phoned her once and text her twice. Initially she had ignored her. Mia never pried into her business and she truly loved that about her. She had always just accepted that sometimes Jessie was a little wild, somewhat mysterious and very secretive. However, when Mia text and asked if she was still alive, she felt obliged to reply and told her that she would see her in work the following day. For the past three days she had taken the two hour round trip to visit her mum hoping to get some answers. It had been six years since she had last been to see her and on the first day she had only just managed to get through the gates before turning and returning home. She had angrily thrown the flowers in the bin before she headed home on the bus. On the second day she managed to make it through the gates but only sat in silence as she stared at her mum's grave. Then every now and again she would trace the outline of her mum's name and the picture that adorned her headstone. No matter how badly her stepfather had treated her, her mum had always loved her. She knew that she had been a difficult teenager and craved her mum's attention and affection. But her stepfather had been jealous of her relationship with her mum and berated her whenever her mum's back was turned. She had once tried to tell her mum, but everything changed after she had miscarried her brother at seven months. Shortly after that, Jessie made the decision to leave home and it had all but torn them apart. Then when she was diagnosed with breast cancer they fought to reconnect, and in the last six months of her life they became closer than ever. On the third day of her visit she had begun talking to her mum, she knew it was Ben's words that encouraged her to do this. She talked until it got too cold and dark to stay. Remarkably, just like Ben had told her, she felt better for it. It had been well over ten years since she had last said the words out loud and it was like a weight had been lifted from her shoulders. On the bus home she text Ben, keeping it simple:

Thanks, x

He didn't reply until the next day as she was getting ready for work.

Oh, so you're still talking to me! Thanks for what?!

Jessie ignored the latter part as Ben didn't need to know the facts just that she wasn't crazy and she was grateful, so she kept the text breezy, knowing it would stop him from enquiring further.

You fancy catching up soon? x

Sounds good.

*

'Morning!' Jessie realised that she sounded too happy, but what the hell she was much happier than she had been in a long time. Those few days that she had taken off had been just what she had needed.

'The wanderer returns!' said Karl, the very camp and hilariously funny barman who worked in Imagination. 'Where have you been my darling? I've missed you terribly!' he continued.

'Not as much as we've missed you!' Karl had been off with the shingles and had been as sick as a dog.

'I've just been taking some,' she paused searching for some inspiration, 'down time.' Jessie replied giving him the hug he inevitably wanted as he had opened his arms to her.

'Down time!' he laughed, 'What were you doing in this down time? Watching too much American TV? That's what they always used to say in LA.'

Jessie smiled to herself. 'Yeah something like that.' Jessie loved Karl; he was guaranteed to give you a giggle throughout your day. He always gushed about his time in LA, keeping staff entertained with stories about celebs he had befriended. Karl wanted people to think he was vain and carefree, but unfortunately that couldn't be further from the truth. He had adored LA, but when his beloved mother was diagnosed with dementia he returned to the UK. By that stage she didn't even know him anymore, but he wanted to be there till the end. Amongst one of the many reasons he cared so much for his mum was that when he came out of the closet she was on his side from the beginning. He got his sense of humour from his mum; when he informed her of his sexual orientation she said to him, 'To be honest Karl, I'm surprised you didn't come out of the womb with a Gucci clutch!'

Jessie had arrived early hoping to have a catch up with Mia before she started but Mia wasn't in yet, so while she waited Karl made them both a cappuccino. She sat at the bar whilst he restocked and went about his work. Mia turned up 20 minutes later.

'Morning Karl,' she said smiling at him; he nodded in acknowledgement as he had a pen in his mouth and both hands filled with bottles. 'Hey Jess, you enjoy your time off?'

'Yeah thanks Mia, it was good. How've you been?'

'Good.'

'No news?' she said as she could see Mia wracking her brain.

'Only Izzy being a snobby cow.' Mia looked particularly angry when she said this.

'What has *Pretty Woman* been up to now?' Jessie said, sounding less than pleased.

'Come on, I'll tell you all about it while we set up.'

An hour later and Imagination was ready to serve lunch. Friday was one of their busiest afternoons. But ten minutes before they were due to open there was a knock on the closed door.

'God, they're bloody eager today,' Jessie said sounding slightly pissed off at the thought of greeting early customers. 'They best be big tippers!'

'Will you get that Jess, I'm busting for the loo and Karl is out the back having a smoke,' Mia said just before she headed through the toilet door.

'Yeah, no probs.' She was trying to undo the two huge bolts on the back of the door when there was another rap on the door. 'Alright, alright!' she muttered under her breath getting more agitated by the minute. She pulled the huge wooden door open only to be blinded by the sun.

'Hey there Jess,' she knew the voice but couldn't see the face. It was only when he brushed past her and she smelt the grassy smell from him that she knew it was Jake.

'Derby, what are you doing here?' she said, bewildered.

'I'm here to fix the door upstairs, didn't Robert say?'

'I've not been in the last few days, I've not seen him.'

'You been gallivanting have you?'

'To be honest, it's not the word I'd use. Anyway, how come you're fixing the door? That surely isn't in your remit as gardener, is it?'

'Oh Jess there is so much more to me than you know.' He said placing his huge hand on her upper arm. 'You want to show me where this door is and a coffee wouldn't go amiss.' His hand was still on her arm and he squeezed it gently in an encouraging manner.

'Still as cheeky as ever I see! Come on, it's up here.'

Half an hour later and Jake had returned downstairs. They were starting to get busy, but Karl would not let him escape and he was shamelessly flirting with him. Much to her own annoyance Jessie kept sneaking glances at him, she wished she didn't want to, but unfortunately she did. Although, the thing was whenever she looked, he was staring at her. She knew she didn't blush and she was always grateful for that,

124

but inside she could feel herself getting embarrassed. She had to give herself a shake – she was working. So, she decided to ignore him for the next half an hour, which worked pretty well. However, she was still surprised to see him sitting on the sofa as she rounded the corner with a tray full of glasses.

'What are you still doing here?' Jessie asked as she placed the tray onto the bar.

'I needed to ask you something before I left.' He waited for Jessie to speak, but as she didn't he continued, 'You fancy going out tonight? Tomorrow night? Or Sunday night?'

'Wow,' Jessie said laughing, 'all three nights?'

'Nope just the one, but you can't be washing your hair every night!' he said throwing her a cheeky smirk.

'Well,' she began to try and think of excuses and looked away from his gaze to see Karl resting his chin on his hand and his arm on the bar, taking in every word. She eyed him, but Karl was no good at taking hints. 'Karl,' she finally said.

'Don't mind me!' he said jovially, clearly loving the entertainment. 'This is better than watching *The*

Morgans.' She knew that this was his favourite American soap, which made her smile.

'What's so amusing?' asked Jake confused.

'Nothing.' she replied, then remained silent.

'Come on Jess, one date, how bad can it be?' Karl interrupted.

'I think that is a back-handed compliment, but I'll take it thanks Karl... come on Jess!'

'Come oooooon Jess.' encouraged Karl.

'Christ! Okay, okay I feel like I've been backed into a corner! How can I say no?'

'Great! Sunday night? You're not working, right?' She shook her head. 'I'll pick you up from yours at 7.30pm and we'll go for dinner.' Before she had a chance to ask how he knew where she lived, Jake leant over the bar and shook Karl's hand. 'Thanks for the help mate.'

'No problem darling, any time.' Karl smiled broadly at him.

Then Jake leant in and kissed Jessie on the cheek. 'See you on Sunday.'

'Yeah,' she replied as she watched him walk out of the door. She turned to Karl to ask what had just happened and saw him staring at Jake's arse as the door closed behind him.

'Well, if you don't want him come Sunday night, I'll have him!' Karl said.

'I bet you would!' she said picking up Jake's glass from the table. 'Anyway what were you saying to him?'

'Ah just that you're a hard nut to crack, so I gave him a few helpful hints, like your rota for the weekend, where you live and...'

'Bloody hell Karl, you probably gave him my blood type too!

'O positive if I'm not mistaken.'

She threw the bar towel in his face but started to laugh.

'Well, if it is that bad, I'm gonna blame you!'

'I can't wait for the next instalment. I reckon you could take *The Morgans* any day Jess!'

*

Two days later and Jess was pacing the floor of her house. She had phoned Mia and asked her opinion on what to wear.

'No, I've tried that on, I look awful in it.'

'I bet you don't Jess!' Mia said, sounding frustrated with her. 'Anyway what's the big hang up? It's just a date, right?' She knew what Mia was getting at, as this is always what she said about every date. She knew that Mia had already guessed that she fancied the pants off Jake.

'You're right. It's just a date. Black trousers and lace top it is.'

'Have a fab night!' Mia said as she hung up.

Half an hour later she was still walking around in only her underwear. Angry with herself, she pulled out an old black dress that was the 'if all else fails' item of clothing that she assumed everyone owned. As soon as she put it on she felt happy, yet cross with herself for not just doing that in the first place.

'Ding dong,' went her doorbell as she was just applying the finishing touches to her make-up. As she answered the door she was pulling on her heels.

'Hey Jess, you look nice,' said Jake.

'Thanks. You don't scrub up so bad yourself!'

'Cheers for that,' he said, although she wasn't sure if he was taking the Mickey. 'Shall we go?'

'Yeah.' Jess closed the door behind her hoping that tonight wouldn't be a total let down although, if it was, at least she got to look at a pretty face all night.

Three hours into their date and Jessie was surprised at the thought that crossed her mind. She was just putting on a layer of lip-gloss and a spray of perfume, and realised she was actually having fun. How often does that happen? How often did she go out on a date with a guy that she liked and then it turned out they were a nice guy. She could say categorically – never. This is too good to be true. Although, it was only their first date, she felt like it was more than that due to all the time they had spent together at Robert's laughing and having fun. She stared at herself in the mirror and made herself snap back to reality. Leaving the bathroom, she decided she would not be swept up in it all and marched back to the table meaning business.

'I got you the dessert menu, you fancy one?' Jake said smiling his crooked smile at her.

'Unless they do chocolate cake, then no thanks.'

'I remembered you telling me that is all you like and yes there is.'

'Oh, right... okay. I'll get that.' She smiled because he had remembered what she had thought was an insignificant piece of information about her. Seriously, there it was again, that damn thought: he's too good to be true!

As Jake paid the bill and suggested that they go on for a final drink, she found herself agreeing. They walked up the street and she let him grab her hand and hold it. What was the harm she thought, as he gave her hand a little squeeze. As they approached the door of the bar, he held it open for her and she stepped in. She nipped to the toilet and as she came back she could see the back of Jake's head. As she approached him she could see that he was talking to someone. A man that she recognised. She would know those eyes and beard anywhere and it sent a shiver from her head to her toes. A wave of nausea passed over her and she felt dizzy. She had to get out of there. She stumbled over to the door as a caring stranger grabbed her arm. She locked eyes with woman who seemed to smile at her non-judgmentally, so Jessie allowed her to guide her outside. Jess found her voice from somewhere and thanked the woman and told her she would be fine. She turned the corner of the bar and went into the alley and vomited. She had felt so good after talking to her mum, but now she was back to square one. As she began her walk home she wondered if Jake had yet realised that she wasn't coming back. Then she felt her phone vibrate in her bag and fished it out. Jake's name flashed on the screen, she pushed it as far down into her bag as she could manage. Frightened he might have left the pub and come looking for her; she pulled off her heels and began to run. New tears were dripping from her eyes, her vision was blurry. But nothing could take away the image of that man that had been etched on her memory for as long as she could remember.

Chapter 9

Mia

Mia stretched as her alarm went off at 6.00am, she quickly smacked the top of it as she hated the noise, but she would rather that than her annoying phone alarm. It was another new thing she needed to invest in, the list was stacking up and she really needed to start ticking things off it. She had decided to get up that early and go for a run, as she needed to clear her head. She pulled on her running gear, quickly brushed her hair and tied it into a ponytail. Grabbing a quick glass of water, she gave an already awake Dusty a few biscuits. She didn't mind going out on an empty stomach, but thought it unfair to expect her dog to. She bent down and attached the lead to her collar. Unfortunately Dusty seemed to be following Mia's mood and looked forlorn.

'Hey gorgeous girl, turn that frown upside down,' Mia said smiling as she ruffled behind her ears. It was fair to say Dusty was as fickle as dogs come, and immediately started bouncing up and down. 'Come on you!' she pulled at her lead but was so absorbed by her own thoughts she didn't even complete a warm up. As she turned the corner to get to the park she started running faster. Dusty loved it. Her mind had begun to swell with thoughts; she couldn't believe that her sister was actually contemplating having an affair. Lucy a cheat? It just didn't ring true. She was so glad that she had come to speak to her first. Although Mia was her little sister, she valued her opinion. Mia had laid down all the pros and cons of going through with it and the destruction it would potentially cause. The cons far outweighed the pros. Her mind ran over the conversation that had happened the day before.

'Lucy, do you think you're just stuck in a rut?'

'I don't know Mia. I love spending time with Sebastian but the guilt afterwards is almost unbearable and the thing is I only started the dancing lessons with him because Ed was too busy.'

'Just stop them.'

'But I love them so much!' she said agonisingly.

'More than Ed?'

Mia hoped that what she had said had struck a chord with her. As much as Ed could be a bore, he was alright as brother-in-laws go plus it was plain to see that he adored Lucy and the kids. He worked hard and made the best life he possibly could for his family.

Then there was Jessie, although she was her best friend she was really struggling to figure out what was going on with her at the moment. She always let things lie with Jess and never questioned her. She remembered the first time she did ask a question about her past and Jessie nearly bit her head off. It was a good job they had formed a firm friendship by then, as it would have seen most people off. Jess liked to think that she was strong and unshakable but Mia knew that deep down she was vulnerable and scared, but scared of what? She wondered if she would ever know. However, one thing that she did know was that Jessie liked Jake and she could see why, he seemed like a genuine bloke. But then it had been three days since their date and she still hadn't heard from her. She hoped it was because she had been happily in bed with him for the last week, but she knew it was unlikely. She was finding it more and more difficult to lie to Robert, making excuses for Jessie was becoming challenging, but he always seemed to believe Mia and she was feeling guilty about it. Jessie's behaviour was getting more bizarre and she knew that she was really the only person she confided in. She had been round to her flat to see if she was okay. She'd rung the doorbell and saw her blinds twitch. She was definitely there so Mia sat on her doorstep for an hour. Every few minutes she would ring the bell, but it began to rain and she was cross with Jess at this point, she refused to sit and get wet. She was at her wits' end with the whole situation and decided she would wait for Jessie to get in touch with her. This was the second time in as many weeks that she had done her Houdini act and she had enough on her plate to be caught up in another drama.

'Earth to Mia.... oi!' Her thoughts were interrupted and she felt an elbow dig into her upper arm. She looked up to see Alex running beside her. She removed her headphones from her ears; she blushed a little as she really didn't know how long he had been running alongside her.

'Sorry,' she almost whispered and then smiled weakly.

'Hey, are you okay?' he asked sounding concerned, she could see his furrowed brow.

'Yeah,' she replied and carried on moving, but he grabbed her arm and managed to get her to stop. Dusty was wrapping herself around his legs and he was ruffling her fur.

'No you're not,' he said brushing a piece of hair from her eye. It made her shiver and again she was thankful for Izzy.

'Just a lot on with work, my head's all over the show,' she lied, although not about the latter part. She wiped all the stray bits of hair from her face feeling the need to do something with her spare hand.

'Is there anything I can do?' he asked attempting to step out over the barricade that Dusty had seemed to make with the circles of her lead that she had created around Alex. Unfortunately he toppled backwards onto the ground. Mia began to laugh as she pulled him to his feet. 'Hey, I made you smile!' he said sounding pleased with himself.

'Indeed you did,' she said, still flashing her teeth.

'How about I cook for you tonight, I owe you a meal. Plus I'll get Ben to make dessert. He makes a great tiramisu, you'll love it.'

'Are you sure?' She asked.

'Hey, I wouldn't ask if I wasn't.'

'Okay, if you don't mind. That would be great. Thank you.'

'Say 7.00pm?'

'Can we make it 7.30pm? I've got to drop Dusty off at my sister's.'

'You off somewhere? Ben and I could mind her you know.'

'Aww thanks, but it's my niece's birthday tomorrow and her dad is *allergic*,' Mia used her fingers to indicate 'to dogs'. But Evie loves them, so every birthday Dusty goes around and stays over for a couple of days, she loves it and gets spoilt rotten!'

'Lucky Dusty, eh?' he smiled at her and she licked his hand in acknowledgement. 'Right, I'll see you tonight Mia, gotta go or I'll be late for work.' He turned on his heels and sprinted in the direction of home. Mia smiled as she watched him go and looked forward to seeing whether Alex could actually cook.

Mia had dropped Dusty off at Lucy's and managed to get a few chores done before heading up to the boys' flat. She was just putting her washing on the clotheshorse and singing to herself as her buzzer went. She looked at the clock in the spare room and saw the time read 7.30pm. Who could this be? she thought. She had to be at Alex and Ben's now, but she had been determined to put her washing out.

'Hello?' she said inquisitively

'It's me.'

'Ben?'

'Will you let me in? I need to see you.' He sounded strange. She buzzed him in but continued hanging her washing out, leaving the door on the latch. She heard the door close and waited for Ben to speak, but nothing.

'I hope that you've made your *amazing* tiramisu. Alex has bigged it right up!' Mia waited for a cheeky come back, but nothing. 'Ben….' Still, nothing was said. So, she made her way to the living room and took in the sight before her. Ben was leaning against the wall near the front door, with his head hung onto his chest. 'Ben.'

He looked up and fixed his eyes in her direction, the lovely sparkle was all but gone, the one that made his face come to life. He started walking towards Mia but stumbled and had to steady himself on the chair.

'Ben, have you been drinking?' Mia said, realising she sounded anxious. He attempted to move towards her again but this time he had to steady himself at the breakfast bar. He was standing fairly close to her now and as he opened his mouth to speak she got a huge whiff of what she thought smelt like brandy. Instead of speaking though, he inhaled deeply and grabbed hold of Mia's hand. She didn't flinch, but instead she led him to the couch and sat him down. She headed over to the kettle and flicked it on and proceeded to make him a strong black coffee with two sugars in to take the edge off. 'Here,' she said passing him the mug and sitting next to him in the corner of the couch.

'Th...an...ks,' he just about managed to say.

'Drink,' she ordered. They sat in silence as he slowly drank his coffee. Finally Mia spoke, 'What happened Ben?'

'Those fuckers...' he stopped and stared into his mug.

'Who Ben? What's going on?' He turned to face her and she grabbed the mug from his hand to stop the coffee splashing everywhere. She placed it to the left of her on the coaster on the arm of the couch, then turned back to face him. 'Tell me Ben,' she said, grabbing his

139

hand. He was now staring at the floor like it had all the answers. She grabbed the back of his neck and forced his face towards her direction. She looked him in the eye and waited for words to leave his mouth but instead he leant towards her and began kissing her. 'Ben... no.' She said as she tried to push him off. Although his movements were slow the weight of him was too much for her to push off. Instead of moving back he had started to kiss her neck and now his body was angled so he was practically lying on top of her.

'Come on Mia,' he said, continuing to breathe hard into her neck.

'Stop it Ben, please.' She could feel her whole body squirming, trying to find some grip with her feet to give herself more leverage, but they kept slipping off the couch. 'Ben,' she could hear the desperation in her voice and had not even realised that she was crying. She could not believe this was happening. This was not Ben, not lovely Ben. It was like he had zoned out completely and didn't know what he was doing. He continued kissing her hard on the mouth and she felt like she couldn't breathe. The taste of her own salty tears and his brandy saliva was making her nauseous. She tried to pull her

140

mouth away, her arms were trapped under him; the sheer force of his body kept her pinned to the couch. She couldn't believe how strong he was, eventually freeing her hands she frantically started scratching at his neck but it didn't seem to work. Instead he just grabbed both of her hands and pinned them down. He was like a wild animal. He knocked the mug from the arm of the couch and it hit the wooden floor. She felt like everything was happening in slow motion, her mind was whirling and she didn't even hear it smash against the floor. Somehow he managed to grab both her arms and he now had them pinned together so he had a free hand. He worked his way down her body roughly grabbing her breast over her dress, immediately she froze. Her voice had disappeared, even if she wanted to speak, she knew no words would leave her lips. His hand travelled down her body, roughly pawing at her skirt. He pushed it up and ran his fingers along the top of her knickers, before pulling them down. She felt a new tear roll down her cheek. She was unable to stop this powerful man, throbbing with adrenalin.

'Mia are you here?' she heard Alex's voice come from the other side of the front door. Ben quickly covered her mouth with his hand, unbeknown to him that sound would not leave her lips anyway. 'Mia,' he repeated again, pushing open the door that Ben in his drunken state had forgotten had been on the latch. Once Alex was through the door she could see the look of panic in his eyes as he could see the fear in hers. He took in the scene, the broken mug, her tear stained face, Ben's feral eyes and without a moment's hesitation he grabbed Ben and threw him onto the ground.

'Mia, are you okay?' he said speaking quickly and sounding distressed. She began pulling her knickers up and her dress down. She nodded slowly.

'Ben, what the hell were you doing?' Alex said angrily as he stood over Ben who was sat on the floor.

'Fuck off Alex,' Ben said, as he used both of his hands to rub his face.

'You've been drinking,' he said as he turned to look at Mia who was sitting in a ball on the couch, hugging her knees, her whole body was shaking uncontrollably.

'So,' he said sounding despondent.

'You fucking prick Ben. I can't believe you'd do this. Get up! You little shit.' Alex said as he kicked Ben in the leg.

'Mia I'm so sorry,' he walked towards Mia, but she felt herself cower on the couch, so he didn't move any closer to her. 'I said GET UP!' he shouted this at Ben and kicked him harder in the leg. Ben tried to pull himself up by the high stool but fell back. Alex grabbed him from under the arm and pulled him to his feet and pushed him to the door. 'Get out!' he continued in his angry voice. 'Mia, I'll get Ben upstairs and come back down and check on you. Will you be okay?' she nodded at him again still unable to form words, and this time unable to make eye contact. The door closed and they were gone, but the door was still on the latch. Mia pulled herself off the couch and closed the door, putting all three locks on. She slid down the door and began to cry big, hard sobs. She cradled her knees and rested her head on them. She didn't know how long she had been there when she heard Alex at her door calling her name. She ignored him, until eventually he went away. She pulled the throw from the back of the chair and wrapped it around her shoulders. Somehow she felt safer by the door, she really needed Dusty with her and now realised how alone she felt. She cried until the small hours, until she was exhausted. She picked herself up in the blanket and walked to her room where she lay on her bed awake until the sun began to rise.

Chapter 10

Ben

'Ah Christ,' Ben moaned as he pushed his temples together. His head was banging. He pulled himself up using the side of his bed. He was trying to piece together the events of the previous night. He hung his head in shame as he tasted the alcohol on his breath. Fuck, fuck, fuck. He wondered what he had done. He had worked so hard to get dry and now he had ruined it all. He pushed himself off the bed to his feet and headed to get himself a glass of water and some painkillers. As he walked into the kitchen he caught sight of himself in the mirror and saw that he had a black eye and then he realised that his ribs were hurting. He lifted up his shirt that hung scruffily from his suit pants and witnessed the bruising that explained his pain; his ribs were black and blue. He pushed the palm of his hand against the huge, purple bruise. He almost didn't believe it to be real. But the pain that shot through his body made him feel faint. He dashed to the sink to vomit. He wiped his mouth with the back of his hand. He filled a glass of water and drank it quickly. He heard Alex's bedroom door open and he slowly turned round to see him dressed in his running gear.

'Hey,' Ben said sheepishly to Alex. He was met with silence. He walked straight past him to fill up his water bottle. 'Okay, I get it. You're angry.' Alex looked him directly in the eye and he could see the disgust behind them. He turned on his heels and out of the front door.

Ben was woken by the slam of the front door. He rubbed his eyes and tilted his head so that he could see the clock in the kitchen. He realised that he had fallen asleep and had been in his comatose state for the last two hours. He pulled himself into a sitting position and watched as Alex drank a whole pint of water and walked straight into the bathroom, ignoring him again. Christ he knew he had been bad last night. But Alex always forgave him. Maybe he was just fed up, but it had been a long time since he had slipped back into his old ways. Ben sat patiently as he waited for Alex to leave the bathroom. He walked out with a towel wrapped around his waist revealing his other scar that sat on his upper arm.

'Alex. For fuck's sake will you talk to me?' Ben said, as he knew that he was all set to ignore him once again.

'Talk to you. I can't even look at you. You fucking disgust me.'

'I had a drink Alex. It won't happen again. Something really bad happened at work.'

'I don't give a shit. Nothing you can say or do can make up for what you did to Mia last night.'

Ben wracked his mind, what had he done? 'I didn't even see Mia last night.'

'Don't give me that. You tried to have sex with her.'

Ben didn't speak. He couldn't. He put his head in his hands. No, he wouldn't do that, he would never do that.

'No Alex. That's not true. It can't be. I would never hurt Mia.'

'I saw you!' Alex screamed at him, 'If I hadn't walked in God only knows what would have happened.'

'No... no... no,' Ben leapt up from the couch and headed for the kitchen sink and vomited again, this time more violently. An eerie silence moved between them. Ben still couldn't remember what had gone on. He could see Alex searching his face looking for answers and most of all for a sense of realisation.

'You don't remember anything do you?'

'Not a thing. Is Mia okay?'

'I went down to check on her last night, after I kicked the shit out of you. Then before and after my run.' Alex stared at his feet, eventually looking up at him and saying, 'nothing.'

'Jesus, what did I do? Shall I go and see her?'

'Do you really think that's a smart move? She was terrified Ben. You almost raped her. You had her pinned to the couch; she was helpless. You know I should arrest you?'

Ben sat down on the couch and Alex mirrored him. Ben felt like his head had actually exploded, the pain from his hangover was now overtaken by a throbbing guilt, guilt for something he couldn't even remember doing. This guilt was a totally new feeling to him. The guilt of drinking was different. The shame was somehow different. He hurt himself when he drank, but now he had hurt someone he cared very deeply for. The silence between him and Alex felt endless. His best friend was completely disgusted with him. How could this ever be made right? thought Ben. He had ruined everything.

'Do it Alex, arrest me,' Ben finally said. Alex stared at him and put his head into his hands. 'Please Alex.' Ben begged. 'It's the only way that things can be made right.'

'Shut up Ben! I'm not going to arrest you. I want to fuckin' kill you for what you did but I just need a minute to think.' The silence floated between them once again. 'I have never been a dodgy cop Ben and you have put me in the most horrendous situation, but unless Mia presses charges then I may not need to arrest you. Get in the shower, clean yourself up and we'll talk over what you remember.'

An hour later and it was clear that Ben had drunk himself into such an inebriated state that he didn't even know how he got home. Alex had been down to Mia's flat while Ben had been in the shower to try and get some answers. She had just told him to leave her alone. Alex saw this was a step in the right direction though as at least she was speaking and it was not a wall of silence. Ben knew the only way he could fix this was to call his sponsor Alan. He would tell him what to do, the thing he knew, without the phone call, that he had to do. The only thing that would make this right. It was time   to   go   back   to   rehab.

Chapter 11

Lucy

'*Ah choo*! See I told you I was allergic!' Ed said, grabbing another tissue from the box and began loudly blowing his nose.

'It's your hay fever Ed! Don't give me that! Dusty is downstairs and she has been as good as gold!' Lucy said, smiling at Ed and pulling him back down towards the bed. He leant over and gave her a kiss. Lucy was so glad that she had spoken to Mia and had seen sense with the whole ridiculous situation that she found herself in. She had made more of an effort with Ed, she had ignored Sebastian's texts and even stopped going to her beloved dancing lessons. Things were really good with her family and she was happy for it to stay that way. Ed's kiss had led into a ten-minute session of foreplay, ten whole minutes, yes – things were definitely on the up! Unfortunately their passion was unduly stopped by the doorbell ringing.

'Who the hell is this? It's 8.00am!' Ed said, clearly frustrated at having to stop.

'Ignore them, they'll go away,' Lucy said through heavy breathing as she grabbed his face and continued kissing him. She then pulled his crotch into hers. But there it was again, the damn doorbell feeling louder than the last time and now Dusty was barking like a lunatic.

'Jesus, someone is persistent,' Ed said as he rolled onto his back. However, Lucy sat up and straddled him and they continued kissing again. But it rang again and this time it woke Oliver. Lucy wanted to run down the stairs, open the front door, push the intruder off the front step and go back to bed with her husband. But, instead, Ed shouted, 'Alright, alright! I'm coming!' before turning to his wife and saying 'I'll get the door and you see to Ollie?' Ed said in a questioning tone, but Lucy knew it was more of a statement. She jumped out of their bed and looked for something to put on her naked body. She grabbed an old t-shirt that only just covered her bottom and pulled on her knickers. She quickly scurried into Oliver's room in the hope that Evie had not been woken by his screams. The kids sleeping in till eight only happened in Lucy's dreams.

'Hey little man. Where is your dummy?' Lucy said looking in his cot and realising that he had managed to knock it onto the floor. She picked it up and stuck it in her own mouth before picking Ollie out of his cot and sticking it in his. She placed him on his mat and changed his nappy, then put him back on her hip ready to begin the descent down the stairs. It took a while for her to tune into the voice that she could hear from the kitchen, she recognised her husband's immediately and then she realised the other was Sebastian's. *Shit. What was he doing here?* She felt her stomach actually do a somersault. She slid down the wall and sat on the stair she had managed to reach before being stopped in her tracks. Oliver sensed her mood and nuzzled into her neck. She could feel her heart pounding against her son's warm body. The noise of her heart seemed to drown out their voices and she wasn't sure if that was a good thing or not. She needed to focus, she actually shook her head, as if that was even going to help, but ironically it seemed to work.

'I can't believe it!' Ed said sounding surprised. Lucy closed her eyes tight in the hope that when she opened them she would be somewhere else.

'I know, it's a great price, isn't it?' Sebastian said sounding pretty happy with whatever he was talking about. She could hear them heading towards the front door and felt herself freeze. Ed had grabbed the door handle and Sebastian was facing the stairs, his eyes darted up them until they landed on her. She couldn't make eye contact with the man she nearly destroyed her family for, and instead she closed her eyes again and kissed Ollie on the top of his head.

'I'll be in touch Sebastian,' Ed said as he stretched out his hand for him to shake it.

'Great. See you Ed,' the door closed and Lucy then realised that she had been holding her breath. She exhaled slowly.

'Hey sweetie, what are you doing sitting there?' Ed said as his eyes met hers, once she had finally opened them. She felt her face force a smile.

'I didn't want to interrupt, it sounded important.'

'Not at all!' Ed said sounding amazed by what had just happened. 'You want a cuppa?'

'Thanks darling, that would be lovely.' Lucy managed to push herself off the stair and make her way down them.

'That guy is crazy! What is he doing calling in at this hour of the morning? All over our shared fence!' Ed said as he opened the kitchen door and Dusty came bouncing out. He walked passed the dog and he flicked on the kettle, folded his arms and leant back on the work surface. 'Lucy, what's the matter?' Ed said as he walked towards his wife. He took Oliver from her and placed him in his high chair and passed him a rusk from the cupboard.

'Nothing, why?' She gulped, and felt like everyone in her postcode would have been able to hear it. He moved towards her and gently touched her face with one hand and used the back of his other hand to feel her forehead.

'The colour has completely drained from your face, sit down.' He led her towards the closest seat around the table.

'I'm totally fine Ed, don't fuss.' He was so good to her. He really did love her and she did him, even though he was, in the words of Mia, 'Boring Ed' at times.

'Well, you sit there and I'll do breakfast for us all.' She watched as he started pottering around in the kitchen and Dusty came and calmly sat at her feet. She knew that things needed to be sorted out, Sebastian coming to the house gave her a wakeup call she needed. Ignoring him was clearly not going to work. She would have to arrange to meet him.

*

'How dare you come to my house! How dare you! Don't touch me and especially not in front of the kids!' Lucy was furious and pushed Sebastian's hand from the small of her back. She stormed off pushing Oliver in his buggy, towards the swings where Evie had already darted off with Sebastian's two children, Emily and Jack. Dusty was loyally walking next to Lucy on the lead.

'Lucy, you weren't answering any of my calls or texts, what was I supposed to do?'

She immediately stopped and spun around, then started poking him in his chest. 'Not come to my house at 8 o'clock in the morning! That was cruel.' He grabbed hold of her hand and she let him as she knew that the children couldn't see them.

'I'm sorry Lucy, I really am.' She could feel her anger subsiding and she looked up at him. Their eyes locked and for a minute her heart skipped a beat.

'Mummy! Mummy!' Evie's shouting broke the moment. She pulled her hand away from his and turned around to see Evie running towards her. 'Mummy, Emily has fallen off the swing and she's crying.' Before Lucy could speak Sebastian started running towards the swings.

'Come on darling, let's catch up with Sebastian and see if Emily is okay.'

An hour later, the three older children sat and ate ice cream while Oliver slept in his buggy, as Lucy and Sebastian watched from a park bench. Dusty was just to the right of them chasing her tail.

'Can you forgive me Lucy?' she paused and thought that he didn't need her forgiveness. She was partly to blame.

'Of course,' she said as she smiled up at him.

'I booked that hotel we talked about,' he said returning her smile.

'What?'

'Remember in the pub, the last time we went dancing together.' He saw her confused face but continued, 'it's for two weeks on Saturday. The kids are going to their nana's house for the weekend.'

'What?' Lucy repeated sounding more and more bewildered.

'I've booked a hotel, you know...'

'Stop talking,' she interrupted him and he did as he was told, 'Sebastian that night in the pub was the reason I stopped doing this. We saw one of Ed's patients. Why on earth would you think that I would go to a hotel with you?' she said, sounding exasperated.

'Because you agreed to it,' he replied with what he thought was a reasonable answer.

'No, I didn't!' she said, realising that she had raised her voice as Evie was looking over with concern. So Lucy casually waved at her to let her know that she was fine.

'You did, anyway we haven't done anything wrong.'

'The moment we step foot into that hotel we will be doing lots of things wrong.'

'I thought this is what you wanted?' Sebastian said, sounding hurt.

'Well, I don't. I really don't.' She looked at him and his eyes looked sad. 'I'm sorry Sebastian, I truly am.' She stood up to go and he grabbed her hand.

'Lucy, please...' her eyes had begun to fill with tears. She pulled away from his grip and shouted to Evie and Dusty that they were going home. Evie obediently ran to Lucy with Dusty in tow, and grabbed her mother's hand. She looked down at her beautiful daughter who was smiling up at her with a huge ice cream moustache.

'Mummy, why are you crying?'

'I'm not darling, it's just a bit of hay fever.'

'Like Daddy?' she questioned.

'Yeah, just like Daddy.' Lucy let the next few tears of guilt drip from her eyes, while making a deal with herself that these would be the only tears she would allow herself to shed over Sebastian. As, if she didn't nip this in the bud now, there could be many more unnecessary tears ahead.

*

'Hey Mia, it's me and the kids!' Lucy realised that she sounded too happy; in reality she felt like shame had taken over her every day thoughts and 'happy' couldn't have been further from the truth. She also knew that turning up unannounced at her sister's to stay may cause some problems, but she had the perfect excuse with Ed being away at his annual conference.

'Oh hi Lucy, come in.' Phew, thought Lucy, she sounded okay. She pushed open the communal front door and walked through to the back of the building where Mia's front door was situated. She expected to see Mia standing in an open doorway but instead she heard her unlocking her door, it was like Fort Knox.

'Aunty MiMi!' Evie said as soon as she saw Mia. She lifted her niece up and embraced her as if she had only just met her for the first time. Dusty was now bouncing around very excitedly seeing Mia for the first time in days. Popping Evie onto the floor Mia lent down and rubbed Dusty's ears. Dusty then proceeded to lick Mia's face, which totally grossed Lucy out. She loved that dog and wished that Ed would cave and let them have one of their own. He was a doctor; he could self-prescribe as many antihistamines as he needed.

'It's so good to see you Lucy,' Mia said, standing up and embracing her sister in a tight hug.

'You alright Mia? I can't breathe!' Lucy half joked as she pulled away from her sister.

'Oh... Sorry.'

'What's up?' Lucy asked Mia.

'Nothing. Nothing at all.' But Lucy knew her sister much better than that. However, she decided now was not the time to go digging. The kids were running amok in her sister's flat and Dusty had just weed all over the floor, much to Evie's delight.

Three hours later, the kids were finally settled and asleep. Much to Lucy's surprise, Mia had been overjoyed at the prospect of them all staying. She knew that it would be a squash as Mia's new place was, although lovely and cosy, really small. Mia had insisted that Evie sleep in her double bed with her, which her aunt-obsessed daughter couldn't have been more excited about, while she slept on the camp bed in the spare room with Ollie in the travel cot. They sat and guzzled wine. Lucy loved it when they got drunk together, but she knew that a hangover with her two gorgeous children was not an option so she had drunk very slowly. Mia was not taking things quite as slowly and had practically drank both bottles to herself, not that she had realised. As Mia drained the last of the second bottle, Lucy took it off her and placed the empty bottle on her breakfast bar, just as Mia's front door nearly rattled off its hinges. Mia's front door was situated right near the downstairs fire exit and whenever someone came in through that door it made her sister's door shudder. Lucy knew this was something that Mia had become very used to and couldn't understand why Mia nearly jumped out of her skin, especially as she had downed at least a bottle and a half of wine.

'What's got into you? You're a bag of nerves!' She saw her sister's shoulders tense up. But she turned around with a huge smile.

'It's just that...' Lucy waited patiently, 'that... I've probably just had one too many wines!'

'I did notice you had drunk far more than me.'

'That's just because you're becoming a light weight!'

'Yeah right! I could drink you under the table anytime!'

'Is that a bet?' Mia asked finally lighting up, it had taken her all night to seem like herself.

'Yep it is! When Ed's back in town then we are going out missy and I'll win that bet!'

'You're on!' Mia said marching over to her and shaking her hand.

An hour later and Mia was asleep on her lap, they had put some girly movie on. She hadn't really cared when Mia had reeled them off. She was itching to tell her about what happened with Sebastian at the park, but thought it was unfair to do so as she had landed on her sister totally unannounced. Tomorrow, she resolved, she would tell her tomorrow.

Lucy had been woken early the next morning but not by her lovely son. For once she was not woken by his screams but by the sun beating through the curtains and as she opened her eyes, Ollie was sucking on his dummy and staring at her. She got up, made him a bottle, gave him some breakfast and flicked on a kids channel on Mia's TV. An hour later and her sister's doorbell was ringing. She jumped up as she did not want to wake Mia, or Evie. A tall blonde stranger faced her at the door. She

163

knew immediately by his scar though that it was Alex, Mia's neighbour.

'Oh, hi.' Alex's smile seemed to fade when he saw Lucy at the door and not Mia.

'Hi there.'

'I'm Alex, Mia's neighbour.'

'Hi Alex, I'm Lucy, Mia's sister.'

'Oh hi!' he repeated but this time in a much more familiar tone. 'Mia has told us all about you.' He said showing the most amazing set of teeth. 'Then that little guy must be Oliver?' Alex said pointing down at Ollie who was now pawing at Lucy's legs. She bent down and picked him up.

'Yeah, this is Ollie, say hello Ollie.' As they both waited patiently, he initially eyed Alex up and then casually turned his head to what was clearly more exciting, *In The Night Garden*. 'And he's usually so chatty!' they both laughed at Lucy's sarcasm. 'Would you like to come in?' Lucy asked, hoping that he would say yes. She was in dire need of some adult company and even with that scar he was still quite the looker.

'No, it's fine honestly,' he said smiling. But there, she saw that look again, he was hiding something too.

Maybe he was seeing Mia, she wondered. But why would she keep that a secret? Or did he have a girlfriend?

'Are you sure?'

'Yeah, yeah, I'm just off for a run actually and was seeing if Mia wanted to come.'

She took in his running gear.

'Oh right, I'll pass that message on for you.' She placed Ollie on the floor as he had wriggled out of her arms and made a bid for freedom. 'Anything else?'

'Nope, just that. I should go. It was good to meet you Lucy.'

'You too Alex, enjoy the run.'

An hour and a half later and Mia was still not out of bed. Evie had long been up and tormenting Ollie for the last 25 minutes.

'No Evie, that is enough!' Evie had grabbed a toy from her little brother and it had made the sitting Ollie jerk backwards and bang his head on Mia's wooden floor. He let out a real howl of pain and she picked him up as huge tears rolled from his eyes.

'Evie! Look what you have done now!'

'I'm sorry mummy.' And with that Evie burst into tears. It was like a pantomime.

'Wow wow, what's going on here?' Mia finally appeared from her bedroom.

'It has all just got a bit out of hand, will you pick her up?' Lucy said, feeling flustered and nodding her head in the direction of Evie.

'Say sorry Evie.'

Lucy was greeted with a very stubborn frown, but eventually the words 'Sorry Ollie,' followed.

'Good girl. Now give him a kiss and no snatching please. Evie I have told you about that before.'

With all the commotion that had taken place that morning Lucy had totally forgotten to tell Mia that Alex had called. She would text her when she got home she thought. She looked in her rear-view mirror at her two precious children sleeping in the back. She couldn't believe the rest of Ed's conference had been cancelled due to the fact that key speaker had been taken ill. A room full of doctors – couldn't one of them have sorted him out, she thought. She hadn't wanted to leave Mia's early, but what could be her excuse, "Sorry love, I need to talk to my sister about the affair I nearly had" She looked out into the darkness and concentrated hard on the narrow windy lane ahead. She thought about her lovely sister, what was she hiding from her? There was something and she was damn well going to get to the bottom of it. But first she needed to sort out a bigger mess – the one she knew all about – her own disastrous life.

Chapter 12

Jessie

Jessie's feet were sore, her throat ached and her eyes stung. As she paced the floor for what felt like the five hundredth time, she caught sight of herself in the mirror. Good God she looked like she'd been dug up. She licked her finger and attempted to wipe the smudge of mascara from under her eyes. Staring at her swollen eyelids she closed them, letting the heaviness force them shut. She held them tight shut until the stinging stopped and tears rolled down her cheeks. Using the back of her hand, she wiped them away and slowly opened her eyes taking in how bloodshot they were. Suddenly a dizzy spell came over her and she had to steady herself on the fireplace, taking another look at herself in the huge ornate mirror. Bizarrely, she was thankful for her phone vibrating on the couch. It had been Jake calling her every 15 minutes or so ever since she walked out, which was only interspersed with texts from him asking if she was okay. She hadn't been able to bear it, but then seeing herself in the mirror seemed just as bad right now. She couldn't speak to him. He could never know. She grabbed the bottle of whiskey that she had started to drink upon entering her flat that night. Swigging from the bottle, she allowed her body to shudder from head to toe and lay on the couch. Vibrating again, she decided to turn her phone off and threw it onto the floor, wanting and needing only silence.

Jessie immediately regretted not closing her bedroom curtains the previous night. Although she surprised herself that she had actually found her way to her bed at all. Pulling the duvet over her head, she rolled away from the glaring light. As she rolled over to the other side of the bed, her shoulder smacked the whiskey bottle and the fumes hit her. She felt her stomach somersault and she leapt from her bed and into the bathroom. Her throat felt raw and painful, but she felt better for getting it all out of her system. Grabbing a hair tie from the sink she pulled her hair back into a loose ponytail, washed her face and brushed her teeth. Heading to the kitchen she knew it was pointless pulling open the kitchen cupboards, unless the food fairy had left her a parcel the night before. She was not disappointed when she saw a lonely tin of green beans and a bottle of tomato ketchup. Her mind wandered as she thought why the hell she had a tin of green beans in her cupboard. She was not hungry, but she did need a cup of coffee. Pushing the cupboard door closed, she leant back onto the work surface and her eyes shifted to the floor where a jar of empty coffee lay next to the recycling bin.

'Fuck,' she said under her breath, 'what were the chances.'

Heading to her bedroom she pulled off her dress from the previous night and pulled on leggings and a hoodie to head to the shop, not before searching through her junk drawer, pushing the batteries and candles to the side and taking out all of the instruction manuals she had accumulated over the years. There at the back of the drawer were the painkillers that she so desperately needed. Throwing two into her mouth, she swallowed them down. Mia admired this skill of Jessie's; swallowing tablets minus the water, Mia had to chew them into a disgusting paste. Opening the front door, the first thing that hit her was the fresh air, which for a split second made her feel slightly better. However, seeing Jake sitting at her feet meant the nausea swept over her again.

'What are you doing here?' Flustered, Jessie rubbed her face. She felt so self-conscious about her make up free face and her bed head hair.

'I was worried about you,' he said, as he stood up and ran his fingers through his hair. Finally looking up, he held her gaze. She felt her face flush and her eyes shot to the ground.

'I'm fine,' she snapped. Realising she sounded aggressive; she put her hands in the pockets of her hoodie. She knew she looked defensive, but that's how she felt.

'You're not, I can see you've been crying.' His tone was so gentle and his movements mirrored this as he stepped closer to her to touch her arm, immediately she moved backwards and realised she had nowhere to go as she felt her heel hit the front door. Brushing past him, she marched ahead for fear that she would say something she may regret.

'Jessie, wait,' he called after her. 'Did I say something to upset you? We were having such a good time.' He followed her, and she kept on walking. 'Please Jess, talk to me.'

She stopped and heard his footsteps hesitate, and then stop.

'I can't Jake, I just can't do this.' He grabbed her arm and spun her round to see tears rolling down her face.

'Jessie, I might be able to help you.'

'No, Jake no one can.' She wriggled free from his grasp and turned on her heels to make the short walk back home. Their chemistry was undeniable and she so desperately wanted to turn and look at his lovely face one more time. But she stopped herself as she knew that she would be met with a look of bewilderment. Could she ever be honest with him or with anyone? She wondered.

'Hey darling! How was the big date?' Karl said, as Jessie walked into Imagination. Walking straight past him and towards the kitchen, she heard him scream in her direction. 'Jessie! I asked you how your date was!' but the volume of his voice was muffled as the kitchen door swung shut behind her. Once in the staffroom, she closed the door behind her without turning on the light. Inhaling deeply, slowly and holding onto the wall she finally turned on the light. She knew how close she was to losing her job and knew that she had to give herself a shake. Robert had phoned her the day before and given her the last warning he was willing to give her. Mia could no longer cover for her; she knew it was getting ridiculous. Throwing her bag and coat into the corner of the room, she pulled off the T-shirt she was wearing and grabbed a work shirt from the eight that were hung up in a row. Throwing her crumpled T-shirt onto her belongings on the floor, she slid on the shirt and quickly fastened up the buttons and headed out into the kitchen.

'Hey Jessie,' she jumped, she hadn't heard him come onto the kitchen as the door had been closed.

'Hi Andrew, how you doing?' she said and flashed a weak smile at Imagination's head chef. He was a dick most of the time, but she knew being a head chef was a stressful position. Yet, his behaviour to most of the staff was outrageous. However, as totally unacceptable as his behaviour was, Robert let him away with murder because he was so brilliant at his job.

'Yeah fine... fine.' He turned away from her quickly, but she still caught sight of the shiner on his left eye. A gambler, that's what he was. Probably someone collecting a debt. It wasn't unusual for Andrew. See, everyone had their problems, she thought. She didn't have the desire or inclination to even attempt to have a conversation with him; she inhaled deeply before entering the restaurant again, prepared for the grilling she was inevitably going to get from Karl.

'I don't believe it for a minute Jessica Cole,' Karl said as he took a huge slurp from his mug of black coffee.

'Believe it Karl, he's just not my type,' Jessie lied but still managed to maintain his gaze.

'Mmmm, I honestly don't know if you're a brilliant liar or you are shockingly telling me the truth?' Shrugging her shoulders she smirked at Karl, even though inside her heart ached just a little bit at what could have been.

'You know me Karl... NEXT!'

'But he's so lovely, handsome – massive hands and feet and well…'

'No Karl, don't even go there!'

'Well, if you're not gonna picture it, then I'll just have to!'

'Go for it, you little perv!' Jessie said throwing the tea towel at his face. Jake had been put into a little box in the back of her head. Her head was full of boxes that had been put there never to be talked about with anyone. Karl was walking a thin line with a large key and threatening to open that box. Jessie was strong though and she knew that she was done with Jake. No question, she had to be.

'Did Karl mention that Mia has taken two weeks off?' Robert said as he sat in his office sorting out changes to the following week's rota and now she knew why.

'What? No.' Realising she sounded confused, but deep down it was embarrassment that had won this emotional war. Why had Mia not told her that she was taking two weeks off work?

'She called me yesterday, said her mum's not great and she's going to Spain for a week. So, you'll have to cover for her Jess. Okay?' She knew that he wasn't asking her, he was telling her.

'Of course, that's not a problem.' She knew this was probably a good idea as she needed to be kept busy. However, what she needed more than anything was to see Mia. The kindest and loveliest friend she had ever had and she hadn't been there to support her. There was something wrong with Mia, taking two weeks off like this was not like her. Thanking Robert for the new rota and walking off, she decided to go and see her friend the following day. She'd get to the bottom of what was going on.

Chapter 13

Mia

Exhaling deeply, Mia slowly closed her laptop that sat on her huge desk. This was her third attempt at writing, but she was struggling to focus. Staring at the wall yet again, it was only the chill that ran down her spine that snapped her back to reality. Her publisher needed the next instalment imminently, and she was determined to make her second book as successful as her first. *Forgotten*, sat on her desk like a trophy, she pulled it over towards her and rubbed her hand across the front. She looked at the title. The irony of the title felt like a dagger in the heart of her writing ability. Not only had she forgotten how to write but she had forgotten how to feel too. There was a vast emptiness inside her that she couldn't explain, a loss, like grief. Resting her head in her hands she knew that she couldn't avoid it any longer. Opening her laptop she began to write an email to her publisher, lying yet again about her non-existent trip to Spain. Telling Claudia that her mother was ill, but upon her return she would have the next five chapters finished. She closed the laptop and walked to the kitchen to make herself a coffee. Her phone beeped in her back pocket and she pulled it out to see Alex's name flash onto the screen.

How you doing today?

Knowing what it would say, she smiled as she read his daily text. Initially she had ignored him, his constant knocking at the door, his persistent calling and his tireless texting. However, when he slid a note under the door telling her that Ben had gone back to rehab, she had decided to acknowledge him, and that was two days after it happened. Yet, a week on and she still had not left the flat, she knew that she had to face the fear and do it anyway. Dusty was driving her up the wall, but at least she had a little bit of patio space that she could run around in.

Okay thanks.

Mia replied with her usual response, not giving too much away but allowing him to know that she was at least not hanging from her shower rail.

Have you been out today?

Alex always replied with the same response. She knew she had to leave the flat and this is why he kept asking. He continued.

Day off today. Just got back from my run and got us two drinks from Costa. Can I tempt you up? Or can I come down? I could take Dusty out for a walk too?

She had put him off so many times when he asked. She was frightened of becoming a recluse. Hesitantly, she sent a text that invited him to her flat. She quickly put on the bare bones of her makeup and ran a brush through her hair. She looked at herself in the mirror and put on some lip balm.

Ten minutes later and there was a knock at the door, which made her jump even though she had been expecting it. Gingerly she walked towards it and peered through the peephole. She could she Alex's huge frame through the door. He was pulling his jumper down over his belted trousers with his free hand. He knocked again and she began to take the locks from the door, leaving the chain until the last, and then carefully pulled the door towards her.

'Hey Mia,' Alex said, locking eyes with her. Frightened to hold his gaze, her eyes darted to the floor.

'Come in,' she said weakly. Dusty moved in Alex's direction and calmly brushed against his legs. She felt guilty that she had made Dusty lose her sparkle too.

'Thanks.' She saw Alex survey the room and he glanced at the sofa almost with a look of disgust. 'So I got you a hot chocolate, with cream and marshmallows. Although I think it's probably cold by now. Stick it in the microwave or in a pan, but then the marshmallows may go funny and that would taste disgusting, well I think it would?' He stopped and looked at her. 'What are you smiling at?'

Realising that she was, her smile broke into a bigger one, it felt good. 'You're waffling Alex, really badly too.'

'Sorry Mia. I'm not really sure what to say. I thought about it loads upstairs. I was expecting you to say not to bother coming in like you normally do and when you said that I could come down, I thought what am I gonna say? Will she want to talk about it?'

'You're waffling again Alex!' he smiled this time. She took a swig of the hot chocolate and put it in the microwave, but picking off the marshmallows before she did so. There was a long silence between them, one which they both allowed. She knew this would heal, their friendship was worth rescuing. She turned and looked at him and she realised that he hadn't taken his eyes off her for the whole of the silence. He smiled at her and she returned it. Yes, this friendship was worth fighting for.

An hour later and they had talked about everything besides Ben. It was the huge elephant in the room. She didn't want to mention him and she wondered if he would.

'It's quiet up there on my own,' she knew that this was his way in.

'Not even with Izzy keeping you company?'

'The thing with Izzy is that… it's well… we are…'

'Engaged?' Mia didn't know where he was going with this, but she thought she'd try and help him along as he was very hesitant.

'Fuck no!' Alex said, sounding totally bewildered by her statement.

'Oh sorry,' Mia whispered.

'Oh God no, I'm sorry. Sorry Mia,' he reiterated, he must have realised that the volume of his voice had frightened her. 'We split up.'

'Really?' Mia's heart stopped for a second. How long had she wanted Alex to actually say those words? Wishing she could feel something but the hollowness she had felt, was like a tidal wave drowning her and she felt like she was being pulled under. 'Since when?'

'It's not important. What is important is that you are okay Mia. What Ben did was unacceptable and he…' his words trailed off due to her intercom buzzing which made her in turn almost jump from her seat. She moved towards the prolonged buzz, someone was eager.

'Hello,' she said hesitantly. 'Come on in.'

'You're shaking Mia. Who was it?' Alex asked, concerned.

She paused for what felt like a long time before she finally said, 'Jessie.'

Alex moved towards the door to let Jessie in, 'Does she know?'

'Do I know what?' Jessie asked inquisitively.

It had been the most excruciating hour for Mia. She had managed to deviate the conversation about Ben, much to her relief. Even when Jessie was digging and she was digging deep. She had commented on the fact that Mia had lost weight. Mia knew she had because she had barely been able to eat in the last few days. She knew one thing though. She had partly enjoyed having her friends around and it was time to get on with her life. Ben had frightened her, he had been her friend and she didn't know if she could ever forgive him or trust him again. However, for now as she knew while Ben was in rehab, she felt safe. It was time to try and get her life back on track.

*

Trembling as he wiped the sweat from his brow. He knew he could no longer pretend to be that man. The blood dripped from his elbow as he tossed the knife into the water. Without looking back, he turned and disappeared into the shadows.

Mia closed her laptop and broke into a smile. She had done it. Breathing in slowly, she pulled her legs into her body and then stretched them out onto the desk. Tilting her head back into the crook of the chair, she did a huge stretch. The last five chapters she had written had been somewhat cathartic. She knew what she had to do now, she pulled on her boots and grabbed her keys and headed up to the top floor.

'Mia?' Alex said, shocked. She hovered by the door waiting to be asked in. 'Come in, come in.' Finding his manners, Alex moved aside and gestured towards his couch.

'Thanks.'

'You want coffee Mia?' Alex said, as he automatically walked into the kitchen and flicked the kettle on.

'Please,' she smiled at him and she saw his shoulders drop.

'You look well Mia,' he paused and then continued, 'different.'

'Thanks Alex. I wanted to talk to you and clear the air.' He poured them a hot drink each and passed Mia hers as he sat opposite her on the couch.

'Okay.' He looked anxious and she knew why.

'I want to talk about Ben...' she paused as she said his name, making Alex think she wanted him to speak.

'He's a good guy Mia, really he is. He —'

Mia cut him off. 'Let me finish Alex, please. I need to say what I came here to say.' He nodded as she continued. 'It's been nearly two weeks since Ben did what he did and I've told nobody. I don't know why I haven't. Maybe because deep down I do know that Ben is a good guy.' Alex looked at her with relief in his eyes. 'I've spent the last week thinking of pretty much nothing else. I have cried every day, not eaten properly and despised Ben for what he did. But then I realised that I don't know *that Ben* who attacked me that night. He was literally a different person, not Ben my lovely friend, but Ben the alcoholic. So, I've come to the conclusion

185

that if I go to the police, I won't really achieve anything.' She looked at Alex, who looked like he was going to speak, but he obviously stopped himself. 'I have to forgive him for what he did because if I don't, then I become a bitter person. I don't hold grudges, that's not who I am. ' Mia stopped as she drank from her mug of coffee, the silence between them was palpable. 'But I'll never forget it Alex.' She locked eyes with him and he clearly understood it was his turn to speak.

'Thank you Mia. Thank you for not going to the police.' He put his head in his hands.

Unaware that all this time her chest had felt tight, it was only after she finished speaking that she realised that the tightness had let go of its grip. She knew it wouldn't be an easy journey, trying to find her old self again and no doubt there would be more tears and perhaps some anger along the way. However, she had finally made the first step to getting some control back over her life and for that she felt proud.

Chapter 14

Ben

Dear Mia,

I know that I am probably the last person you expected, or more importantly wanted to, hear from, but this is all part of the healing process not just for me but I hope in some way for you too.

I've been away for twelve weeks now and it has given me lots of time to think, but I only wish I knew where to begin. Of course, it should be with an apology. I am truly sorry for what I did to you Mia. I can never take it back and I am so ashamed of my behaviour. There are no excuses for what I did, but I wanted to explain. So that you know what happened on that day and why I became so out of control.

I had been to my regular AA meeting the day before it happened. Nothing had changed and I spoke to all the usual people and left feeling positive. However, the next day at work things did change. I had bagged this big contract and business was doing so well, you know the Hunt contract, the one I told you about? I went to meet with the new clients that day and there in the office was one of the addicts from my AA meetings. Clearly neither of us had expected to see the other and I think the shock was written across both of our faces. The next hour was so awkward and I didn't actually know what to say, I was hesitant over my words and made myself look like a fool. They took me for lunch and later that afternoon upon returning, the company told me that they no longer required my services. I knew it was because my AA guy had told them something. He had totally blown the circle of trust that is essential in our meetings. The thing that got to me the most was that he is also an addict. Who was he to judge? I was shown out of the meeting and waited for him outside. He was terrified when he saw me and his explanation was that I wasn't right for the job. But I could see the truth in his eyes. An addict had destroyed another addict, I couldn't believe his disloyalty. I was furious and thought what was the point? So I headed straight to the nearest pub and drank brandy until I could no longer see straight. Some things I can remember from that night and others I can't. This is how I was for years Mia – I was a drunken mess. I just can't believe I let myself down so badly again; I had been dry for months. On that night I do remember making a conscious decision to come to your flat and not ours, as I knew that Alex would kill me. However, everything after that is hazy. I hope you do not think this is an excuse Mia. I truly do not remember a thing. Only because Alex told me, do I know the whole story. I am so sorry Mia, I really am.

In the last twelve weeks I have been to many therapy sessions and when I leave tomorrow I plan to go back to my meetings more regularly. I've talked lots about my childhood, but I realise now that I have to stop blaming my past for my future mistakes. I need to start taking responsibility for my own actions and decisions. Mia if you need to go to the police (Alex told me you're not), but if to make this okay for you, then you must. It's your prerogative. You owe me nothing and you need to be able to move on with your life. That is why I want you to know that I will not be returning to our apartments. Alex tells me how well you're doing and I don't want to jeopardise that. I'm moving away Mia and I'll build my life somewhere else. My sister has invited me to New Zealand. She's found a local AA meeting for me to attend pretty much as soon as I arrive. Plus I'll finally get to meet my nephew, which I'm really looking forward to.

I am so sorry and I wish you the best of luck in the future Mia, you deserve it. You're such a wonderful girl.

Take care,

Ben.

Chapter 15

Lucy

Lucy paced the floor, she knew that she had to go on this night out. Emma, Lucy's oldest friend, had been harping on for weeks that she couldn't remember the last time that the four of them had been out together. It was about time they all put on their glad rags and made the effort to be human for the evening. Emma, was the cool, calm and collected one, well, she was single, childless and up for just about anything but missed her friends, who sometimes forgot that they were more than just mums.

Clare, the group's self-appointed organiser, was regimental about everything and this date had been in everyone's diary for months. There was no backing out now. Clare was one of those well-meaning but annoying mums who thought that she had the answer to everything. Sophie, on the other hand, couldn't be more different. She was trying to juggle four kids and seemed to be falling apart at the seams.

Deep down, Lucy had to admit she was half looking forward to getting out and getting some head space. Evie had been sick for the last week and she had seen more vomit in the last five days than she believed she would ever see again in her whole life.

'Wowser Ollie, doesn't Mummy look nice?' Ed turned to Ollie who couldn't take his eyes off of the sequins on Lucy's dress, which were catching the light. Lucy smiled at her husband as she slipped on her shoes and kissed him on the lips. Walking to the bathroom she cleaned her teeth and ran the brush through her hair again. 'What time are you meeting the girls?'

'Five o'clock,' she shouted from the en-suite.

'That's early!' Ed sounded surprised, as surprised as she had been upon hearing the time. But Sergeant Major Clare and her two year-old son, Thomas had their routine, so screw everyone else. It was a five o'clock start or no start at all!

'I don't understand why you're not having a drink? Get a taxi,' Ed encouraged her.

'I told you I can't. What if Evie's sick again and I have to be firing on all cylinders tomorrow?'

'I have the late surgery tomorrow. I can go in later and anyway she's totally fine.'

'I haven't ordered a taxi now,' she said as she applied the delicate pink lipstick onto her full lips. 'But thanks darling. I won't be too late. I'll see you tonight.' She leant in and gave Ollie and her husband a combined hug as she did not wish to reapply her lipstick after another kiss. 'Evie?' Lucy shouted as she made her way down the stairs. 'Mummy's going now.' Why had she just spoken about herself in the third person? She hated it when people did that, so corrected herself, 'I'm going now darling. See you later.' She walked in to the living room to see her daughter asleep on the couch. Bless her she thought, she was worn out. Her cheeks were flushed with the heat so Lucy pulled the snuggle blanket from her legs, and brushed her cheek with the back of her hand before she left the room.

'So Lucy, how's Evie feeling?' Sophie asked as she knocked back her second glass of wine in as many minutes. She looked around the table at Emma and Clare to see their look of concern too.

'Yeah... she's... erm... getting better.' Lucy took in the sight before her. Sophie was her friend from toddler group; her four kids between the ages of 18 months and 8 years were draining the life out of her. She looked exhausted despite the amount of makeup she had trowelled on.

'Must be handy your hubby being a doctor,' Emma said, giving Lucy a look that seemed to mirror her thoughts and this was followed by a subtle wink.

'Yeah, it totally is.' Almost forgetting that she was a nurse too but realised that was why she had winked. She had a Doctor for a husband; apparently it was like winning a gold medal, well in her circle of friends. Except Emma, who didn't give two hoots.

'Should we move on? It's dead in here,' Sophie asked.

'Yeah let's.' Lucy thought that maybe dinner would be good. It may make Sophie, the runaway train, slow her drinking down a bit.

Causally walking down the street, Lucy inhaled the night air and looked up to see one bright star shining in the sky.

'You okay Luce? You seem in a world of your own tonight,' Emma said as she smiled at her and put her arm through Lucy's and held her gaze.

'Just tired Em,' she had known Emma since high school and, besides Mia, she was her best friend. They went way back. She wanted to tell her that her world had become a little messy and she wasn't really sure what to do about it. Then she considered that discussing it wouldn't achieve anything. It was over before it had begun with Sebastian. After their confrontation in the park he had put the house up for sale and as good as done a moonlight flit with his children. No explanation, he just left and she had not heard from him for months now. She realised it had been a blessing in disguise. A clean break had been just what they needed. So Emma was asking her a question that she was not 100% sure how to answer. However, she knew nothing good could come from even uttering the words and anyway, the door was now closed on that chapter of her life. She didn't want to share the fact she nearly became that person who betrays their family.

'I know you.' She paused, waiting for Lucy's acknowledgment. 'Are you sure?'

'Totally,' she threw Emma a wink and knew that would suffice for now.

'Jesus girls, will you give me a hand with this light weight?' Clare, the sensible one of the group, half mouthed and half whispered in their direction. Lucy and Emma broke out into a quicker pace to catch her up. Clare stopped to fix her shoe at a bus stop when all of a sudden Sophie burst into tears.

'What's the matter Soph?' Emma said, putting her arm around Sophie as she plonked herself onto the bus stop seat and cupped her head in her hands. Clare looked up from fixing her shoe totally bemused, in fact, they all were.

'Sophie, what's the matter?' Clare said repeating Emma's question.

It felt like an age as they waited for her to reply. A number of people had walked past the bus stop, clearly also wanting to know what was going on. Lucy had become distracted by the very attractive man behind Emma. He had no shirt on and his jeans hung so low you could see those muscles that sat just above the waistband, Lucy always wondered what their purpose was, besides looking very sexy indeed. She was just thinking if she pulled his pants down then what might be there...

'Didn't you Luce?' Emma was looking right her, she however was still looking at the half naked man behind her. Even though it was just a large billboard of a man promoting some aftershave or other, she was still having her own little fantasy.

'Erm...'

'You felt overwhelmed when you had Ollie? And Sophie has four, she must be at her wits' end. Plus it's okay to cave Sophie, you're not Wonder Woman!'

'Totally Soph, kids just take over your life...' Lucy inhaled deeply and continued before Clare could interject, 'and yes of course for the better, but sometimes you do want to give them back but then you can't ever remember your life without them.'

Sophie's huge sobs had started to subside.

'I feel like I'm drowning.'

Hence the bucket of wine she had already attempted to drown herself in, Lucy thought.

'It's okay to ask for help,' Lucy said, digging in her bag for a tissue. She found one that looked unused but very crumpled. Handing it to Sophie, she attempted to clean up the makeup smudges from under her eyes. Emma took it from her and wet it with her mouth and started wiping the huge mascara streaks from her face. Emma was the only one of them who wasn't a mother and although she always said children were not in her plans, Lucy thought that she'd make a great parent.

'Come on, let's go and fill our boots with some food,' said Clare.

'I can't like this!' Sophie said astounded.

'Yes you can, I've as good as fixed you!' Emma looked at Lucy and Clare in the hope they'd back up her lie, which they did.

'A bit of lippy and you'll be fine!'

'I'm not sure girls.'

'Come on you, we need a night out!' Clare said, linking Sophie.

They all began walking towards the little Italian on the corner when Lucy felt something crack the side of her head. Initially she wasn't sure if she was hurt. Then she felt her hairline, which felt wet. She got a whiff before she saw the egg yolk slime on her hand. Then another egg landed right in front of her feet and splattered onto her bare legs. Sophie and Clare turned around and burst into a fit of hysterical laughter. Wanting to burst into tears, she decided that she needed to do what Emma had also started to do now and laugh out loud.

'Little bastards!' she screamed at the car that had returned for a look at their eggy masterpiece. They we're beeping like lunatics.

'Come on you,' Emma grabbed, Lucy noted, her clean arm and escorted her to the Italian and the toilets to clean up.

Fifteen minutes later and nearly another hair wash and leg scrub and she was almost as good as new. Emma always carried her perfume with her, so she managed to make the egg smell, somewhat more flowery than before.

After a very lovely evening of drinking – oh yes, she had decided on a drink after the debacle of the evening – eating and lots of laughter (and ensuring that Sophie was okay) they headed home in a taxi. Lucy realised how lucky she was to have such wonderful friends; they were a mismatched bunch who she had managed to coax into one little friendship group. Their memories as a foursome were all pretty new, but this night had definitely left its eggy mark. She just hoped her head wouldn't be too scrambled in the morning!

*

Lucy woke up with a start but she couldn't piece together her dream and felt like she couldn't breathe. She realised as she looked back and saw the time on her alarm clock it was because she hadn't heard her kids. She swung around in a panic and saw the note Ed had left on his pillow for her.

Lucy, thought you might appreciate the lie in and the peace that would follow – the kids are with my folks. I said you'd pick them up at 3.00pm. Looks like you had fun last night! Love Ed x

She looked back again at the clock and realised that it was only 10.00am. She smiled to herself, oh she would enjoy the peace. Then only after further sleep would she worry about having to see Ed's obnoxious parents.

Fate had intervened when Mia had called her and, being the brilliant sister that she was, she went and picked Lucy's car up from where she had abandoned it the previous evening as it was her day off. When she had persuaded Lucy to go and get the kids with her, she thought she was onto a winner, and then when she actually went in and got the kids from the dreaded in laws she knew someone was smiling down on her. She had waved over enthusiastically at Cynthia who seemed to be smiling back through gritted teeth.

'Mummy!' her daughter shouted. As she saw Evie bound towards her with excitement she felt the guilt creep in – she felt like a bad mother for going out and getting drunk. Then she reminded herself what a rarity it was.

'Hello darling! Did you have a lovely time at Nanny and Pops'?' She turned around to see her daughter strapping herself in. Gosh, how grown up she was becoming. Of course Dr Daddy had been right too, she looked great, not a spec of vomit in sight. She turned and saw Ollie fast asleep in Mia's arms. It was magical to watch her with her niece and nephew. One day she would make an amazing parent. Lucy watched as Mia put Ollie into his car seat without him uttering a sound. Driving back, Lucy and her sister took in the peace of Ollie's gentle snoring and Evie munching on the jellies her auntie had bought her.

Once back in the comfort of her house, she put the kettle on and pulled her hair back into a loose ponytail. She had left it down in the hope that Cynthia hadn't been able to spot that she had left the house without a stitch of make up on, a sin in Cynthia's book. Evie had settled herself in front of a princess cartoon and Oliver was amusing himself with some building blocks. Although every now and then the infectious music would catch his attention and he would get caught up in the pink dresses twirling in front of his eyes.

'What about Spain, Luce?' Mia said cupping her coffee in both hands as she wrapped her arms around her knees.

'What about it Mia?'

'Let's go and see Mum and Dad with the kids,' Mia said and Lucy smiled at the thought.

'That'd be great!' Lucy replied eagerly.

'Wouldn't it? It'd be lovely. Some sun...' she trailed off waiting for Lucy to say something, but as she was not forthcoming she continued. 'Mum and Dad would love us to go over. They've been hounding us to come. I think Dad needs a break too.'

'It sounds great. Let me just run it past Ed. I didn't last time. You know it wasn't the right time.' Mia gave her a knowing nod and flashed a fake smile. 'Are you gonna tell me what's the matter?' Lucy said as she put her hand on her sister's shoulder as she walked towards her.

'I don't know what you mean.'

'You do. There's something different Mia. You can tell me. I won't judge.' Mia's eyes started to gloss over with tears.

'Mummy! Mummy! Smell my finger!' Evie ran back into the living room and pushed her finger under her mum's nose, by this time Oliver had crawled towards Mia and she had lovingly picked him up.

'What is that?' Lucy thought she was going to baulk.

'I wiped my own bottom!'

With her finger apparently, thought Lucy. She didn't know whether to applaud her daughter's independence or vomit. She slowly began to realise that her daughter may not be a quite as grown up as she first thought. But Evie had left her auntie in hysterics. The gloss of tears in Mia's eyes a moment ago had turned into tears of joy. They both laughed hard. So hard Lucy thought she might actually wee a little, while Ollie and Evie both just stared in bewilderment.

Chapter 16

Jessie

'Hey Mia, you fancy meeting for a coffee?'

'Sure, you free now?'

When Mia said yes, she waited for her to suggest her local cafe. They both loved the cakes there. She put the phone down, delighted that on a very rare occasion they both had the same day off and finally they would get to spend some quality time together. It had been weeks since they had actually just sat and chatted. She felt like Robert had been punishing her for letting him down so many times in work, as the rota had barely featured them on the same shift. Unfortunately, she hadn't thought that Mia would actually be free right now. She was sitting in her jogging bottoms and hoodie, so she quickly threw on her jeans, a lose-fitting T-shirt with her favourite biker boots. She brushed her teeth, turned the telly off and pulled on her jacket before heading out of the door.

'You've got froth on your nose!' Jessie said as Mia broke into a huge grin and removed it with the back of her hand. She eyed her friend and thought how much brighter Mia had seemed in the last couple of weeks. Mia had never confided in her, she had felt hurt initially as she knew there was something wrong with her closest friend. However, she had never told Mia her secret so how could she expect Mia to tell her? 'So how was Spain? How's your mum? You look great by the way.'

'Yeah she was good thanks Jess. The warm weather certainly works wonders for her. She's still a bit of a handful for my dad – he loves it when we're out there. I think he wishes we could go over more often, but he understands that with work, it's too difficult.'

'He knows you can't, but that's great about your mum and I bet the kids loved it too.'

'Ollie was in his element in the pool, but wait till I tell you what he did, it was hilarious.' Jessie waited for Mia to carry on and felt the warmth radiating not just from her glowing tanned skin but also from her ease and smile. She felt relieved that her lovely friend seemed back to her normal self.

206

An hour later and Jessie and Mia were both laughing at something rather disgusting Evie had done. So much so that they had not even noticed him walk in. Mia stopped laughing quite abruptly, then quickly and extremely cheerily said 'Hi!'

Jessie turned around and as she caught sight of his hands she knew who would be staring down at her. Her heart had already jumped into her throat and her mouth was almost dry.

'Mia,' he smiled in her direction and then refocused his attention on Jessie. 'Hey Jess, how you doing?' She felt her face flush but managed a reply.

'Good. You?'

'Great thanks. Long-time no see. Been busy?' Jess wasn't sure if it was a rhetorical question so ignored him in the hope that it was. 'So how's work girls?' Realising that this was a question for both of them and seeing Mia begin to talk she felt her shoulders drop. In a daze, she excused herself and walked towards the bathroom and slowly locked the door behind her. She headed towards the mirror, and used both hands to lean on the sink before removing them and tightly rolling them into fists.

Realising how clammy they were, she wiped them on her jeans. Even her head was clammy. She grabbed a tissue and wiped her brow. Ten minutes later, she thought she had given Jake enough time to leave and left the haven of the bathroom. Even though her wish had come true, she felt sad to see Mia sitting alone sipping her coffee.

Jessie hung out of Mia's patio door inhaling her cigarette as she watched Dusty charging up and down. It made her laugh. The patio was so small she wondered if Dusty ever got dizzy. Less than 20 seconds later, Dusty lay down at her feet and groaned.

'Hey Dust, you okay?' She smiled at her knowing she wouldn't get a reply even though she lifted her head in acknowledgement of her question. Dogs were so clever she thought, especially Dusty. She took the last drag of her cigarette and stubbed it out in the plant pot that Mia had provided for her, clearly sick of her stubbing them out on the ground.

'You want a drink Jess?' She thought about it for a moment, not sure whether to go home, but then decided to accept her offer.

When Mia handed her the coffee she broke the silence with a question. 'How long is it since you last saw Jake?'

'It's been ages.' She now wished she'd gone home after she had put out her cigarette.

'I saw him a couple of weeks ago.' Mia said placing her coffee on the breakfast bar as she pulled herself onto the worktop letting her little legs dangle free.

'Really?' Jess had tried to sound nonchalant but realised it had not worked. What she really wanted to ask was: why didn't you tell me?

'Yeah, Robert asked me to go and see to Harvey when they were at the Lakes for that weekend. Remember?' Jess nodded not having a clue when they had made their umpteenth trip of the year but clearly the conversation had bypassed her. Maybe it had been when she'd been hitting the bottle hard, her memory was always a bit fuzzy when that happened.

'He was asking after you Jess.' She practically ignored Mia, but this didn't stop her continuing. 'He was worried about you.' Jessie had moved around in her chair, it must have looked like she was squirming to Mia, but it only seemed to give her more leverage to carry on. 'He told me what happened that night, I explained that you're not 'girl next door' material and that's what he said he liked about you.' For the first time Jessie looked up at Mia who was smiling encouragingly. 'I've never asked you Jess, but I'm asking you now.... She paused, 'talk to me... Please.'

Jess didn't speak and neither did Mia, it felt like an eternity. Then she mustered, 'I can't Mia.'

'I get that you like to keep secrets, I really do, but Jess... Whatever it is, it's got to stop holding you back from a potential future with someone. I'm only saying this now as I've seen the way you look at Jake. It's totally different to the way I've seen you look at anyone.' Jess felt herself begin to flush and wasn't really sure what to say as Mia was right. She really liked Jake, so much so, that she'd tried really hard to forget him. Eventually Mia spoke again, 'Jess?'

'I've never told anyone.' Looking up she stared at Mia, she held her gaze while Jess said nothing until finally she continued. 'EVER.'

'Okay, so don't tell me. Let Jake be the one person you tell. He really likes you Jess, he as good as told me.' Jess had bowed her head again, feeling that Mia could sense her shame. Mia's words had brought a flicker of a smile to her mouth, but still she did not look up at her friend. A tear rolled down her cheek. She let her lovely friend sit down next to her and pull her in towards her. Jess put her head on Mia's shoulder and for the first time let herself really cry in the presence of someone.

*

Jessie had felt lighter after crying to Mia, like a weight has been lifted from her shoulders. Although she knew deep down the weight was still there, she felt a little better. She also knew that if she really wanted Jake, then, for the first time in her life, she would have to be truly honest with someone about her past. She'd deleted Jake's number from her phone, but had written it down before doing so. Calmly she got off the couch and went to her bedroom and began rooting in her underwear drawer – nope not there. So, she moved onto her sock drawer, she still couldn't find that scrap of paper so she began scooping her socks onto the floor. Panicking she started pulling her socks out of the balls they were in, until she got to the last pair and she caught sight of the piece of paper under a pair of dark green socks. Her heart was beating so furiously that it worried her. She knew that she needed to tell Jake no matter what. Whether he accepted her with her secret, well, only time would tell.

Part 2

6 months later

Chapter 17

Mia

'That's wonderful! Thanks Claudia. Shall I come to the office next week? Yes I can do Tuesday, at 10.00am. That's no problem. See you then.' Mia hung up and placed her mobile onto the breakfast bar and found herself actually doing a little dance in her living room. She had finished the last chapter of her new novel the previous week and sent it to Claudia who had raved about it. She had loved it more than her first book. Mia was very modest but couldn't deny she loved hearing people praise her writing.

She wanted to share her happiness (even if he would never know why) with someone and the first person she thought of was Alex. She text him.

Hey, what you up to tonight? Fancy dinner at mine andmaybe going to the pub for a drink?

Mia had pottered round the flat for an hour and had begun baking a cake, when her phone vibrated in her back pocket. It was Alex calling her.

'Hey Mia,' he sounded muffled like he was on his hands free.

'Hi Alex. You get my message?'

'I did yeah, that'd be great but I don't finish work till 8.00pm. So do you wanna just go for a drink?'

'Or maybe just dinner? I'm baking a cake; it's in the oven as we speak.' Mia said as she crouched down to look at the cake through the oven glass.

'Check you out baking! What's come over you?' Alex said with sarcasm running through his voice.

'I'm a good cook and you know it!' Mia said smiling.

'Oh yes you can cook, but bake... Oh I'll wait and see!'

'You're so cheeky PC Plod!'

'Eh that's detective to you! And on that note I've got to go. Incoming call from the station. See you just after 8.00pm,' and with that he hung up.

Dusty had been happily chasing birds that kept landing on top of the small railings in the patio area and Mia had been glued to some daytime TV trash that she couldn't believe was even allowed on the air. The burning smell had gone undetected as she was so engrossed in finding out who Kyle's dad was. Could it really be the haggard, dirty looking guy who was old enough to be Karen's father? But then Tony, her actual husband, wasn't much better. He seemed to have lost one of his front teeth and had a dodgy comb-over that was really greasy. This was great research, she told herself. It was only Dusty's barking that broke her thoughts and made her realise that she could smell burning.

Quickly, she jumped up and ran towards the oven as smoke billowed out. She grabbed a tea towel and pulled out the cake that was as good as cremated. She flung it onto the side and hopped onto her work top to open the window, she started wafting the smoke alarm with the tea towel like a lunatic, which had started howling about 10 seconds after Dusty's alert. The wafting seemed to be making only the slightest bit of difference to the alarm on the ceiling of the kitchen, so she grabbed a chair from the study to stand on to waft a little closer to it. Eventually, it stopped. Mia climbed down from the chair and sat down for a minute to catch her breath, she hadn't realised how vigorously she'd been waving that tea towel. Dusty was now sat at her feet looking very upset, she hated loud noises. Mia patted her knee and Dusty lifted her head and placed it on her lap. Stroking her ears to calm Dusty and herself, she finally turned to look at the mess of her cake. She got up and stood over it. It was definitely not edible. She closed her window, grabbed her keys, Dusty's lead and her purse, slipped on her shoes and headed to the corner shop to see what she could pass off as her own delight. Before leaving she turned the telly off, the credits were flashing across the screen. Damn cake, she thought, now she'd never know who Kyle's dad was.

'This is really lovely Mia – you can bake!'

'I told you so,' Mia felt bad lying to Alex but she also thought this little white lie couldn't really cause any harm. She'd made sure that the Victoria sponge cake packaging was well and truly in the recycling bin outside. She watched as he almost inhaled the cake, clearly enjoying it. He'd eaten it so quickly that he'd left some crumbs on his face. She leant over and brushed them from his cheek. He twitched, startled that she had touched him. Mia then realised she had touched his scar.

'I'm sorry,' she said as she quickly pulled away, but he grabbed her hand, which made her look up at him. The warmth of his huge hand made her tingle all over. Not able to hold his gaze she let her eyes drop and then he quickly pulled his hand from hers. Unsure of what had just happened between them she started to clear the plates away. She wondered if she appeared as flustered as she felt.

'Mia, its fine.... It's just that...'

She ignored him as he began to speak. 'Let me get those photos I said I'd show you of Spain. They're in here somewhere.' Mia went into the study and leant against the cold wall in the darkness. She didn't know how to feel. It had been months now since Ben. She really liked Alex, but perhaps she was getting the wrong signals, like she had been with Ben. Realising she had been in there for a while she flicked on the light and began searching, she knew she'd left them in here somewhere.

'Can you still not find them?' Alex asked as he entered the room and threw her a big smile showing off his glistening teeth. Things must be okay she thought.

218

He'd been so good over everything, he'd really looked after her since that night and as good as lost his best friend because of it. She realised that she wouldn't let her silly feelings get in the way. He obviously just wanted to be friends and she didn't want to lose that.

'Well, I thought they were in here.' She scanned around the room, taking in the mess before her. When she sat in this room it was all about the desk, the laptop and her thoughts. She could quite easily erase everything else around her, which now she thought she must have done. A flicker of embarrassment entered her eyes as Alex took in the sight before him.

'Not got round to this room yet Mia?' he said as he began to chuckle.

'You could say that!' she said and mirrored his chuckle.

Mia watched as Alex sat on the edge of the desk and picked up a book from the pile that lay before him, her heart skipped a beat. He began to flick through it. 'So you finally got around to reading it?'

'Yeah.' Mia turned away pretending to still be searching for the photos. She'd lied twice in as many hours to Alex. She could feel her blushing face begin to subside.

'It's great, can you believe it was the brother? I thought it was the dad for sure,' Alex said and she could still hear him flicking until finally he stopped.

'Got them!' Mia felt a rush of relief, she wasn't even sure that they had been in that room.

'Oh my God!' Alex looked from the wall to the front of the book repeatedly. He'd finally cracked It. He began reading, holding the book open like some sort of trophy, 'For my Granddad, who always believed in dreaming big.' He then walked over to the frame on the wall, one of the things she had put up the first day she moved in. It held a picture of her and her amazing granddad, Frank, and next to it was a hand written note which Alex read out loud. 'Never give up kid, dream big.'

'I was getting worried about your detective skills,' she smiled nervously.

'You?' he said sounding astonished. He flicked to the front of the book. 'You're Richard Aims!' She watched as he ran his hand over the cover.

'Yep.' Mia clutched the packet of photos to her chest and exhaled deeply. It was a funny feeling, a sense of relief that finally someone knew, she wasn't sure if deep down she had wanted someone to find out and that someone she had wanted to be was Alex.

'Mia Richards.... Richard Aims, how did we not see it?'

'Why would you?'

'Mia, you're so good! This is amazing!' Mia felt her face flush.

'Well, I've just finished my second book. My agent seems to like it. Hopefully you will too. Come on let's look at these,' She said waving the photos in front of Alex's face. He followed her quietly but apparently his brain had been flying with questions.

'So, does anyone know that you're "Richard"? he asked excitedly.

'Nope.'

'Not even Lucy? Or your parents?' he asked in astonishment.

'No, not even my family.'

'Wow!'

'My agent, Claudia, obviously knows. But no one else needs to know, do they?'

'I suppose not, but why wouldn't you tell anyone? And why write as a man?'

'It was my agent's idea, she said that as the book's very gruesome it may appeal more to a male audience. I trusted her judgement, and I'm so glad I did.'

'But why don't you at least tell people you write?'

'Why should I? It's my own little haven that no one knows about. It's silly really, but if I tell people then it becomes all about the money and how well it's doing, for me that's just an added bonus. I write because I love it. It's my passion. Plus, people are so quick to judge.'

'Like Izzy in the park,' Alex said, sounding embarrassed. Mia couldn't believe he had remembered.

'Yeah, like Izzy,' she stopped herself, she wasn't in the habit of pulling people to pieces, although in her head she had done that many times to Izzy.

'I was so embarrassed of her that day; she never thought before she spoke,' Alex said. This always happened when he spoke about Izzy, he lost his sparkle. His enthusiasm for Mia's writing had all but disappeared.

'Oh it's long forgotten,' Mia lied. Good God, another lie, she thought.

'Well, I'm sorry. I didn't ever say that and I know she never will have.'

'You don't have to apologise for her Alex. Honestly, like I said, it's forgotten.'

'So tell me, when is the next book due out?'

'Not been given a date yet, it has to go through so many different channels. You'd be surprised.'

'Really?' Alex said sounding surprised. 'What's it called?'

'At the minute *Book 2*,' she smiled as Alex looked confused. 'As in, I don't have a title yet. I find it one of the hardest things to come up with.'

'I'd find writing, what is it? About 100,000 words?' Mia nodded, 'the hardest part.'

'I absolutely love that part!' she said grinning from ear to ear. 'Meeting your new characters, getting to know them and thinking where they may end up.'

'Mia, it's so amazing watching you talk with such passion!' He smiled right back at her. His sparkle was back, she thought warmly.

'I do have a big passion for it and that's why you've got to promise that you won't tell anyone,' she said clasping her hands together in a prayer gesture, as if she was begging.

'Okay, okay,' he said rolling his eyes in pretence, 'but promise me one day you'll tell your family? They'd be so proud!'

'One day,' she said, still smiling.

'Oh and while we're on favours...' He paused and gave her a huge smile. 'If I keep quiet...' She waited patiently for what he was going to say, she felt a little nervous. 'I want your first signed copy of *Book 2*.' Mia began to laugh. 'I'm serious, one day you could be worth millions and I want a piece of that!'

Chapter 18

Ben

From: Benjamin Webster

To: Alexander Jones

Re: The surf's up!

15.05.15

Alright mate, how's things going? Sorry it's taken so long to reply to your email, been mental with work. We've just finished a big renovation on a minted couple's house. You should see it. They've got this 25-foot swimming pool in their back garden. Their kid swims for the country or something, apparently he's good enough for the Olympics. How's work going for you? You wrapped that case up yet, with those fuckers in Vice?

I can't believe David and Jane have been so good to me. How long have I been staying at their gaff for now?! But I finally have enough for a deposit to rent this place around the corner from them. I'm pretty happy to be close to them – Jane was insistent. She knows that I need someone to keep me in line. She knows that was you for all those years; she said it's about time she did her part. Feel like a tit though Alex, like I can't be left on my own. Feel like my friggin' nephew has bigger reins than I do. Although I know where she's coming from, she just doesn't want me going the same way as Dad. He was only 4 years older than me when he managed to destroy his liver and himself. It's his twenty-first anniversary next month. I can't believe it. I'm determined to not end up like him.

Can you believe David took me on with my past record?! Although I think Jane badgered him into it. She said they've talked about letting me invest in the business in another couple of months. She said I have to be dry for a year. I can't mess this up; she said if I invest and balls it up its Jamie's future I'm messing up. My big sister is very clever to use my nephew as leverage, but she knows how much I adore him. To be honest, it's all working out well (although I'm not sure I deserve it). I still haven't had the rest of my money from the business. Pete's being an absolute dick about it; he's so frigging pedantic. I know I caused lots of problems just leaving like that but I think he thinks I did it on purpose. To be honest I thought he'd be glad to get shut of 'the drunk'. Anyway, hopefully it'll be sorted ASAP. I'm loving this new direction with work; it's so much better than sitting at the computer all day and going stir crazy. No doubt it's this nice weather too, I imagine this manual labour is a bit shit in the lashing down rain of the UK.

You heard from Izzy lately? I still can't believe she hooked up with that 50-year-old from her work, but I suppose it makes sense for her. I met this lovely girl in one of my meetings, but both of us know that nothing can or will happen between us. We both know that it's too dangerous. She's great company and it's nice that she doesn't judge me in anyway. She's been dry for 10 years. She's amazing, puts me to shame really, but I suppose we all deal with our demons in different ways and at different times. There's no set way to handle an addiction, one day at a time, so Mike, my new sponsor, keeps telling me.

How's Mia doing? I know I ask every time I email and you always say she's fine, but I still worry about her. I can't believe she never told anyone Alex, not even Jessie or her sister! I know if she'd told Jess, she'd have hunted me down and killed me with one look. She really is fine, right?

I started surfing about three weekends ago now and it's bloody brilliant. I was pretty shit at it at first, but apparently it's all about having no fear. I've got bruises all over my legs, but I'm definitely getting better. You should see Jamie – he's brilliant. Not at surfing, he's too little for that but he does this thing called body boarding. He certainly has no fear of the water but I suppose that's because he doesn't understand about the undercurrents. He had a scare last month, went right under the water but David made him go back out there the following day. He was terrified at first, but he was right to do it, imagine having that fear all your life. He was back on his body board after about 20 minutes as if nothing had ever happened!

Anyway mate, sorry for rambling, I won't leave it so long next time. In fact, once I'm settled into my new gaff and got the Internet set up, we can finally sort Skype out.

Take care Alex, Ben.

Chapter 19

Lucy

'You clever boy Ollie!' Lucy clapped her hands together as she pointed them in her son's direction and watched him clumsily walk towards her and stumble into her arms. Something else Ed had missed, she thought to herself, as Ollie beamed at her and proceeded to stick his finger in her mouth and pull her lip to the side as if she'd been caught with a fish hook. Ed had missed Oliver saying 'Dada' the week before last because there was a number of staffing issues that had arisen and, as one of the more senior partners, Ed had stayed late most nights. Mostly, by the time that Ed arrived home, Lucy was sparked out on the couch. Recently, things had been really good between them but she was starting to feel the distance beginning to grow. She went about her usual nightly routine and, after putting Evie to bed and reading her a story, she gave Ollie his bottle. He then fell asleep in her arms and now her left arm had gone dead. She hated that feeling; she often got it in her leg after Ollie had sat for too long on

230

it. Once, when she had attempted to stand on it, she'd twisted her ankle really badly. Slowly, she began to wiggle her fingers and move her wrist underneath Ollie in the hope that he would not wake —thankfully he didn't. She walked upstairs with him and laid him in his cot. He stirred a little and flipped himself over. She waited and watched as he nuzzled his face into Vincent, his favourite teddy bear. Content that she could walk downstairs without a wail making her turn on her heels half way down, she closed the door over and began her descent down the stairs. When she reached the bottom stair, she saw a shape through the beautiful stain glass window of her front door. She felt her heart lift as she waited for Ed to put his key in the door and walk in. However, the silhouette began to move away from the door and then move towards the door again. Maybe he'd left something in the car, she thought. So she opened the door to greet him. But she was met with the back of a man she knew, but it wasn't her husband. Although she recognised that mop of dark curly hair anywhere, she knew it well enough because she had run her fingers through it more than once. The man turned around quickly and locked onto her gaze, she felt like a rabbit caught in the headlights.

'Hi Lu...cy.' Sebastian said as she saw him swallow hard.

There was a long pause before Lucy spoke.

'What are you doing here?' She thought her heart was going to explode out of her chest.

'I don't know,' Sebastian said sounding flustered.

'What?' Lucy knew she sounded annoyed even panicked. 'Why are you at my house Sebastian?' she reiterated the question but phrased it slightly differently in the hope that he might snap himself out of the ludicrous trance he seemed to be in.

The house phone ringing broke the silence. She jumped and turned to answer it, leaving the door wide open.

'Oh hi darling.' Lucy caught sight of herself in the mirror and ran her fingers through her hair. 'Yeah, that's fine,' she continued. 'No, honestly, it's okay, I'll eat on my own. See you later.' Slowly she turned back to the front door after trying to gather her thoughts for a moment and there facing her was only darkness. Sebastian had gone.

*

Going back to work had been a decision that she and Ed had discussed at some length. She had loved every minute of being off with Evie, but with Ollie it had been different. She felt ready to go back to work and what with Evie starting school that September, she thought it was as good a time as any to do it. Sebastian had arrived the night before she was due at the surgery and her head was in a spin. She knew how lucky she was to be working in Ed's surgery, but then that was a perk of having your husband as a partner in a practice. Her old colleagues had been very envious.

'Off the shift treadmill Lucy, it can't be bad!'

'I know girls, fallen on my feet marrying a GP.'

It was now a running joke, but many female doctors hated it. She once heard one say, 'It's the only reason that nurses do this job, to marry a doctor.' If she hadn't been about to drop Evie from her womb, she would have torn a strip off her but a contraction had kicked in and saved Lucy's dignity (although Evie hadn't) and that doctor's throat.

'But then I imagine working day in day out with your hubby would be a pain in the backside!' Rita was the sister on Lucy's ward and had been happily married for forty years, but then perhaps that had been why. Rita's words were now ringing in her ears. She really could have done without seeing Ed today, never mind every hour on the hour in her consultation room.

'Ed, don't fuss!' she had snapped at him unnecessarily, realising how horrible she must have sounded as he looked at her like an injured puppy. 'It's just that I don't want your staff thinking you are showing me any sort of favouritism.' She feigned a weak smile and he walked behind her and began to massage her shoulders.

'Stop stressing,' he said calmly.

Her eyes began to well up. Don't cry, she told herself. She felt bad as Ed stood there massaging her shoulders when all she could think about was why Sebastian hadn't replied to her text. She gently placed her hand on his as a thank you and indicating for him to stop. He bent down and carefully brushed her hair from her neck and kissed it. She grabbed the back of his neck, pulling him in closer and inhaled deeply. Snap yourself out of this Lucy, she told herself.

'Not sure nooky on your first day is acceptable Nurse Brown!' He pulled away and kissed her on the top of the head. 'You need anything, just give me a shout darling,' and with a big geeky grin, the one that she had fallen in love with, he was gone.

Lucy put her head in her hands and swallowed hard to stop herself from breaking down on her first day of work. With perfect timing there was a knock at the door. 'Come in!' she sounded overly cheery she realised, but then knew that Mrs Ward wouldn't even notice. She might have been a frequent visitor to the hospital when her beloved Sidney was ill, but she was still as deaf as a post.

'Oh dear, don't you look marvellous!' It was more of a statement than a question.

'It's great to see you Betty, you look really well!' She had insisted that all of the nurses and doctors had called her that, they had become like her family over the years as Sidney had been in and out of hospital with his reoccurring cancer. His final fight had come to an end just before she left to have Evie. They had been an inspirational team, one she had admired and hoped she and Ed could mirror one day. 'So, you're just here to have your dressing changed on your leg?'

'Yes dear, such an idiot I am! I caught it on the oven door when it was open...' Although Betty's voice hadn't trailed off, Lucy's thoughts had. She would text Sebastian again after work and tell him to not come around to the house again or get in contact – there was no need. She had moved on and was happy with Ed. One day, she and Ed would be like Betty and Sidney, but she had to start making the right decisions before that could happen and this was going to be her first.

*

'At last!' Lucy said kicking off her shoes and flopping onto the couch.

'You did it! First full week down,' Ed said as he handed Lucy a glass of wine and she pulled herself up towards it.

'Thank you,' she smiled as her husband sat at the other end of the couch and she stretched her legs out so that they were on his knee.

'You shattered darling?' he said rubbing the bottom of her legs.

'You know what? I'd say I'm more tired having the kids than a full week with patients!' They both smiled at one another, knowing she was probably right. 'Although, I've missed them very much.'

'You were okay about my folks taking them? It was a nice surprise?' he said looking at her anxiously.

'Of course!' She said throwing him a grateful smile. 'It's so quiet without them!'

'But more time for us to have some uninterrupted nooky, no kids, no patients ... ' he had lent over to her and was kissing her hard on the mouth, his big lips felt so good on hers. She stopped momentarily to put her wine down then moved over to straddle him, continuing to kiss him hard. He grabbed her around the hips and pulled her towards him even further. They kissed like teenagers for what felt like hours. Then Ed grabbed her by the hand and they went upstairs. Although they were finishing off a long, tiring week, they still managed to find the energy from somewhere to make them both have a very good night's sleep.

'Come in,' Lucy said as she typed her next patient's name into the system. 'Mr Grove, how can I help?' She spun around on her computer chair to see Sebastian standing at the door. 'What the hell are you doing here?' She stood up but then froze to the spot, unsure as to what she was going to do. 'Sebastian!' she shouted without realising how much she raised her voice.

'I don't know. I'm sorry Lucy.'

'My next patient is due in,' she hesitated but then blurted out, 'any minute now.'

'It's okay, Pam knows me and said I could nip in for 5 minutes.'

Dear God, Lucy felt like wringing Pam's neck about now, regardless of what an excellent and extremely efficient receptionist she was.

'She said you have a gap.' Lucy eyed the clock above the door and of course Pam was right.

'So what is it Sebastian...? You leave practically in the middle of the night, then you turn up at my house and then leave mysteriously and now you turn up at my work unannounced! What is it that you want Sebastian?'

238

She felt her face flushing and she could hear the anger in her voice.

He walked towards her, touching her hands to calm her down. It stopped her dead in her tracks, she felt calmer and then he leant forward until their heads were touching. When she wasn't angry with him or shouting at him then he managed to bring an inexplicable air of tranquillity to any room or situation. He let go of one of her hands and touched her face, using his thumb to gently brush her lips. She inhaled deeply and felt like the only noise she could hear was her heartbeat. The silence between them seemed to fill the room with words that had gone unspoken for months. In that moment, the answers she had so craved when he had left, did not matter. She didn't know how long they stood there for, but it felt like an eternity. Then the realisation hit her: what was she doing? She was in work and her husband was four doors up the corridor.

'No,' Lucy said and she seemed to startle herself as well as him. She backed away from him and sat down in her chair. He looked hurt. '*What* is it that you want Sebastian?'

'I left Lucy, I did what you asked.'

'I know! So why come back?' She sounded angrier than before. Only now she realised how hurt she'd been when he'd up and left without a goodbye.

'Because I love you...' It was like she'd been hit by lightning. He loved her? That couldn't be possible she thought. '...and that is the reason I walked away...' he paused briefly, 'because I love you.'

She realised that her knuckles had gone white as she had gripped the arms of the chair so tightly. 'So why come back?'

'...Because...'

'Why now?'

'...because... I'm dying Lucy.'

Chapter 20

Jessie

The light beaming through the crack in the curtains had managed to work its way up from Jake's thighs to rest on his belly button. She held her gaze on his outie, she had never seen an outie in her life until she had started sleeping with Jake and it truly did fascinate her. According to Jake they were somewhat of a rarity and he'd tried, somewhat unsuccessfully, to make her believe that he had swallowed a marble in his youth and it had gotten stuck just at his belly button, making it protrude.

'Seriously Derby, do you really think I'm gonna believe this clearly made up story?' she had said laughing as she tried to poke it back in.

'Well, I did when my brother told me that he'd made me swallow it when I was a baby, just to test the theory. I believed him until I was about 10, and that only changed when we went swimming one day. That's when I saw my first other outie. I said to this kid, who was about 13, you swallowed a marble too? Pointing to his belly button...' Before Jake could finish his sentence Jessie had burst into a fit of laughter. She flung herself back onto the bed and covered her face to try and control her giggles a little.

'Oh Jake, that is hilarious.' She had moved her hands away and looked up at him. He had pretended to sulk, only she knew that look far too well now and moved towards his belly button and had kissed it firmly with her mouth saying, 'Well, marble or not I still love it!'

Jessie now made circles around his belly button with her fingertips and she then followed the line of hair up towards his chest that eventually met a mass of dark hair at the top. Her eyes finally fell onto his rugged face and as she took in his overgrown stubble, she smiled and touched it. She knew this wouldn't wake him; she was unsure whether a runaway train running directly across his face would even wake him. It was ironic really how much he'd let his stubble grow, nearly into a full beard, he was so precious about his gardens yet he had let his facial hair get wildly overgrown, but she didn't care. She looked at his rising chest aware that they both really needed to get up for work. So she leant over, not even caring about her morning breath, and planted a kiss on his lips. Nothing. So she threw back the covers and straddled him and leant in for another kiss. Still nothing. Jesus, she thought, is he dead? No, he couldn't be, she'd just watched his chest rising and falling. Perhaps he was unconscious, although she never really did understand that concept. She wondered whether, if he was unconscious, he would still be able to breathe but just couldn't wake up. She felt her mind going into overdrive and she began to panic. So, she put her hands where his heart should be beating, but before she could check for a heartbeat, he'd sat up like a zombie, causing her to fall backwards and planted a kiss on her lips.

'Checking for a pulse there Coley?' he said pinning her hands down onto the duvet, half of it was covering her face. He let go of her hand to push the duvet away from her cheek. This only gave her ample opportunity to twist his nipple, which he disliked greatly.

'Ouch!' he squealed and she laughed in return. 'I'm gonna get you Jessica Cole!' he shouted as he began chasing her from the bedroom. She ran into the living room, but he managed to grab her by the waist and started kissing her neck. She laughed and she knew he had won, as whenever he did that, her legs always went to jelly as if her whole body was melting. He had a way of touching her that made her feel warm inside; she'd never been touched so gently by a man before and my God did she love it. She turned around and they began to kiss passionately. He lifted Jess onto the worktop and nearly knocked a full glass of water over as he did so, not that either of them would have noticed. He began lifting her old, huge T-shirt above her hips, breasts and finally over her head. He ran his hand from under her chin until he reached her breast and began gently caressing each breast in turn. Then he kissed her neck and lifted her from the worktop and carried her back towards the bedroom. They walked past the huge clock that covered nearly half of a wall.

'Oh shit Jess!' he quickly said in what seemed like a blind panic. 'It's gone nine! I have to be there at half nine today as that couple are going away and they want the last part of the job doing!' He released Jess from his hold and placed her gently on the ground as he ran into the bedroom. She had been left standing in her living room with only her red kiddy knickers on. Mia loved to laugh at her kiddy knickers as she had so aptly named them. Yes, these red ones that she was wearing did have butterflies on and the others that she owned may have had flowers, bows or spots on. However, there could be no arguing that they were the most comfortable knickers she had ever owned and anyway didn't they always just end up on the floor somewhere? She made her way back to the kitchen and picked the T-shirt up from the floor and pulled it over her head, flicked on the kettle and watched Jake as he pulled on his boots. 'No time for a shower?'

He shook his head and then quickly ran over to her and planted a frantic kiss on her lips. 'See you tonight?'

'Yeah, I'll meet you at Imagination at 8.00pm?' Jess said as she watched him head to the door.

'I'll pick you up!'

'It's fine, honestly, it's massively out of your way. I'll just see you there.' He hovered in the doorway and paused as if he was about to disagree with her. 'Go Jake, or you really are going to be late!'

'Oh here she comes, the gorgeous birthday girl!' Karl said with such delight and what she thought was a hint of pride in his voice. Jess couldn't be sure that he wasn't going to start applauding.

'It's not my birthday Karl!' she said heading towards him as he passed her a whiskey and coke. She loved that Karl knew her drink of choice — regardless of the occasion or the mood, he could always get it spot on. For some reason he had given her whiskey, that was her drink when she was feeling melancholy. When it came to her birthday, her darkest day, there was only one reason to drink, and that drink would be whiskey. That was why she had asked for this reservation to be made two weeks after her birthday, so she could get herself out of her annual funk. Surprisingly, she had not been as bad as usual this year and she knew that was down to Jake spoiling her. He had given her some new, lovely memories to hold onto over the last six months since they had been dating. She grabbed hold of the beautiful Tiffany heart necklace that hung around her neck. She had told him about the necklace her mum had given to her on her twelfth birthday and how she loved it. She had not told him the part about her stepfather ripping it from her neck the following year and throwing it into the canal near their house. She couldn't believe that he had even remembered the story, but when he gave it to her he had said he'd hoped it looked a little like the one she lost. Christ, her mum couldn't have afforded Tiffany; his gesture had set her heart alight. She had not felt happiness like it for many, many years.

'Well, that's why you're here,' Karl said, sounding annoyed as she attempted to correct him.

'Thanks,' she said, as she picked up the whiskey and began to sip it slowly. Although she had been with Jake for months now, she knew that tonight would not be the night that he saw her annihilated. She had bought a new bright red dress that clung to every curve on her body and she was going to enjoy him undressing her later. 'I know that's why I'm here Karl and it's such a lovely present from Mia.' She lied. But what could she say to her best friend, "really Mia, the place where I work ... for dinner?" How ungrateful would she sound and, to be fair it had been a billion years since Robert had let them taste any food from the restaurant and she had been dying to try the new fish on the menu. You could only pick at little bits here and there before it became noticeable and the head chef, Andrew, was a prize tool.

Brilliant, but the personality of a frustrated 15 year old who couldn't get laid.

'Wow!' Mia appeared from around the corner looking as perky as ever. Her friend approached her and drew her into an embrace. 'You look sensational!' Jessie could feel herself blushing the colour of her dress. 'You know who you look like....' Before Mia could finish, Karl had interjected, but in unison they said,

'Jessica Rabbit!' Mia and Karl fell about laughing and Jessie tried to hide the smirk that had entered the corner of her mouth, the look she had been going for. Granted, not as glam as her dress stopped at her knees, unlike Mrs Rabbit's dress.

'Anyhow,' Mia continued, 'let me take you to your table, follow me.'

'Why are you being so formal?' Jessie laughed as she picked her bag up from the bar and rolled her eyes at Karl who was grinning from ear to ear. Then as they rounded the corner, she saw Jake sitting at the only occupied table at the restaurant. It was only then she realised that the restaurant was quiet, there wasn't the usual humming of other customers chatting – only the dulcet tones of Michael Bublè coming from the speakers. He stood up as she walked towards him. 'What's going on?' Jessie asked, looking very confused.

'I booked out the restaurant for us,' he said, smiling at her as she clung onto the back of the chair.

'Why?' She turned to Mia for support, but she had gone. Oh shit, she thought, what was he playing at?

'Let's order, then I'll tell you,' he passed her the menu. Her palms had begun to sweat and the menu slipped from her grasp. She looked down at the menu but did not read it.

'Oh Jesus, I know this menu like the back of my hand. I'll have the pâté to start and the lemon sole for main.'

'You're spoiling it Jessie,' he said looking a little forlorn.

'Spoiling what?' She sounded cross.

'Christ Jess!' He stood up and walked towards her, as he dug into his pocket she began to speak, almost unaware of what was coming out.

'No.' It came out as a whisper at first, then she repeated it louder twice more. 'No... No.'

'No what?' He pulled up a chair next to her. 'You don't even know what I'm going to say!'

'I can't marry you Jake.' She spat the words out without even thinking. 'No Jake, the answer's no.'

'For once, Coley, just shut up,' he's said smiling at her. Then, finally, he pulled out the mystery object from his pocket and there she saw a key hanging from a Derby's Gardening key ring. 'All I was going to ask was, will you move in with me?'

Jess felt her shoulders drop what felt about 15 feet and she exhaled, which made her realise that she had been holding her breath. 'What?' She sounded confused, but she knew she wasn't. She also knew she had to speak although she thought that she might cry.

'Move in with me Coley. We are great together. We practically live together as it is. Let's do this!' She smiled so hard that an actual tear rolled down her cheek. 'Wow and *now* I see you cry for the first time. Not what I was hoping for to be honest.' His thumb rubbed away the tear before it passed her lips.

'Yes!' she said, feeling the happiest she thought she had ever felt in her whole entire life. He embraced her and pulled her face towards his for a kiss.

'I can't believe you thought I was gonna propose!' He was looking at her now but still holding her face, 'Do you think I don't know you at all?' he said sounding pleased with himself. This time she pulled him in for a hug. Tears ran down her face, she hoped they'd pass for tears of joy. Not tears of sorrow, that really he didn't know the worst thing about her and if he did, would he still want to be her roomy?

Chapter 21

Mia

'I know Lucy, can you believe it?' Mia sat on her bed and was attempting to kick off her left trainer with her right foot, she had managed the other one but this just wouldn't budge and it was starting to hurt her foot. She held the phone between her ear and her shoulder as she leant down to undo the laces. 'Lucy, are you still there?'

'Yeah, that's great Mia.' Lucy exhaled deeply after her statement.

'What's the matter with you? Huffing and puffing.' Mia said as she walked back into her living room. Dusty was rubbing her nose against the patio doors. Mia walked over to them and knew Dusty would want to get out to do her business. They had just run all the way around the park, but like some humans, she preferred to go in familiar settings. Mia smiled as she watched her dutiful dog dash into the corner of the patio and stare at her until Mia turned away.

'Nothing.'

'Oh come on Lucy, this is Jess. You always have an opinion on Jess and her love life and it's not usually so...' Mia hesitated, searching for the right word, 'kind.'

'What?' Lucy snapped.

'You know what Luce, I've got to go. The buzzer's just gone and I need to pick up.'

'Okay, bye.'

Mia felt terrible lying to her sister, but with the mood she seemed to be in, probably because she was so tired now that she was back at work, she didn't want to annoy her, jokingly or otherwise. Mia walked over and checked that the kettle had enough water in before she flicked it on. She grabbed her favourite mug, with the huge handle, so she could get her hand right in. She often wondered why mugs were made with such small handles. Cups, yes, as they were fancy and had a saucer so that if the little handle got too much you could put it on the saucer and rest your achy fingers. But mugs, they were for putting your whole hand in, getting a firm hold on it and then finally relishing the warmth that it so generously offered. Once she had settled her hand into its usual place that fitted almost like a glove, she grabbed her phone with the other hand and looked to see if she had any messages. There was one from her dad, telling her it was raining in Spain, "which is bloody marvellous for your mother" and could they Skype tomorrow night. She replied, trying to sound up beat and told her dad she would look forward to Skyping. Another text from Lucy, apologising for being a grouch and finally one from Jessie explaining that she had spent the last 15 minutes trying to get into Jake's, and she was surprised that the door was still on its hinges! She was so elated for Jess; she had eventually found happiness. She imagined this had come after she had told Jake the truth — whatever that may be. Jess had found contentment; she was relaxed and maybe the weight that had dragged her down all of these years had finally been lifted. Mia knew that she would never know her best friend's secret. Meeting Jess all those years ago in Imagination had come with a few unusual dos and don'ts for their friendship. The biggest don't was to ask about her past and she had always respected that. However, she still couldn't help feeling envious towards Jake, in whom she had finally confided. However, she was delighted that Jess had been able to let her barriers down and let someone in. Her mind began to get carried away with a fairy-tale ending for Jessie and Jake. Although after her outburst at the restaurant she knew that wasn't going to happen, well at least the fairy-tale wedding.

'Fuck me Mia, I really thought he was going to propose!' she had said to Karl and Mia while Jake was at the toilet.

'Oh we know darling, we were listening around the corner!' Waving his had around as if to say, "what did you expect?" Jessie shot him a look as if to say, "How dare you!" But the three of them burst out laughing, as they knew Jessie would have done the same had the shoe been on the other foot.

'Oh Jess, you really are happy aren't you?' Mia had asked clasping her hands in front of herself and bringing them up to her mouth.

'Alright, alright you two! Looking at me like I've just told you I'm pregnant or something. We are just moving in together, it's no big deal!'

'Oh you're such a spoil sport Jessica, let us at least enjoy this moment even if you won't!' Karl had said with a smile.

'Seriously guys, do one! Or no tip for you!'

Karl and Mia did as they were told but not before Karl stuck out his tongue at Jess, which she mirrored back.

'Now gorgeous, just you to sort out!' Karl had said as he picked up his bar towel and casually threw it over his shoulder.

'I'm good as I am thanks Karl,' Mia said as she had rested her elbows on the bar and watched Karl make her a latte. She wondered how he knew the exact coffee drink she wanted. Everyone knew she was a coffee addict, but she had toyed with having a cappuccino or a latte. Sometimes she thought he must be able to read minds.

They had sat on the couch near to the entrance. The beauty of your best friend's boyfriend hiring out the whole restaurant, was he wouldn't care if you sat and had a well-earned coffee break.

Karl had turned his body to face Mia. 'Nope, I'm not having that. Someone as gorgeous as you should not be on their own. It's a crime!'

Mia had laughed.

'I only speak the truth Mia, you turn heads young lady, you don't know it, but you do.' Mia had stopped laughing now and was blushing, oh was she embarrassed. 'But don't you worry Mia, Cilla is here. God rest her soul.' Karl stopped to move his top lip above his teeth and all of a sudden turned Scouse, 'so our Graham let's find someone as gorgeous as Mia!'

They had giggled uncontrollably, but behind the giggle she knew she had to stop Karl in his tracks. Last summer he had attempted to set up the young bar girl, Michelle, with his cousin's friend and dear God she knew Michelle wasn't a looker but the friend practically had a bog eye, it wasn't his fault and he was a lovely guy, but his eyes looked like they were fighting for the corners. Karl had himself down as somewhat of a matchmaker, when really that couldn't be further from the truth. She couldn't allow Karl to set her up, it would be disastrous. Instead, she knew exactly what she needed to do – it was time to tell Alex how she really felt.

*

Mia had decided to go for a run in the attempt to clear her head and build up some courage. Once she returned from the park with an exhausted Dusty, she picked out her all-important outfit and jumped in the shower. She blasted her hair with the hair dryer to give it the wavy affect, one that looked casual and carefree. It was only as she looked at herself in the mirror and saw her minimal make up that she had her first doubt – she wasn't sure if this is what she should be doing.

She pulled off the pink T-shirt she'd been wearing; the whole look had been too girly, she'd decided. Instead she opened her drawers and found a red vest top and pulled it over her head. She ruffled her hair again as it had fallen on her face due to the changing of her top. She looked at herself in the mirror again and smiled. She felt confident in red, she never knew why, but she did. She had gained her confidence back. She had doubted whether the shorts had been too much, but then she wore them all the time, how they could be too much. Rooting through her makeup bag she finally found the Vaseline she'd been searching for and gently rubbed it onto her lips. Her plan had worked. Dusty was fast asleep after their energetic hour around the park. Her energy had been infectious – Mia practically sprinted the whole way. She imagined if she'd timed herself that it may have been her personal best. Dusty had flaked out as soon as she had jumped in the shower, she was glad one of them was calm after their mad hour. She watched for a minute as she saw her chest rise and fall. Finally, deciding that she had procrastinated long enough, she closed the door behind her and began her journey up the flight of stairs.

Mia knocked at Alex's door and waited. He didn't answer, which only made her heart beat faster. She knocked again, thoughts flashing through her brain: maybe he was out, or asleep or in the shower. Stop it, she told herself.

It was time to give up, he clearly wasn't there and just as she turned away and was about to descend the flight of stairs, she heard the door being unlocked.

'Oh hi Mia!' Alex sounded genuinely shocked at her presence and she could see why, he was stood with just a towel around his waist. So he was in the shower, she thought.

'Hi...' She realised that her voice had barely come out of her mouth and then she proceeded to shout the rest of the sentence, 'Alex!'

'Are you okay?' Alex moved to the side of the door as if to invite Mia in. She walked past him and felt like she was holding her breath but smiled and nodded. 'I'm gonna go and throw some clothes on. Stick the kettle on Mia?'

'Okay,' she finally managed to say.

She hadn't expected Alex to be half naked and it had thrown her, especially after she had seen that scar on his upper arm. She watched as he walked away, observing the drips of water trickle down his back until he finally went into his bedroom. While she made their drinks and went over to the couch, she tried to get a grip of herself.

After a couple of minutes, he came out wearing shorts, a T-shirt and flip-flops. He grabbed a hoodie from the back of a chair, put it on and zipped it up as he walked towards her. She handed him his cup of tea and swigged far too much of her coffee. It burnt her mouth bringing tears to her eyes, it was even too hot for her.

'Are you okay Mia? You're acting... Weird.'

Oh bloody marvellous, she thought and panicked. Just calm down, she told herself. She knew she was being strange. Rein it in for 5 minutes, she thought.

'Dusty was sick last night and kept me awake a lot of the night.' This was a good start she thought, lying to him, this wasn't reining it in - this was the opposite. She was an awful liar but not when it really mattered. However, with men she seemed to stutter and stammer and become this person she didn't recognise.

'So where is she?' Alex asked looking concerned.

'Who?' Asked Mia.

'Dusty!'

'Downstairs, she's totally fine now. She just managed to get some of my chocolate and it didn't agree with her, but she got it all up, so she's fine now.' She hoped to God that wasn't just a myth that could really be true. She heard people saying that you shouldn't feed your dog chocolate and she never had, just in case. She was waffling and it was because she was lying and wasn't 100% sure about where the story was going or how it was going to end. 'I think she's learnt her lesson though.'

'Oh that's good. To be honest though, I never had her down as a chocolate lover!' Alex was attempting to crack a joke, but Mia could see he looked like he was squirming and he moved to sit next to her on the couch, 'Mia there's something I need to—'

The TV blaring out rudely interrupted them.

'You must have sat on the remote!' she said smiling. He pulled it from behind his back and waved it in the air as if he'd won a prize, then went to turn it off. 'No! Don't,' she said almost shouting. 'Don't turn it off please, I totally forgot that my dad asked me to watch this programme this morning on SAD, you know what my mum suffers with?' She looked at Alex searching in his eyes that he knew what she was talking about.

'Yeah yeah, sure.'

'Great, that's probably why he wanted to Skype me tonight – to see if I watched it. That was lucky wasn't it?' she said removing her flip-flops before she curled her feet up onto the couch under her bottom. She felt her shoulders drop and a sense of calm rushed through her, she'd hold off until she'd digested this information and then she would 'talk' to Alex.

Mia hadn't anticipated that the show would be littered with other stories and she'd have to wait for the 15 minute slot on SAD, but it had been interesting. Alex had made them breakfast and it had been delicious. She ran her finger around the edge of her plate picking up the last remnants of the tomato ketchup and licking her finger.

'Jesus Mia.' She caught Alex staring at her.

'Count yourself lucky I didn't lick the plate!' she said cheekily although her face blushed slightly.

'I didn't mean that!' he said smiling, 'I was talking about that,' he said indicating the television.

'I know, it is terrible and people just think you make it up.' She leant forward and put her plate on the table. 'Mum was that bad,' pointing to the telly as if to make a comparison to what they had just seen, 'that's why they had to go away.' She crossed her legs and faced Alex on the other chair. 'What that doctor said was interesting, about it being hereditary, well the depression part. My nana was always depressed, my mum practically raised herself and her three brothers, but then she always thought she escaped the worst of it, but clearly not with SAD.'

'It's not like you'll get it Mia, you bloody love the rain and the cold!' She chuckled, he knew her well. Running in the rain was up there with writing and meeting new people, as her three favourite things to do.

'That is true!' Alex moved towards her and put his hand on her knee with made her flinch.

'It must have been hard when you were kids though?'

'Harder for Lucy I think, she took the brunt of it all and protected me, funnily enough just like my mum did with her brothers.'

'Has she ever... you know...' Alex was clearly lost for words.

'Tried to kill herself?' Mia helped him out. He nodded. 'Not to our knowledge, but then Dad is amazing with her. Not like that woman, Sandra was it?' Mia looked at Alex for confirmation, he nodded. 'No one took any notice of her, no wonder she got herself into that state. Dad adores Mum, warts and all. His only problem is that he wants me and Lucy and the kids over there, but he knows that's not fair.' Mia jumped up, she wasn't sure now was the right time to say anything. It kind of felt inappropriate and she had lost her nerve. She would have to save it for another day.

'What are you doing?' Alex asked.

'Making us a drink, you want one?'

'Yeah, I'll do it though.' Alex got up and walked towards the kitchen taking Mia's mug out of her hand.

She followed him and hitched herself onto the worktop, allowing her legs to dangle as she watched Alex move swiftly around the kitchen. He handed her the coffee, but managed to spill a little on her leg.

'Ow!' Mia squealed.

'Oh shit, I'm so sorry Mia!' He quickly ran the cloth under the cold water and pressed it onto her bare thigh. The red mark was subsiding as he held it on the burn. He moved back over to the sink and turned on the cold tap and began soaking the cloth again, he gently wrung it out before he placed it on the red mark again. The iciness of the water took her breath away. 'I'm so sorry,' he repeated. Their faces were so close that she could feel his breath on her cheek. Finally she turned to face him and their eyes locked. Slowly, he moved his free hand up towards her face until it touched the corner of her mouth. 'Red sauce,' he said. But she didn't care. She thought her heart was going to burst out of her chest. He moved slowly towards her, those few inches between them felt like miles. She closed her eyes and felt his hand on the base of her neck, then finally felt his lips press against hers. Mia moved her hands around his neck and began to run her fingers through his still-damp hair. He moved his body as close to the worktop as possible, which pushed her knees apart and pulled her body towards his. Her breasts were pushing up against his chest. She moved her hands from his hair to his bottom and pulled it towards her crotch. She could hear the heavy breathing between them but that was all she could hear. She hadn't heard the door, she was too caught up in what was happening, but Alex clearly had. He pulled away from her and she saw what she thought was a look of fear in his eyes. When she turned her head towards the reason she understood why. She felt her stomach flip and a wave of nausea hit her throat. There in the doorway stood Ben.

Chapter 22

Ben

'Shit,' Alex panicked.

'Hi mate,' he said to Alex and then he paused before he said her name, 'Mia.'

She did not turn round; she had seen him in the doorway and turned away, terrified. He had caused that look of fear and he hated himself for it. He was lost for words as he took in the sight before him. Mia was sat on the worktop, her tiny frame looked tense as she stared down at the floor. Ben watched as Alex moved his hands from Mia's thighs and seemingly, nervously ran his fingers through his hair. Eventually he moved away from Mia, from in between her legs and he walked towards his friend. Ben moved halfway to meet him and shook Alex's outstretched hand. He expected a hug, as it had been almost a year since they had last seen each other. However, the circumstances were not what he had envisaged upon his return.

'It's good to see you,' Ben said, feeling the sweat on his friend's hand.

'Yeah, you too Ben.' Ben could see an anxious look in Alex's eyes. 'I didn't realise you were coming back today.' Alex stopped as he heard Mia climb down from the worktop. Ben watched as she walked out of the apartment barefoot without acknowledging either of them. 'Mia wait... please.' Alex shouted as he ran towards the door and stopped in the doorway. 'Oh hi Jimmy,' Alex said to his neighbour.

'The postie delivered this letter to me Alex, but it's your name.' Jimmy lifted his glasses up and looked more closely at the address showing Alex it too, 'looks like a misprint on the address.' Ben saw Jimmy through the crack in the door; he looked a little out of breath from his climb up the stairs.

'Thanks Jim.'

'No worries. Mia okay? She looked like she was crying when I passed her on the stairs.' Jimmy looked concerned then shrugged his shoulders as if to indicate that he had no idea why. There was a long pause and Ben realised that Alex either didn't know what to say or was contemplating going after her.

'Hiya Jim!' Ben moved from behind the door into view.

'Ben! It's good to see you mate.' Jimmy moved towards Ben and hugged him. 'What are you doing back?' Ben watched as Alex left the flat and assumed that he'd gone to see Mia. Jimmy watched as Alex left and repeated his look of confusion, shrugging his shoulders yet again.

'Few things to sort, you know, not everything can be sorted by email.'

'Even in this day and age! That's crazy!' Jimmy said, as he patted Ben on the back.

'You want a coffee Jim?' He seemed to take in Ben's luggage.

'Looks like you're just back kid,' Jimmy said, pointing to Ben's case.

'Yeah, not long ago actually,' Ben said flicking the kettle on.

'Don't worry about a drink for me, I'm good thanks. You get yourself settled.'

'You sure Jim?' Ben said, as he followed Jimmy to the front door.

'Honestly, but pop down when you've got some free time, I'd love to hear about New Zealand. Alex has kept me posted, but it'd be good to have a catch up.'

'Will do Jim,' he turned before he left and shook his hand.

'Welcome home mate! It's good to see you.'

Ben closed the door behind him and felt pleased that at least somebody seemed genuinely pleased that he was home.

'Ben! Where are you?' He could hear Alex shouting from the living room as he got out of the shower. 'Ben!'

'Jesus Alex, give me a minute!' he shouted back through the wall. He pulled on his boxers and walked into the living room where Alex was stood, anger written across his contorted face.

'Why didn't you tell me you were coming home early?' he paused, but only briefly, and just as Ben was about to answer, he began again. 'Months it's taken me for Mia to be alright and now we are back to square one. For fuck's sake Ben!'

'I did, I emailed you on Tuesday about it. I take it that you haven't read it?' He could see that Alex didn't really care about the email he was more concerned about Mia and just looked straight through him. 'She looked okay to me, you seem to be taking care of her.' Ben winked at

Alex, but this was like red rag to a bull. Alex flew at Ben and grabbed him by the throat, pushing him up against the wall. Ben didn't retaliate, he just let him, his guilt allowed him. Alex's anger seemed to have subsided as he let go of Ben's neck and Ben began to cough, gasping for breath. But Alex was not done. He punched him, hard in the face. Caught off guard, Ben fell to the ground. He sat on the floor, waiting to be kicked or punched further but when he looked up Alex was sat on the couch breathing heavily but staring at him. The pair were silent for several minutes. 'I'm sorry, that was in poor taste.' Ben said and Alex looked up at him, his eyes glazed over. 'What? I said, I'm sorry.'

'She's not okay Ben. She wouldn't let me in. She just ignored me, but I could hear her crying.' Alex put his head in his hands.

'I am sorry.' Ben stood up and walked into his bedroom, not knowing what else to say, instead he got into bed and wished he hadn't bothered flying half way around the world.

Ben felt like he had slept for days but when he woke up he saw that it was dark. He looked at his watch and realised that he was still the same day, but just much later. He could hear the TV on in the living room. He lay silently as he listened to the shouts from the television. He wondered how best to handle the situation with Mia and Alex. He would only be around for a few weeks, but he had so badly wanted to see Mia and make things right, but he wasn't sure if that was even possible after both of their reactions earlier that day. Alex had explained that she was great, she was like the old Mia, but had he royally fucked that up in one moment? It was time to find out, he thought. Ben got out of bed and pulled a T-shirt over his head, he felt the tenderness around his eye as he did so. He knew it was what he deserved. But now was the time to go and take the rest of the abuse Alex had in store for him. He wondered if Alex and Mia were together, it had looked like they were hooked up from what he had seen when he walked in. Time to face the music, he thought as he pulled the door open and saw Alex slumped on the couch.

'Alright mate?' Ben said as he walked to the kitchen to put the kettle on. 'You want a brew?' Ben could see that Alex had been drinking whiskey. He'd always been pretty good with his alcohol consumption when they lived together and hadn't kept alcohol in the apartment. However, he'd been gone for a long time and he'd expected changes. The good thing was that Ben was not craving it. He could smell it, but he wasn't dying for a drink. Perhaps that hypnosis that Jane had pushed him into was working.

'Come on Jane, that is complete bollocks and you know it!' he had mouthed the profanity as Jamie was waiting patiently by his mum's legs.

'Honestly Ben, you know Wendy's sister,' Ben nodded the obligatory nod, thinking he barely knew who Wendy was, never mind her bloody sister. 'Well her sister's nephew, it was his best mate and it worked on him,' Jane had said as rubbed sun cream into Jamie's arms, he was itching to get outside, he'd been off school with the flu and now he was like a caged animal trying to escape. 'Jamie! Don't forget your sun hat!' He had hurtled towards the door only to have to turn on his heels, as Jane had thrown his hat Frisbee style towards him. Being only five, he attempted to catch it but missed. He picked it off the floor and put it on his head as if nothing else in the world mattered more and proceeded to bolt out of the open patio doors.

'That sounds like one of those bloody urban legends,' Ben said as he flicked the channel on the TV. Jane moved to stand in front of the television and he slid along the couch to try and change the channel through her.

'I don't ask for much Ben, I never questioned what happened in the UK and why you felt the need to leave everything. But now I am asking for something. I REFUSE to watch you go down the same path as Dad. He destroyed our childhood Ben, and I will not allow him to do the same to your future.' She stopped and took a deep breath.

'I wondered if you were going to come up for air then sis?' He smiled and she returned it.

'I'm serious though Ben, please just try this for me?'

'Good God woman you have that look in your eyes when you wanted me to drive you somewhere when we were kids. You're doing your stupid sad eyes!'

'Pleeeeeaaaaasssssseeee?' She clasped her hands together in front of her chest like she was praying.

'Alright, alright, I'll do it. But don't come crying to me when I have come to you and to say I told you so!'

'Yeah, yeah little bro, of course you will.' She turned and flashed her sad eyes again. He lifted one of the cushions and threw it at her. They both laughed and she turned to him again and smiled before mouthing 'Thank you.'

He inhaled the whiskey fumes again and smiled as he thought about how Jane would react to this news. There would be no 'I told you so', well only her to him.

Ben poured Alex a coffee. He hadn't answered him but thought that perhaps he would appreciate it. As he walked over to the couch, he handed it to Alex who ignored him, so he put it on the coaster in front of him.

'I'm sorry,' Alex said as he turned to look at Ben. 'I was totally out of order for hitting you.' Ben wasn't sure what to say. 'I was pissed off with myself and took it out on you.' Alex took the whiskey glass from his chest and drained the reminder of it by tipping his head back. He placed the glass back on the table and picked up the mug of coffee, raising it in Ben's direction. 'Cheers.'

Ben raised his tea in Alex's direction, but stayed silent. The silence remained for a good ten minutes or so. 'Any word from Mia?' Ben broke the silence. Alex picked his phone up from the table and pushed the home button as it lit up his face.

'Nope.' He threw it back onto the table. 'I can't believe I didn't tell her you were coming.' He flung his head back onto the couch.

'I thought you mightn't have got round to it when I saw her face.'

'I swear to God Ben, there's been so many times. Then this morning, she came to see me. I thought this is a sign. Ben gets back tomorrow, I'll tell her now. It's the perfect opportunity... but then I burnt her leg and then we kissed.'

'You burnt her leg?' Ben looked confused.

'Yeah, by accident and then we kissed after that and now she'll never kiss me again for lying to her.'

'She will mate, just give her time. Plus, I'm only here for a few weeks, when I'm gone, it'll get back to normal, surely?'

'I hope so mate, I really do hope so.'

*

Three weeks had flown by and Ben was actually a little sad to be leaving the UK again, he had seen loads of his old friends and bumped into Jessie with her boyfriend, Jake. She looked fantastic, glowing almost.

'We should meet up properly before you go back. I'll speak to Mia.' Clearly Jessie was still in the dark about what had happened and he was not about to start filling her in. Plus, he also knew that he wouldn't see them again. It's something that he had said to most people when he saw them, but realistically three weeks was not a long time.

He headed up the stairs to their apartment having lingered on the bottom flight, contemplating whether he should knock on Mia's door. Alex had told him not to, but it was his last opportunity before he flew tomorrow. He was glad that he hadn't when he put the key in the door and saw Alex and Mia sat on the couch. Granted, not sitting on the same couch but at least he must have had a conversation with her to get her to be sitting in their apartment.

'Hi Mia.' Ben realised that his voice sounded pleased.

'Hi Ben.' Mia looked up at him and smiled. Not the smile he remembered, one that was full of life, it was weak. He felt responsible for that.

'Do you want a coffee Mia? Alex?' Ben placed his shopping bags onto the worktop.

'Sit down Ben, Mia's not staying.' His heart sunk even more, he felt like he was drowning in guilt.

'Oh right... okay.' He headed over to the couch that Alex was on and sat next to him.

'You look great Ben.' Mia spoke softly and sincerely.

'Thanks.' He would have normally returned the compliment, but this was so far removed from a normal situation.

'I shouldn't have walked out that day...' Mia continued, but before she could finish Ben cut in.

'It's okay...'

'Let me finish Ben, please.'

'Sorry.'

'I shouldn't have walked out. I was just so shocked.' He could see Alex looking at Mia. There was a look of hope in his eyes, but it was enveloped in pain. 'Of course, I didn't know you were coming back here as, for whatever reason, Alex hadn't gotten around to telling

278

me.' She paused briefly as her eyes darted to Alex and they both looked at the ground. 'But I have come so far Ben, don't get me wrong, it's taken a long time. But I realise now that I can see you... I mean I can be in the same room as you. I've seen you loads of times leaving the apartments... and it made me realise that I needed, no wanted, to come and say a proper goodbye.' Ben's heart lifted. 'What you did to me that day... it wasn't you. I know you have demons Ben, but don't we all? Unfortunately for you though, you have to wear yours like a coat of armour for everyone to see. You can't hide from your secret, can you?' Ben looked at Mia astonished by what she was saying, but he shook his head in answer to her question. 'I do forgive you Ben, because life is too short to live in the shadows of the past. We can't change it, but I admire you for not giving up on wanting to fight your demons. I know deep down you are a good man. Whether we ever meet again Ben, I want you to know that I forgive you.' She stood up and walked towards him. He stood up too as she showed him her outstretched arms and he embraced her tiny frame.

'I am sorry Mia.'

'I know you are Ben, I really do.' He was lost for words, it was like Mia had saved him from drowning, and he didn't deserve her kindness. The guilt that weighed him down for the last year had been lifted; he finally found the words that would never really be enough.

'Thank you.'

Chapter 23

Lucy

'How was she?'

Lucy put her bag onto the front desk in the reception area as Pam swivelled around in her chair. 'She was okay,' Lucy said trying to hold it together, but she felt her bottom lip begin to quiver and cursed Ed for not being there. According to Pam, he'd been called out on an emergency as soon as he'd set foot in the door that morning.

'But *you're* not are you?' Pam ushered her towards the door and called into the back office, 'Nicola, I need 10 minutes, come and take over please.' Nicola dutifully stood up without hesitation and scuttled towards the seat that Pam had just left.

'Come on you. Let's get you a cup of tea.'

Lucy watched as Pam moved swiftly around the staffroom kitchen. She was a big lady with a warm heart; Lucy was only now discovering the latter. She had always come across as somebody who was fierce and certainly somebody you would never dare to cross. You needed that on a surgery reception desk because Lucy had often witnessed the grief that she took. She got the blame for everything; the fact that the traffic had been bad on the way there making patients miss their appointments, when their prescriptions weren't quite ready, or that their own doctor was off sick. Heaven forbid that they were not the only sick people in the world. She needed her fierce side most of the time, but she had a caring side that outweighed that. She saved it for the kind and pleasant patients and apparently for Lucy right now.

'It's okay Lucy, it'll get easier.'

'But she looked so sad when I left her, although she didn't cry,' Lucy said hoping to cheer herself up a little.

'Look Lucy, when I left our Tom at the school gates for the first time, it broke my heart. Not his, he skipped off and never looked back.' Pam placed the mugs in front of them as Lucy drew hers closer to her body. 'It's not that I wanted him to be upset, I just wanted him to be bothered that he wouldn't be spending the day with me...' Pam pulled out the chair and sat down next to Lucy, '... and now, at 31, with this bloody economy, I can't get shut of him!' They both laughed, but Lucy could tell she was delighted to be doing his washing, cooking his tea and taking care of him. Lucy wiped the tear from her cheek and took a swig of her tea. 'But seriously Lucy, it will get easier to leave her. She may have been at that window looking sad but I bet, once she turned around and saw the amount of toys that she could play with and the new friends she could meet, she would have had a big smile instead of that frown. Distraction... that is all that kids need.' Pam took a swig of her drink, 'plus she has Mrs Daniels doesn't she?' Lucy nodded. 'Kindest woman you will ever meet.'

'Oh that's good to know. Thanks Pam, I know you're right.'

Pam stood up and finished the rest of her drink; Lucy had barely touched hers. She began washing her mug as Ed walked in.

'Pam, Lucy.' Ed still had his Doctor voice on and it made Lucy inwardly smile.

'I'll leave you two to it,' Pam said as she left the room.

'Thanks again Pam,' Lucy shouted after her, but Pam did not turn around, just waved her hand in Lucy's direction as she headed for the desk with her game face back on.

'How was your call out?' Lucy asked as she watched Ed make himself a drink. She stood up, feeling that it was about time that she did something seeing as she'd come in an hour late so that she could take Evie to her first day at school.

'Awful.' Ed didn't elaborate.

'Oh,' Lucy didn't really know what else to say. 'All okay now?'

'No, I had to get him to the hospital.'

'Anyone we know?'

'Sebastian.'

Lucy felt like her heart had just hit the floor. She moved towards Ed and hugged him. She allowed herself to shed a little tear, knowing that her daughter's first day tears would mask not only the real reason but also her guilt.

Lucy had somehow managed to get herself through the rest of the day and was annoyed that she couldn't go and pick Evie up. It had meant so much to her to see her daughter into class on her first day of school this morning. She would have loved to be the one waiting at the school gates at the end of the day too. However, Ed had arranged his afternoon around it and it wouldn't be fair to try to steal the pickup shift too. Also, she had no gaps that afternoon. Luckily, her 4.15pm cancelled at short notice and she told the front office that she would catch up on paperwork. However, she found it a great time to make a call to her daughter to find out how her first day went and another call to Mia.

'Hello.' Mia answered the phone, more quickly than she had expected.

'Hi Mia, what you up to?' Lucy was making idle chitchat when really she just wanted to get down to brass tacks.

'I'm just pottering today, I told you that earlier when I text you to ask how Evie was this morning. You okay?' Mia sounded genuinely concerned.

'Yeah, yeah I'm fine.'

'Tell me you didn't Lucy, you promised.' Mia paused and a silence fell between them, 'Tell me you didn't sleep with Sebastian?'

Ignoring her question, Lucy ploughed on, 'Can I ask you a favour? I need you to do something for me tonight.'

'Lucy!' Mia sounded really angry all of a sudden.

'Do this for me and I promise I'll tell you everything.'

'I can't believe that I'm doing this for you Lucy! 'I'm lying, I love you, but I'm going to have to lie to Ed now, to his face. I know he can be dull but he is still the father of my niece and nephew!'

'And I'm your sister!'

'Don't you shout at me! Don't you dare shout at me, when I'm the one doing you a favour!' Lucy realised how angry her sister was and that their screams had gotten louder and louder and somewhat out of control. It was ridiculous; the whole situation was ridiculous.

'I'm sorry, I'm really sorry Mia.' Then the tears came and they flowed, she sobbed like she hadn't done in a long time. She cried when Sebastian had gone all that time ago, but not properly she felt too guilty mourning the loss of a relationship that barely ever was, guilty about her kids, her husband. But now she was crying for Sebastian, for his kids who had lost their mum and were now going to lose their dad. She had a pain in her stomach, like an empty hollow feeling. She hadn't realised that Mia had pulled over into a layby. It was only when she felt Mia's arm around her that she knew they were at a standstill. She let the minutes pass as her sobs subsided into nothing but heavy breathing. The silence between them was nice after all of the screaming and sobbing. Mia put her hand on Lucy's leg but did not look at her, before she turned the key in the ignition and headed for the hospital.

'Thank you for this Mia, I'll be back in an hour.'

Lucy watched as her sister drove off then she headed up to oncology. She knew this hospital like the back of her hand, she had worked there for five years and there had been very little change since she had left. She got into the lift. Luckily she had missed the visiting hour rush, due to all of the pandemonium in the car. She pushed the button for the tenth floor and watched as the numbers flashed before her eyes one by one. It stopped at the fifth floor and she watched as a woman popped her head in.

'You going up or down?'

'Up,' Lucy answered and smiled. The doors closed leaving her alone in the lift. She found herself thinking about the time they had all gone to Dublin for Mia's birthday and Jessie had pushed all of the buttons on all of the lifts. She often wondered how lifts confused so many people.

Ding. The lift had arrived at the tenth floor and, in a haze; she headed to the reception desk. 'What room is Sebastian Forsyth in please?' She was relieved that there seemed to be all new staff and nobody recognised her.

'It's room 2, just where his mum is coming out of,' the nurse said as she pointed in the direction she could see Mrs Forsyth.

'Lucy,' Sebastian's mum said in an almost whisper, as she moved towards her, 'Oh Seb will be so delighted that you came.' She drew Lucy towards her for a warm and gentle hug. 'Go in my love, I was just about to go and get a drink and stretch my legs.'

'Thank you.' Lucy gently pushed the door open to see Sebastian sleeping. She had seen him less than a week ago and the change in him was astounding. He was gaunt and hollow. She sat down in the chair that was

288

still warm from Mrs Forsyth. She leant forward and held his hand. He flinched but did not wake. She leant further forward and stoked his hair. This was like the last time that they had seen each other – Sebastian had been lying in bed and she had been stroking his hair.

'This has been lovely,' Sebastian had said as he touched her face. She stood up and walked into the bathroom. She had known that if she stayed in the room he would see her tears. She wiped them away as she looked at herself in the bathroom mirror.

'Really lovely,' she replied once she had composed herself and walked back into the bedroom. 'It's time to re-enter the real world now though.'

'That's true, we need to check out, let's get sorted,' he had replied.

Now Sebastian began to stir and eventually opened his eyes. She didn't know how long she had just been looking at him. A weak smile crossed his lips and he managed to squeeze her hand.

'Hello,' he said softly.

'Hi, what happened?' Lucy said feeling a lump creeping into her throat.

'I just felt really tired this morning.' He stopped. The words seemed like such an effort. 'Mum insisted on getting the emergency doctor out,' pausing again briefly to catch his breath. 'I'm sorry. I didn't know that it would be Ed, I'm sorry.'

'Don't say sorry, its fine. How are you feeling now?'

'Tip top,' he began to laugh but broke into a tirade of coughing. She jumped up and ran around to pick up a glass of water with a straw in and made him sip it slowly. His breathing was heavy but it began to slow and ease.

'Lie down,' she said as she found a cloth and a basin by the side of his bed with cold water in it. She wrung out the cloth and gently placed it on his forehead. Sweat had appeared on his brow from the hacking cough that seemed to tire him even more. 'Who has the kids?'

'Linda.'

She heard Mrs Forsyth say as she entered the room again with two cups of coffee. 'Oh that's good of her,' Lucy said as she let Mrs Forsyth passed to sit by her son. 'Linda's always been a good neighbour.'

'I gave her a quick call and she said that they're okay to stay over tonight just until your sister arrives tomorrow afternoon,' Mrs Forsyth said, handing Lucy a cup.

'When will you get out Sebastian?' Lucy said as she took a sip of her coffee.

Mrs Forsyth threw her a look of confusion, almost disdain, as her phone began to ring. 'You can't have your phone on my love.'

Lucy cut Mia's call dead and quickly text her apologising and saying she'd be five more minutes. She realised then that she had been gone for 90 minutes that time had flown by. She felt like she was drowning, asking stupid questions and acting like she'd never stepped foot in to a hospital before. Denial was her only explanation.

'I'm going to have to go Sebastian. I'll come again in a few days,' she touched his hand and lent over and kissed him gently on the cheek.

'I love you,' he whispered in her ear. She smiled back at him and brushed his face with the back of her hand.

'It was lovely to see you my dear.'

'And you too Mrs Forsyth. I'll see you soon.'

'I'll walk you out.' Lucy smiled back at Sebastian and watched as the door closed behind her, until she could no longer keep the locked gaze they had been holding. They waited in silence for the lift to arrive. 'You do know that he's not going to make it out of here Lucy?' she watched as Sebastian's mum's eyes glazed over.

'What?' she replied, letting denial yet again be the protective fence that had kept her safe since he had told her about his illness.

'Did he tell you? He's been given days?' she could obviously tell by Lucy's face that he had told her nothing of the sort. Months, he had said months. But days, no that couldn't be true. Lucy began to cry, she couldn't stop and Mrs Forsyth embraced her.

'I'm sorry, I shouldn't be crying this must be awful for you... and the children.'

'We've had a long time to process this; he's been terminal for a long time now. The children will live with me in Scotland. I'm cross that he wanted to come all the way back here when he was not up to it and now it looks like this is where he will spend his last few days. Not in Scotland, which has been his home for such a long time.'

The lift door opened for the second time, her phone was vibrating in her pocket, her mind was swirling. 'Can I come tomorrow please?'

'Of course you can dear, he lit up when he knew you were coming.' Lucy hugged her again before she stepped into the lift and wished her a goodnight. Lucy found Mia's car in a daze, she heard her voice but nothing was going in.

'Lucy! It's been two hours, you said an hour. Now you definitely need to spill, all the details.'

'He's dying Mia, he has days to live... and I love him. I love a man that I can never be with.'

Chapter 24

Jessie

'Oh Jesus!' Jessie had attempted not once, but twice, to open the front door. She now knew that she should have placed the carton of milk onto the front step before she had tried the second time. She was stood looking down at her feet and then at her legs, watching the milk trickle down her jeans and begin to soak in. 'For fuc...'

'What happened?'

Jessie looked up as she heard the front door opening and there in front of her was Jake, looking slightly dishevelled. He bent down and picked up the carton that had burst all over the step and poured the remainder of the milk down the grid, then put the carton in the recycling bin.

'What do you think genius?' Jessie said as she passed Jake on the way to the bin. She began to take her boots off and then pull her jeans down. Jake often ignored her jibes, he was so laid back, thank Christ she thought, she wasn't sure how he put up with her. He often joked about the fire in her belly, that it never really was extinguished.

'Hang on Jess, let me close the door before you strip off in front of the whole street!' He pushed the door behind him and kissed her on the lips. She hadn't properly taken her jeans off, they were round by her ankles. She thought that she was going to topple over and grabbed hold of Jake's neck. He took full advantage of this opportunity, as she knew that he would. He pushed her up against the wall and began kissing her neck. All of a sudden, it didn't matter that her legs were wet from the milk and that she probably smelt, she just embraced it and just let Jake do what Jake did best.

'Hey, what are you doing?' Jess said as she rubbed shampoo into her hair.

'I'm getting in with you.' Jake smiled as Jessie leant back against the cold tiles to let him get wet under the shower. He still managed to sneak a cheeky kiss on her lips as he went passed. 'I put your jeans in the washing machine and put some oil on the door. It shouldn't be quite so difficult to open it now.' He smiled at her as she watched him rinse the shampoo out of his hair. He was so quick, she thought. 'Swap,' he said as he moved her by her waist towards the showerhead.

'Thank you,' she said as she let the hot water beat down on her back. She had forgotten that Jake was even in the shower with her. When she finally opened her eyes Jake was rubbing shower gel all over his body, but his eyes were fixed on her. 'What are you after?' Jessie rubbed the water from her eyes.

'What makes you say that?' he asked swapping places with her again to rinse the suds off his body.

'You have that look in your eyes, I know that look now.' They passed for the final time and as they did, Jake grabbed her bottom and she laughed. He then got out of the shower and wrapped a towel around his waist.

'Before you say no, I want you to think about what I'm going to say.' Jake began to spray deodorant as she scrubbed her face with the face wash.

'I knew it! I knew you were after something!'

'My mum asked us around for dinner today and you don't have an excuse.' This was not the something that she had thought he was after. 'We were spending the whole day together, so you have nowhere else to be today.' Jess got out of the shower, wrapping a towel around her head and one around her body, and walked straight into their bedroom. 'Don't ignore me Jess.' She sat down on the end of the bed and he sat next to her. 'Please, please come with me. Mum is dying to meet you, especially since we've moved in together.' She rubbed her hair with the towel then threw herself back onto the bed, letting her wet hair spray behind her. Jake stayed looking straight ahead, he didn't flinch, she could see his back from where she was lay – his shoulders were dropped, he looked deflated. He was so good to her; she just knew she had to go. It had been conniving what he had done, but clever too. This was the only way that he would have a chance of getting her to go. She knew she couldn't make any more excuses.

'What time?' Jess said closing her eyes tight. She felt him move on the bed, he had swung his body around.

'You'll come?' he said sounding excited.

'Yes,' she said forcing out a smile. He leant forward and kissed her on the lips.

'Thank you.' He said as he left the room, grabbing a shirt on the way to the ironing board. 'We need to leave in 45 minutes.'

'Oh this is such a delight to finally meet you Jessica,' the huge woman said as she embraced her in a big hug.

She didn't tell Anna, Jake's mum, that she detested being called Jessica. She didn't want to hurt her feelings, so she decided to keep quiet. Surprisingly, she had loved spending the afternoon with Jake's mum. She was a charming woman who appeared to have the heart the size of England. She had worn her paisley apron since they had walked through the door and her bouncy hair only matched her bubbly personality. Her ruby red lipstick had not moved an inch from her lips since they arrived, which was quite some skill considering they had eaten a whole, delicious roast dinner. Jake must have spoken to his mum and asked her not to mention her past. She was very grateful that Anna had respected that and only asked about her work and their new living arrangements. She had been panicking the whole journey over in the car.

'Trust me Jess, you'll love my mum, everybody does,' he smiled and grabbed the back of her neck acting as some reassurance. 'But my dad, not so much. People often wonder how they ended up together. They practically live separate lives. He'll join us for dinner, but then he'll go back into the front room with his pipe and we won't see him again.'

She had felt relieved knowing that is wasn't just her family that was odd.

'You will come again, won't you Jessica?' Jessie nodded and smiled, thinking she really would like to come again. 'You must visit again Jacob. I have had the loveliest time,' Jake's mum said, embracing them together.

'Sure Mum, of course we'll come again,' Jake said kissing his mum on the cheek. As they walked hand in hand towards the car Jessie turned around and kissed him on the lips. 'What's that for?'

'Just because.'

'Just because what?' He looked at her confused. She smiled, ignoring his question. If he could allow her into his very strange family set up then maybe it was time to open the door to a few of her skeletons.

'I'd like you to meet my mum.'

'Oh Jess, why did you never say? Now I feel stupid.' Jessie led Jake by the hand through the cemetery until they reached the right grave. She stayed silent. She was often at her quietest here out of respect. 'You let me go on about how cool it was gonna be to meet your mum. I'm sorry.'

Ignoring Jake, she said, 'Here she is. Sharon Cole, or Shaz to her friends.' Jessie bent down and pulled out the dead flowers from the vase and placed them onto the ground as she fixed the others. She laid her hand on top of the headstone and shut her eyes speaking to her mum in her head. "You'd have loved Jake mum, he'd have made you laugh and he takes very good care of me." Jake hadn't spoken for a while and she turned around to see him staring right at her. He must have realised that she liked the silence.

She stood up and he pulled her into him, he had his hands wrapped around her waist and she laid her hands on top of his. She felt his breathing, slow and steady in her ear. 'I love you Jessie Cole.' She felt like her legs had gone from under her, like they had gone to jelly. She

300

wondered whether he had just said that because of where they were, like a pity "I love you". She didn't care whether it was or not, standing there made her feel so far away from her mum, even though she couldn't be any closer. She turned around and kissed him on the lips.

'I love you too Jake.' She hugged him so tight to stop herself from crying. 'Come on let's go.' She grabbed his hand and with her other hand she picked up the dead flowers. She stopped and looked longingly at the headstone and before she left said, 'I love you too Mum.'

She could hear Jake at the bar, 'A whiskey and ice please mate, and a pint of bitter.' She had sat in a tucked away corner where they could get some peace and quiet. Jake hadn't seen where she had gone, so looked a little lost carrying their drinks until he saw her hand waving in the air. They hadn't spoken much in the car. She had needed the silence to get her whirling thoughts straight. 'Cheers.' Jake said as he sat down and they touched glasses.

'To our mums,' Jessie said smiling.

'Our mums,' Jake nodded in acknowledgement. Jake began to speak and then stopped himself.

'It's okay, you can ask.' Jessie said as she felt the burn of the whiskey as it trickled down her throat.

'But you don't like me asking about your past,' Jake said as he took a huge swig of his beer. Jessie smiled as she leant forward and wiped away the excess beer that had clung to his moustache. He started again and stopped again, but Jessie's smile meant he knew he should carry on. 'You always gave the impression that your mum left you. Oh God, that sounds terrible, I mean you know, ran away.' Jake took another swig of his drink; in fact Jessie noticed that he'd nearly finished it. Maybe he was nervous, she thought. He was waffling and hesitant and that was not like him at all.

'Did I?' Jessie tried to wrack her brain about what she had said that would have given him that impression. 'No, it was me. I ran away.'

'Really?'

'It was a month before my 16th birthday and I just couldn't hack it anymore.' She felt a wave of nausea in the pit of her stomach. Had she become courageous because he had said those three little words, was she that naïve? Jake was looking at her with a look of concern in his eyes.

'It's okay...' she felt his hand touch hers, '... if you want to stop.'

'No, I don't. I want to tell you.' And she really did want to tell him, and like a tidal wave taking over her body, she began to talk and realised that she couldn't stop. 'Growing up it was just my mum and me and I loved it. I've never known my dad and nor have I ever wanted to.' Jessie took a sip of her whiskey and continued, 'Then when I was ten, my mum met this guy, Stuart, and six months later they got married. Initially I liked him, he would buy me things, keep me sweet, you know because of Mum.' Jake nodded fully engaged in her story. 'But as the years went on I realised that he didn't give a shit about me. I was surplus to requirement. Then every chance he got he would wind me up and treat me like an absolute dick.' Jessie could feel the anger raging inside of her at the thought of her stepdad. 'I hated him.'

'Did he ever, you know... touch you?' Jake asked looking anxious about her answer.

'No,' Jessie said leaning over and touching his arm. He seemed to exhale with relief. 'No, never. I would have ran away much sooner had he done that. He was horrible to me – called me a fat, useless prostitute. You name it, he'd think of a cruel taunt for any situation. I know I was a sensitive teenager who had a wild streak by this point, but I didn't deserve the verbal abuse he gave me. And he was clever, Mum never once heard him speak to me in any other way than in his pleasant "You got enough money to go out tonight Jay?" tone. I fucking hated the way he called me Jay, as if it was just our thing. I hated it.' She picked up the bar mat and began to pick at the corner of it. 'He was a deceitful bastard.' She stopped overwhelmed by her emotions. She wiped a tear from her eye before it slid down her cheek. Jake leant over and gently touched her face with the back of his hand. She downed the remainder of her whiskey.

'You want another?' She shook her head and he remained seated, clearly waiting for the rest of her story. 'Then things seemed to get better, my mum got pregnant and they couldn't have been happier. He began to be nice to me, but it didn't last long and I realised then that he hated me because it meant that my mum had been with another man. He adored my mum, but I was always there reminding him that she'd been with someone else. They found out at the 20-week scan that they were having a boy. Daniel would be his name. Once he found out he was having a boy and they'd given him a name, it started all over again. I'd be replaced; I wasn't needed around there anymore. They'd have their perfect little family which didn't include me.'

'How did your mum not know?' Jake asked confused.

'She was head over heels in love with him. I'd never seen her so happy, and she deserved some happiness in her life. So I just kept quiet. Plus he worked away for 3 days a week, so it meant I got time with her on my own, it's how I survived working towards those days when it was like the good old days.' Jake smiled at her, she could feel the pity exuding from him and she didn't like it, but she knew now she had started this story she was determined to finish. 'Then, seven months into her pregnancy, she miscarried.'

'Oh God, that must have been awful,' Jake said rubbing his beard.

'It was. We all went to pieces, but none more so than Stuart. His anger was bottled up until one day, when he took it out on me. He hit me so hard that I flew across the room and he screamed that it was my fault that Daniel had died.' Jessie couldn't look up at Jake, she felt ashamed. 'Then and there, I knew I had to leave. I was making this situation 10 times worse for them. He blamed me, for no reason, and Mum had to deal with that. I left for all our sakes.'

'Jessie that is horrific, he sounds like a prick.'

'He was.' She ran her fingers though her hair and exhaled deeply. She sat back in her chair, knowing that she had to go on, but couldn't find the words. Jake helped her.

'How did your mum die?'

'Cancer. It's the most horrendous disease. There was nothing of her at the end. She still had her beautiful face, but she was a bag of bones.'

'Did you see her before she died? Or did you walk away for good?'

'If Stuart had his way, I wouldn't have ever seen Mum again, but when she was diagnosed she asked him to find me. It was difficult. I was in and out of hostels and eventually ended up squatting. But even though I had to see his face every day I got to see my mum's, and it was worth it.'

Jake moved his chair around so that he could be next to her. 'Jess, I'm so sorry.'

'There's something else.'

'There's more?' Jake asked in disbelief.

'My mum didn't have much, she left me a little bit of money in her will, but the one thing she did want me to have was my Grandma's ring, which she wore every day.'

'This one.' He pulled the necklace from under the scarf she was wearing and found the ring that was dangling on the end, sitting neatly next to the heart he had bought her for her birthday.

She nodded in acknowledgement. 'But of course when she was gone, actually getting the ring was not as easy as you may think. Stuart wouldn't give it to me. When I asked for it at the funeral, he said that it had been buried with her. I knew that wasn't true because I had asked the undertakers. So a couple of days after the funeral I waited outside the house until he'd gone to work and I let myself in. I was gonna find that ring.'

'And you did!' Jake smiled thinking that this was the good news in the story. It pained her that he thought this was the end of her story.

'I did, yeah. I searched high and low for this ring and somehow I eventually found it. Little did I know that he would come home in the middle of my search. I actually thought he was going to kill me. He started throwing things at me, anything he could find. He called me a cheeky bitch, thinking I could go into his house and take what I wanted. I was in the bedroom and he began chasing me down the stairs, but he grabbed me by my hair as I got my hand on the front door. I remember the feeling of pure fear in the pit of my stomach. I truly thought he was going to kill me. I grabbed whatever I could get my hands on, which was a glass vase that had condolence flowers in. I found all of the strength that I had and flung it at him, cracking him over the head.'

'Good girl!' Jake seemed pleased.

'I managed to get out of the door and run, but I didn't know that he was running after me and being dazed, he clearly didn't see the car that was coming and it hit him.' Jessie put her head in her hands and inhaled deeply to stop herself from crying.

'But Jess...'

'Let me finish.' She removed her hands from her face and looked straight at him. 'Remember our first date?'

'Err, yeah, but how is this at all relevant?' He smiled nervously.

'We went for a drink in that bar after we ate?' she watched as Jake thought about it for a minute.

'Oh yeah and you left me standing there like a dick?' he smiled at the memory and put his hand around her shoulder, she shrugged him off.

'You remember?' he nodded looking worried. 'You were speaking to that guy at the bar?'

'Jesus Jess, I am so confused with where this is going and how you expect me to remember the guy at the bar?'

'The guy in the wheelchair.'

'Oh him! I know him.'

'That's him.' Jessie actually thought she might vomit onto the table.

'Who?'

'The guy in the wheelchair.' She felt like she was going to stop breathing. 'I did that to him, I put him in that wheelchair.'

'What?' Jake looked so utterly bewildered.

'That's Stuart,' she said. She watched as he opened his mouth to speak and she never expected those to be his words that left his mouth.

'And that's also my uncle.'

Chapter 25

Mia

Mia had made herself her first cup of coffee of the day and had curled up in her huge love seat that she had recently bought. She had considered at the time that it may be slightly too big for her tiny flat, but had loved it so much that she had bought it anyway. She would have to do some rejigging of the furniture, but that would come later. She had only just ripped off the cellophane that sat like a moat around the bottom of the chair. The chair was facing her patio doors and she had opened the curtains wide to let the beaming sun into her living room. She got the sun at the back of her flat in the morning and at the front in the afternoon. She had been gutted that she hadn't known this before she moved in; if she had viewed the place with her parents they would surely have asked. But with them being in Spain, she had house hunted alone and, in all honesty, had not done so badly. She loved her little flat. So whenever she could she made the most of the sun in the back. Mia looked out as she saw Jimmy walking past. It was early so she thought he must be heading out to the shops to get the paper. She wondered about Jimmy and how straight-forward his life probably was. But then she thought he could be in the same game as everyone else – looking like everything was normal when really life his was in turmoil. Was he hiding some dreaded secret too? Mia was struggling to get her head around everyone's stories. How on earth Lucy had found herself in this mess with Sebastian and now she was absolutely distraught. How was she possibly keeping this from Ed and the kids? All the way home she had cried in the car, and Mia had no words. She loved her sister so much, but she couldn't bear the thought of the devastation that this craziness may cause her niece and nephew. She stayed silent that night because she could see how upset Lucy was and did not want to start reeling off her true feelings on the matter. She never understood what led people to see their lives down two paths and choose the one that lead all the way down to a huge red button that had 'self-destruct' written on it. Was it that they believed that their happiness outweighed everyone else's pain? Or did they lose their moral compass whilst losing their senses? Or do these people, including her sister, live in denial of what the outcome may be?

Mia's phone had rung twice that morning and it had been Lucy, but she wasn't quite ready to speak to her. She realised that her thoughts had been rushing around in her head and she was starting to feel angry about the whole situation. She knew that if she spoke to Lucy right now, she would let a tirade of abuse come out and she still wasn't sure that was what Lucy needed right now. Instead, she ignored the phone ringing for the third time and thought about her own problems. Even with Ben's arrival, she had not been able to forget the kiss she and Alex had shared – it had been wonderful – but nothing had been mentioned since. Ben's flying visit had thrown everything into chaos and it had been important that she had sorted things with him while he was still in the country. She had never been the type to hold a grudge but in this case she felt she had every right to. She still couldn't believe that he had not found the strength to tell her that Ben was coming home. She was so angry with Alex. They normally text every day and Alex was still doing that, but her replies were less frequent. She was unsure of Alex's motives now, she was not blind to their chemistry, but she wasn't sure whether it had been a distraction so he did not have to tell her about Ben. Or was it a real desire? The way he had looked at her and kissed her that morning, she hoped it was because of the latter. Her buzzer interrupted her thoughts.

'Of course, come in Jake.' Mia pushed the button and let him in.

'Hey Mia, I'm really sorry to bother you.' He sounded flat and Jake was always so upbeat.

'Not at all, come in, would you like a drink?'

He stepped in but shook his head to decline the offer. 'No thanks Mia, I was just wondering if you knew where Jessie was?' Mia now noticed the look of worry etched on his face.

'Yep, she's looking after Robert and Annie's dog.' Mia was really confused, if they lived together why had she not told Jake? She continued anyway, 'His mother is celebrating her 80th in Portugal, you know she lives out there?' It was rhetorical question really, which was good as Jake did not reply. She carried on, 'they asked me to look after the dog, but I couldn't and when I suggested Jess to them Robert bit my hand off.'

'Right, thanks.' Jake turned and put his hand onto the door handle.

'Jake what's happened?' Mia said touching his arm.

'She told me Mia, what she did to my uncle and in true Jessie style...'He paused briefly and inhaled, Mia knew it was not for added affect, although that is the impact it had. 'She ran away. She ran away from it all and I've not seen her since.'

'You've lost me?' Mia said looking at Jake really confused.

'It doesn't matter.' Jake looked nervous thought Mia, he must now have realised that Jessie had never told her, whatever she had told him. 'I've got to go,' he said and lent forward to kiss Mia on the cheek, 'thank you.'

She closed the door behind him and looked to the sky, now Jessie was in a mess. It was all going so well. What on earth could have happened with her and his uncle? One thing that she did realise was that it was more than likely to be the thing that had held Jessie back in all of her relationships. She closed her eyes and prayed that he had not abused her, however she could not think what else it could be. She just held onto the tiniest bit of hope that whatever it was, they could work through it. Jake was the best thing that had ever happened to Jessie. Unfortunately, if she wanted to push you away, then sometimes, no matter how hard you held on, it was a lost cause. She wondered if Jake would be strong and patient enough to push through. She turned away from the door and caught sight of herself in the mirror, she held her own gaze to stop herself from bursting into tears. Why couldn't things for once in her life, and the lives of the people she loved, just run smoothly? Her phone rang again and she saw Lucy's name flashing across the screen, she was cross and answered the phone quickly.

'What?' Mia shouted down the phone, even catching herself off guard with her own attitude.

'Why have you not been answering?' Lucy asked, through huge sobs.

'I'm sorry Lucy. What's the matter?' Mia said hearing the distress in her sister's voice.

'He's gone,' she howled in pain. 'Sebastian has gone.' Christ, Mia thought, they had only seen him last night, but her sibling bond kicked the betrayal to the curb.

'What do you need Lucy? What can I do to help?'

316

'Thank you Mia. Thank you so much.' Lucy said as she embraced her sister. 'Are you sure you don't mind?'

'I want to help.' Mia said as she picked the kids overnight bags up from the hallway and walked over to her car. Lucy followed her. 'What are you going to do?'

'I'm going to go and see him in the undertakers.'

'Oh.' Mia couldn't believe what her sister had just said.

'Don't Mia, you promised no judgements.' Mia slammed the boot down and walked around to the driver's side. 'And don't look at me like that.'

'I'm not looking at you like anything.' Mia wanted to go and give her sister another hug, but she couldn't bring herself to. She knew a man she loved had just died, but she couldn't bring herself to feel sympathy in regards to this situation. It was just so wrong. She looked in to the car and saw her niece's innocent face looking up at her and pulling tongues in her direction. She threw her a huge smile back and finally stuck out her tongue, which in turn made Evie giggle. She was so excited about seeing Dusty, and Ollie seemed to be laughing because Evie was. Keep it together Mia, she said to herself, she opened the door and finally spoke.

'I'll drop the kids off tomorrow at 3.00pm, I'm in work at 4.30pm, that okay?'

'That's great. Thanks again Mia. I appreciate this so much. See you tomorrow darlings!' Lucy said, forcing a smile out at her two beautiful children sat in the back of the car, blissfully unaware of their mother's potentially detrimental actions on their lives.

'Bye mummy!' Evie said still super excited, but Ollie had clearly become bored and nodded off. Oh the joys of being a baby thought Mia.

'Bye Evie. Have fun!' Lucy replied.

Mia drove off and caught sight of her sister in her rear-view mirror. She watched as her sister covered her face with her hands and knew she was clearly crying. Her heart sank for her sister, but her head made her continue to drive on.

'It hurts Auntie Mimi!' Evie had cried for a good two minutes and she was starting to realise that people were staring at them. She had fallen over, in the park, chasing Dusty and now poor Dusty was feeling Evie's wrath. How fickle children were she laughed inwardly. Evie wanted Mia to shout at Dusty, but she had refused, it had not

318

been her fault, Evie had just grown tired and dizzy chasing her. Dogs loved to run around in circles, but little children did not know this. She knew this was why Evie was kicking up such a stink because Dusty had got the better of her, however she was not about to let Evie's stubbornness win this battle. Evie had the potential to be a little diva given half the chance and she was not about to let it escalate under her watch.

'Hey now little one, what's with all those tears?' Mia knew that voice and turned around to see Alex looking down at the situation.

'Dusty tripped me over!' Evie said pointing to her knee where there was the tiniest amount of blood.

'She did not young lady!' Mia said realising she sounded very cross. Alex looked at Mia with a smirk on his face. She returned his gaze and rolled her eyes up to heaven. Dusty looked forlorn on the grass and was resting her head on her paws. Alex patted his thigh and she soon ran over to flirt.

'Hello gorgeous girl!' Alex said playing with her ears. 'You been causing bother, without even knowing it?' Ollie was nearly out of his buggy trying to see Alex; he was leaning so far forward trying to get in on the action

319

that Mia thought that the pram was actually going to topple over. Alex obviously had the same thought and quickly leapt over to Ollie and started talking to him. Mia watched on and smiled.

'Can I get him out Mia?'

'Yeah,' she said as she continued to watch him. He was hunched down unstrapping Ollie from his buggy. His running gear looked so good on him and she loved seeing him all hot from his run, his hair went all floppy.

'Shall we go for a walk to the café?' Alex suggested.

'Yeeeeaaaah! I can get a lolly ice!' Evie said sounding extremely excited.

'It's a bit cold for a lolly,' Evie frowned at her aunt's response, 'maybe a cake?' asked Mia.

'Yeeeeeaaaah cake!' Yep, so fickle were children.

As Alex waited at the counter with Evie for her to make a decision, Mia sat with Ollie on her knee. She looked out of the window at the lake that was in the middle of the park. Ducks were flapping about as people threw bread into the water, she laughed as one hit a duck on the head and it appeared to get a little irate, flapping its wings like a lunatic.

'You'll never guess Mia, Evie went for the cookie, you know the first thing she chose!' Mia smiled as she took the coffee from Alex's hand.

'Thank you.' She gave Ollie his bottle of milk that Alex had also returned with, which was now at the right temperature for him to drink. He sat quietly on Mia's knee feeding himself as Evie tucked into her cookie, every now and then taking a slurp from her glass of milk.

'It's good to see you Mia,' Alex said holding her gaze and sounding genuine.

'You too.' She couldn't lie to him. 'How's work?'

'Good.' He stopped whatever he was going to say but then he decided to continue. 'That day Mia, when Ben arrived.' Her eyes shot to the floor, but she didn't even know why. 'I meant to tell you, you must surely know that.' She looked up and nodded at him. 'And that moment when he walked in… well, you know …'

'Why have you got that funny mark on your face?' Evie was staring at Alex's scar as if she was expecting it to talk back. Who knew how long Evie had been staring at it, making the decision in her little head to ask this question. She had clearly thought the question would be better asked once she had finished her cookie and given herself a lovely milk moustache. Mia wanted the ground to swallow her up. She was mortified.

'Evie, you can't ask questions like that!' Mia said, mouthing sorry to Alex. Although, Evie had asked the question that she herself had wanted to ask for a long time.

'Why not?' Evie looked confused.

'It's okay Mia, Evie can ask.' He leant forward and touched Mia's hand, making butterflies dance in her stomach. 'I had an accident and something happened to my face.' Mia wasn't quite sure that she believed that answer, but she had a feeling that the real reason should not be shared with a four year old.

'Can I touch it?' Evie asked innocently.

'Evie NO.' Mia actually thought she had died a little inside.

'Of course you can.' Alex looked at Mia and mouthed, it's okay.

She watched as her niece stood up on her chair and began to follow the path of his scar from his eye to his mouth. As she approached his mouth he pretended to bite her finger and she burst into a fit of giggles it made Ollie giggle too. Alex picked her up and gave her a piggyback all the way home as Mia pushed Ollie in the buggy. They got to the front door and Mia unlocked it as Dusty and Evie burst in, oh Dusty was back in Evie's good books now. Mia had Ollie on her hip as she turned to go into the flat. Alex brushed a piece of hair from her eye that she was struggling to move with Ollie on her hip. A shiver ran from the tip of her neck all the way to her feet. In return she copied Evie's earlier actions and ran her finger from the top of his scar all the way to the bottom. But he did not attempt to bite her fingers; instead he let her run her finger over his lips. She watched as he closed his eyes. It felt so intimate and intense she could have stayed in that moment forever, she too with her eyes closed.

'Can you smell that?' Alex asked Mia.

'Yeah, it's not me!' she said sounding astonished.

'I think it may be the little guy sitting on your hip!' She had almost forgotten he was there, but with the smell coming from his bottom, there was no doubt that he was there in all his glory.

Chapter 26

Ben

This was now the third time that Ben had attempted to Skype Alex. The first time he had tried, the connection was so poor it was like a snowstorm on the screen, so he had decided to move into another room. The second time, he had successfully connected. However Jamie, his nephew, had insisted that he come and help him move the huge spider in the bathroom. He was a man and he could handle anything, but spiders he was admittedly shit scared of. But then Jane had entrusted her son, his nephew, into his care for the evening and he was pretty sure she didn't want to find him dead the following morning because the only poisonous spider in New Zealand had bitten him. Tentatively he walked into the bathroom to see the biggest spider he had ever seen in his whole entire life sitting in the bath. He felt nauseous at the sight and he could feel the hairs on the back of his neck stand up. He knew that Jamie did not need to know this. Looking carefully at it, as if the pair were going into a battle to the death, he did think that it couldn't be one of those rare katipo spiders, the ones David had told him about. He said they were more like a myth in New Zealand and that there was no solid evidence that anyone had died from their bite in the last 100 years. Although this information did not fill him with confidence. An irrational fear was still an irrational fear.

'What are you going to do Uncle Ben?' Jamie innocently asked, looking at his Uncle like he had all of the answers.

'Well Jamie, what is it that you came in here to do?'

'Have a wee,' he said looking at him confused.

'Well, then you have a wee and I'll stand guard.'

'Can't you just take it out of the bath? Mum just picks them up and tosses them outside.' Oh nice one Jane, bloody Steve Irwin's twin sister, he thought. Even as a kid she wasn't frightened of anything. He remembered only too well the teasing that he used to get while she ran around after him with the spider in her hand. Even when she was in a restaurant 10 miles away, she still managed to make him look like a dick in front of his nephew.

'Well buddy, it is well past your bedtime and I'm gonna Skype a friend, so I'll deal with it later.' That was partly the truth – a little white lie never hurt anyone. However, if he did return later he wasn't sure what he might find. He had visions of the spider soaking in a lather of bubbles, with candles and a glass of wine, it was that bloody big.

'You could have got it by now,' Jamie said flushing the toilet, which made the spider scurry up the side of the bath. Ben moved far more quickly than he had anticipated. 'Are you scared Uncle Ben?' Jamie said smiling.

'Have you washed your hands? And brushed your teeth?' he said trying to ignore the question. 'Chop chop!' Why the fuck was he saying, *chop chop*?! He could feel the beads of sweat gathering on his forehead, he needed to get out of this bathroom and quick.

'I'm done. I brushed my teeth earlier. Will you read me a story before bed?'

'Another one?' He watched as his nephew stood staring at him with his puppy dog eyes. 'Sure, why not?' He found it difficult to say no to him and thought a story might calm his nerves before Skyping Alex. He watched

326

as Jamie skipped to his bedroom while he took one last look at the spider. As he closed the bathroom door firmly behind him he felt a shiver run all the way down his spine.

'Jesus Christ mate it was huge!'

'Was it really Ben? You know what you're like when it comes to spiders. Jane was always the one sorting them out.' Alex looked at him and smirked.

'Honestly mate... like the size of my fist.' He watched himself and saw his fist in a ball pointing it towards Alex and realised that wasn't the truth at all, but he wasn't about to go back into the bathroom and find out it's real size.

'Right okay.' Alex clearly had not bought his lie, but continued on. 'How's it going? AA? Kim? Things moved forward with her?'

'You know what, everything is good. AA is better than it's ever been. Kim left and...' Ben saw Alex look confused. 'Oh no, it's not better because she left.' He stopped himself before he continued. 'Well, actually it is. But it was her suggestion. She moves AA meetings once a year, she's been dry for over 10 years now and she says it helps to keep her on her toes. Plus she says that if she moves, she feels like she can offer more support to more people.'

'Oh right, so are you still trying to make a go of it?' Alex asked him.

'Yeah, we are taking it slow; I've been dry for a year now. But I like her and I don't want a repeat performance, you know what I mean?' Alex nodded, but his eyes darted to the floor. 'Anyway, how are you and Mia?' He had as good as mentioned her, why not do it again?

'She's doing alright, well kind of…. Dusty was really sick.'

'What?' Ben felt his heart drop, that dog was her world. 'Is she okay? Dusty… and Mia?'

'All's okay now, but Mia found a tumour on Dusty's neck and they weren't sure if they could operate. But as she's so young they thought they should give it a go and she seems to be making a good recovery. A slow recovery, but she's getting there.'

Ben wanted to ask if anything had happened between the two of them, after that day that he had walked in on them kissing. He hoped they were happy together and he hadn't spoilt things yet again. However, he now felt broaching the subject was inappropriate and insensitive. There was an awkward silence between them, unusual, but since Mia, to be expected. A swift change of subject was needed.

'Any news on Izzy? You heard from her?'

'Nope, thank Christ.' The pair of them smirked. 'She's still with that old guy.' Alex said. Ben did not like to say that he had seen her in a copy of one of Jane's *Today* magazines with one of the richest men in Scotland. All she ever wanted was to be spoilt and with this guy, that was most likely to happen. He was old, old enough to be her father.

'I'm happy for her,' Alex said almost through what looked like gritted teeth.

'You sure about that?'

'I'm just happy that I don't have to put up with her anymore.'

'I couldn't agree more!'

'What about work? That alright?' Alex picked up his drink. Ben could see it was one of his famous smoothies. Ben had tried one once and gagged so hard he actually thought he was going to be sick.

'Yeah, same old same old. I'm successfully fighting crime.' Alex smiled at Ben and winked at the same time.

'Whilst in training for the marathon I see?' That is what the smoothie always meant.

'Yeah.' He picked up his glass again and tilted it towards the laptop screen. 'Cheers.'

'Did you get in? Have you heard yet?'

'Not yet, but because I've ran a few with good times, I'm pretty much guaranteed a place.'

'Glad to hear it. How do you do it? What is this, your fourth one?'

'Fifth.'

'I couldn't.' He said shaking his head. 'One I'd get bored,' he paused briefly, 'and two, I wouldn't have the stamina!'

'Ah you would be able to do it! I couldn't do what you do week in and week out, get battered on that rugby pitch. I mean I wouldn't want to ruin this perfect face.' They both laughed, but Ben felt awkward. Alex had been the best looking guy at school by a country mile. Although, even with that scar, he was pretty sure he'd win that award even now. However, talk of that scar and everything that went with it had always been an out of bounds subject. When everything happened, Alex asked him never to talk about it again and he never really had. Ben ran his fingers through his ever-growing hair. 'You still pretty much the local hero then?'

'I scored the winning try yesterday.' Ben couldn't believe his luck when he came to New Zealand and started playing his beloved Rugby Union. It was huge over there and he was somewhat of a local celeb, only for his Sunday league team granted, but then what did he care. It felt good, really good.

'Nice one! Hey mate, looks like you've got a visitor.' Ben turned round far too quickly thinking it was the spider, only to be met with Jamie at the door rubbing his eyes.

'What's the matter little man?'

'I need another wee Uncle Ben and I don't know if you got the spider?' Ben turned to see Alex breaking into a fit of laughter.

'Well, on that note, you best go and sort out that tiny spider you saw.' Alex gave Ben a thumbs up for encouragement.

'Cheers mate.' As Ben turned his back to Jamie, he threw Alex the middle finger.

Chapter 27

Lucy

'How are you feeling now darling?' Lucy could not bear to turn around and look at her husband, as she knew the guilt would be etched on her face. She could also feel how puffy her eyes were and he would know she had been crying. Instead she moved her hand to touch his leg as a gesture of acknowledgement for his kind words. He placed his hand on hers for a few seconds and then moved it until it was on her forehead.

'Do you still have a headache?' He moved his hand down the back of her head and stroked her hair. She nodded her head in the hope she could keep it in the pillow. 'Well, Mia has taken Evie to school but she has had to drop Ollie off at my mum's as she has to take Dusty to the vet's today for her check-up.' Lucy felt a wave of guilt pass over her. Mia was looking after her kids as well as her sick dog. But the guilt only lasted a minute as a stronger wave, one filled with grief, passed over her. 'This is the third day you have had this bad head Lucy, if it continues I'm going to have to insist that you get out of this bed and let me examine you properly.' He leant over and kissed her on top of her head and she grabbed the back of his neck and pulled him in to her, in some vein hope that this would appease his worries. 'Sleep well lovely.'

'Thank you,' she managed to say. She waited until she heard the door close before she let her tears begin again. She had played seeing Sebastian for the last time over and over again in her head. She remembered their locked eyes as the hospital door closed on their final look. It had been the last time she had seen his smile. When she had returned the next day, she had come to terms both with how sick he was and the reality of losing him, but these last few days she knew she would cherish a chance to say a final goodbye.

She had felt nervous as she mounted the escalator looking for the oncology ward. The previous night had been a total blur and she had stumbled into the hospital anxiously searching for Sebastian. The thought of seeing him, even in these circumstances, made her smile. She walked passed the reception desk where there was a melee of staff behind the counter. Briefly she looked up to see one of the nurses with tears rolling down her cheeks, for a split second she thought about how hard it must be for nurses in the oncology ward and she remembered the horror of death that she saw from working in the hospital. The patients who died and passed on were at rest; the horror was the anguish of those devastated families left behind. She did not miss those dark days. She knocked gently on the door and walked in. She had expected Mrs Forsyth to be sitting at her son's bed, but when she turned around and saw Sebastian's mother's face, Lucy knew it was all over. She could already see the grief etched in the old lady's eyes. Her eyes looked red raw as if they were stinging, and the light caught her cheeks that were wet with tears.

'Oh Lucy.' She had hold of her son's hand.

Lucy couldn't form the words that she so needed to. She felt like someone had come into her chest and had a tight grip on her heart, then suddenly an overwhelming feeling of nausea passed over her. However, Lucy still walked around the other side of the bed in a zombie-like state and grabbed hold of his hand. It felt cold. 'When...' she couldn't finish the sentence.

'Early hours of this morning, they called me...' she paused briefly. 'I came straight away.' She stopped again

334

but this time brushed a stray piece of hair from his forehead. 'His breathing had become very laboured.' Inhaling deeply, she gathered her words and Lucy realised how much of a struggle if was for her to speak. 'But it was peaceful.' Then she began to weep. She was a quiet and inoffensive lady but Lucy realised that she mustn't have really cried before because the weeping became big hard sobs that she didn't appear to be able to control. It broke Lucy's concentration on Sebastian's face. She walked around and embraced Mrs Forsyth. Eventually her sobs became less and less, quieter and quieter, until everything was still again. Finally the silence was broken. 'You shouldn't have to say goodbye to a child. It's not right.'

'I know… I know.' Lucy held her as they both sat and watched him.

'You were very special to him Lucy, he told me so. Even last night. He'd be glad that you are here now.'

Lucy wanted to explode. She had held back her tears feeling that she had no right to cry like his mother, but that had appeared to push her over the edge and she began to cry, silently to herself. The tears ran down her face. She knew he was now at peace, no more pain or suffering. Instead, she became that devastated person who was left behind, that one who knew about the horror of death. She never thought when she comforted relatives in hospital that one day she would be on the other end of that suffering.

*

Ed had insisted that they should both go to Sebastian's funeral. She was planning on going on her own, to be able to stand at the back of the church and finally grieve properly. She was so angry with Ed for taking this away from her as now she knew she would not be able to.

'Darling, it's fine, I'll go on my own,' suggested Lucy as she put on her lipstick.

'He was my patient and our neighbour. We should both go,' he said as Lucy watched him attempting to find his black tie on the tie rack. Eventually he pulled it out and he started putting it around his collar. Keeping quiet she went into their en-suite and inhaled deeply. She looked at herself in the mirror, just today she thought.

She just needed to get today over and done with and then things could get back to normal.

'I knew it! I knew there was something!' Lucy had never seen Ed so angry. She looked down at her hands, which clutched around the kitchen chair, and her knuckles had gone white. She realised that she actually felt scared of her own husband. 'I was so embarrassed Lucy, crying as if you were the grieving widow, you cried more than his own mother, more than his own bloody children!' He picked up the nearest thing he could and threw it at her. Luckily, he missed, but the mug hit the wall and had smashed into tiny little pieces. She wanted to speak but looked at his contorted face and the fear inside of her wouldn't allow it. Her mind was racing, but outside of her head there was stillness between them. Tentatively, looking up she realised that Ed had been watching her. Not able to hold his gaze, she thought it best to continue to look away from him, in the hope he would speak first. Instead he stormed out of the kitchen and went upstairs. Exhaling slowly, she released her grip on the chair and ran her fingers through her hair. She looked at the destroyed mug on the floor and saw it as a metaphor for her marriage: a broken, ruined, mess. Ed had made assumptions but he didn't know the full story. He had made an instant decision about what he thought had gone on. Her eyes began to glaze over with tears and she shook her head bringing her focus back to the horrendous situation she was in. It was only then that she saw the picture of Ed, Evie and Ollie on the fridge and she understood that her children must come first, not her selfish lust for grief. She began climbing the stairs, taking two at a time. Desperate to fix the mess she had caused.

'What are you doing?' Lucy surveyed the scene before her. His clothes were messily thrown into a suitcase, there were shirts hanging out, socks thrown on to the bed and he was walking out of the bathroom with his wash bag. Her stomach fell to her feet, she knew this was her fault and she felt helpless to stop it. She stood watching him and waiting for an answer, but he just continued. After a minute or two, she spoke, 'Ed! Don't ignore me.'

'What does it look like Lucy?' he threw his wash bag on top of the suitcase as they both stared at it, like it had all the answers.

'You can't leave Ed, please... think of the kids.'

He looked at her with disgust on his face, but finally spoke. 'Oh I am thinking of the kids, not that you seem to have done that. You should be the one leaving, you cheating bitch.' Lucy inhaled sharply, the shock of Ed calling her a bitch took her breath away and she began to cry.

'I didn't cheat Ed,' she said through stifled sobs.

'Did you sleep with him?'

'No.' He paused and held her gaze, she did not look away.

'Did you want to?' Her eyes darted to the floor. 'You're a liar Lucy. A liar and a cheat. How can I ever trust you again?' He was struggling to shut his case as he had packed in such a rush. He continued rambling, 'I knew there was something. He was always just popping around here for the oddest of reasons. I suppose I trusted you, what a fool I was. The pair of you were probably laughing at silly old Ed. Too busy going to work and supporting his family to even notice.' She didn't speak as she watched him finally manage to get the clasp closed. She had moved to stand in the doorway in the hope that this would stop him from leaving. 'Move.'

She lifted her head up and met his gaze. She could feel his breath on her face. 'Lucy move, or I swear to God...' The rage was back in his face. She stepped aside and he brushed past her, knocking her back onto the doorframe. He paused momentarily at the top of the stairs and her heart lifted. 'Don't come into work tomorrow, you'll be busy explaining to the kids why daddy isn't here. Don't forget to tell them the part about you being a slut.'

'Ed, just let me explain. You haven't heard the whole story. Please.'

'So you didn't sleep with him Lucy. That was clearly because he was too sick. Something was going on and you chose your desire for him over our family.'

'That's not true Ed. I chose you. I chose you and the kids.'

'Because cancer didn't give you a choice. That is why you chose us, so don't stand there and lie to me yet again. Just remember Lucy, it's the events in our life that shape us but it's our choices that define us.' He descended the stairs and slammed the front door so hard Lucy thought the glass in the middle would shatter. She didn't know what to do. She knew Mia would be back with the kids in a few hours. So she headed down the stairs to sweep up the smashed mug, she got halfway down the flight and the realisation hit her. She slid down the wall as tears began to roll down her face. This pain was worse. This was a different sort of grief. She had potentially lost everything because of a choice that she had made. This time she felt as if her heart had been ripped clean out of her chest and was no longer beating. She had let her choice define her and now everything she loved so dearly was slipping through her fingers and she wasn't sure how to fix it.

Chapter 28

Jessie

'Are you sure you don't mind Jess?' Robert asked as he looked at her intently. Annie had barely spoken to Jessie since she arrived and was currently busy rubbing Harvey's face as he excitedly wagged his tail.

'Robert, I've told you four times, since I got here. It's fine – honestly.' She imagined that Robert was more concerned with how bad she looked for the sake of Harvey. If she looked this bad, could she be trusted to take care of their precious dog?

'It's just that Mia is busy looking after her sister's kids when she can, isn't she?' Jess knew that it was a question but it was like he was looking for clarification. She did not know the answer as whenever she got caught up in her own life, she knew she became withdrawn and an awful friend.

'Yeah, of course,' she mumbled knowing that she probably sounded unconvincing. 'Like I have already said, it's no problem.' She was starting to lose her patience and knew she was beginning to sound irate.

'Right, come on Robert, we'll miss our flight.' Annie finished her sentence with a smile thrown in Jess' direction, but not a thank you. She was so damn rude that Jessie was dumbfounded. The emptiness inside did in fact keep her speechless. Usually she would have thrown a sarcastic 'you're welcome' Annie's way, but she couldn't be arsed. Together they walked through the hall to the front door. She watched as Annie tottered on her too high heels, as Harvey didn't leave their sides. Harvey knew that they were going away, Jessie could tell, dogs were so astute. After some kerfuffle at the car, she finally waved them off and closed the door behind her. She realised as they had been talking earlier, that Mia had never told Robert that she had helped her look after Harvey before. They only seemed to trust Mia with him, but she was glad when she had said yes because she had met Jake. Just the sheer thought of him filled her with sadness and guilt. Jessie was using Robert and Annie just as they were using her; it seemed like a fair deal she thought. Even if they knew nothing of it. Desperation had been their

343

calling card that day after Mia had let them down. This was very out of character for her, so there must have been something bad going on. When they were showing her around the house, she felt it unnecessary to tell them that she had bounced up and down on their bed, ate ice-cream out of the master bath and had mind blowing sex with Jake on their rug in the huge hall that was the epitome of elegance at the front of the house. Her own desperation had met theirs with a grateful heart. She had so badly wanted to get away from it all and this had been a brilliant opportunity for her. Although, Jake had not actually been back to the house in days she was fearful that he would and she would have to regurgitate the whole story again. But with days of thinking time, she imagined his initial shock had turned to anger and who could blame him?

Jessie had decided that she would stay at Robert and Annie's. She'd had too many nights in the hostel. She knew it was wrong but then she was sure there were more inappropriate things that she had done in this house before now. Robert's house was enormous, but somehow she felt safe there, the stillness and vastness made her feel a world away from everything. The solitariness of the house out in the middle of nowhere, away from her worries made her finally feel free. She knew that she would have to face reality soon, but not just yet.

Jessie was flicking through one of Annie's many magazines absent-mindedly. One of the models reminded her of Mia. She thought about her friend and now realised why she hadn't seen Mia on any of the day shifts, as usual her selfishness had meant that she hadn't even asked her where she had been or what was going on. But the longer she thought about it, the more she knew how unusual it was that Mia had not been in contact with her. She would have at least had a text from her once a day, with the usual, 'Just touching base Jess.' However, they had been like ships that passed in the night, but now after Robert's update about Mia, she felt that she should text her.

Hey Mia, how are you? Is Lucy okay?
You seem to have the kids so much, x

Mia replied.

Just some problems between Lucy and Ed. I'm just helping out. I'm sure they'll be fine. How's Jake? X

Yeah all good thanks. See you soon, x

She felt her eyes prick with tears and she made an excuse to escape. Too many tears had been shed, not just over the last couple of days, but over the years. She had finally told someone, found the courage to share the truth and as expected it cost her the happiness she had so dreamt of all her life. She would never make that mistake again – never trust anybody with her secret. Secrets should be hidden, put in a box far away at the back of the brain, where they were locked and the key was thrown far, far away.

Robert and Annie had decided to stay on another week, which was a luxury you could afford when your mother lived in Portugal and you had your own business in the UK. She played along that it was somewhat of an effort, but deep down she was delighted. It meant she would be in the house for a whole month. Although elements of the house were a little pompous for her taste, it verged on sheer perfection, *House and Country*'s dream day out. Its elegance made her feel as if she were in an old house in the movies, sweeping curtains covering stain glass windows, hundreds of varied cushions – patterned and plain – scattered in countless huge rooms. That morning she woke up in the huge bed and stretched out her arms, feeling the pang she had felt every day for the last few weeks – the emptiness of not feeling Jake next to her. It made her jump out of bed. She pulled her joggers and T-Shirt onto her nearly naked body and caught a glimpse of her long hair in the mirror. It probably needed a brush through it, but then she had very little intention of leaving the house on her day off. She made her way down the wide set of stairs holding onto the smooth oak banister. She was met by Harvey, who was wagging his tail madly. She had really fallen for this dog. She had been with him 3 weeks and he had been great company, just what she had needed. She had got herself into a nice little routine. Jessie flicked on the TV and filled Harvey's bowl with water and dog food. She always held her breath when she opened the dog food tin and scooped it into the bowl. The smell made her feel nauseous. She flicked on the kettle and opened the back door so Harvey could go to the toilet if he needed. She went into the living room and lay on the couch with her tea and toast. She wondered if Phil and Holly on *This Morning* wanted to giggle at their guest — a woman who lived as a real life princess. Jessie was smirking, however she was still engrossed as they showed footage of the would-be princess' house and her wardrobe filled full of huge princess gowns. Each room was dedicated to a different princess. The living room had just been transformed into *Frozen*; Jessie couldn't help but think how cold it looked. She sat open-mouthed at the huge portrait of this princess wannabe hung above her fireplace with a long blond wig on dressed as Elsa. Absolutely ridiculous, she thought. Then the camera panned to Phil, somehow he was not laughing. They were so professional those two. Her thoughts were only broken by a voice at the door, a voice she knew so well. Her heart had all but stopped.

'Robert? Annie? Are you there?' said the voice that sounded like it had entered the house. Jessie jumped up and ran to hide behind the nearest wall she could find.

Her heart was racing and the hairs on her neck stood up. The pockets of silence were only interrupted by the voices on the television. 'Is anyone here?' it felt like an eternity, but she knew she had to speak, she turned the corner and they locked eyes.

'I am Jake, I'm here.'

Chapter 29

Mia

Mia had been staring at the ceiling of her bedroom for well over half an hour now. It was a rarity when she allowed herself the time to be still and take some time to reflect. She was wondering how she had managed to miss such a big part of the ceiling when she repainted, so she picked up her glasses from the side in case that altered what she saw. Deep down she knew her glasses would not make the slightest bit of difference and she would most definitely need to rectify the patchy paint job. Mia picked up her phone and saw a WhatsApp message from her mum, her parents had become obsessed with it since they had both upgraded to a smart phone. There was a photograph of her dad sitting on the veranda reading the newspaper as the sun was setting. He had his thumb up, in acknowledgement of her mum taking the picture, but he was clearly engrossed in his paper. Mia sent a quick reply saying that she hoped the weather was still as beautiful as ever. Before locking the screen, she checked the time and realised how early it was. She wasn't usually awake at this hour unless Dusty was nuzzling at her door. However, it had been many weeks since Dusty had woken before her. The medication she was on was making her sleep for hours at a time and she had not stirred through the night for weeks. As if Dusty could read her mind, she heard the door gently open and she sat up to see her slowly walk into her bedroom. Mia always slept with her door closed, but since Dusty had been unwell she had left it open and even had allowed her onto the bed. She jumped up without even being asked today and laid her head on Mia's legs. Mia knew that she was getting better; she just wished that she was well now and back to her old self. Dusty was like a different dog now, she had lost all the 'spring' in her springer spanielness. Mia stroked Dusty's ears and, for a moment, forgot. Dusty whimpered in pain as she had touched her wound were the vet had cut out the tumour.

'I'm sorry,' Mia put her face next to her beloved dogs. 'I'm sorry Dusty,' she repeated. She closed her eyes and for a minute thought of what might have happened if Alex had not found the lump on her neck. She shivered as though someone had just walked over her grave. She had been so caught up with supporting Lucy and looking after her niece and nephew, that Dusty seemed to have become Alex's concern and not hers. He had taken her out with him every day for his usual jog, really taken care of her while she had other priorities. She would never forget the look on Alex's face when he had to tell her what he had found...

'You dropped Evie off at school?' Alex had asked all sweaty from his run.

Mia handed him a glass of juice and smiled. 'Yeah, no tears today.' Mia didn't enjoy lying to anyone but her niece had sobbed every day since Ed had left the martial home and today was no different. She had cried because she wanted to see her dad, while Ollie was none the wiser. She had not confided in Alex, as she was unsure of what it would achieve. Plus he didn't need to know that her big sister was ruining her own life.

'And Ollie, no Ollie today?' She tried to read his face; he seemed unusually sombre. Not more bad news, she thought.

'No, I'm in work later so I dropped him at nursery and the in-laws are picking them both up.' She had sat in the love seat by now and Dusty lay across her feet.

'I need to tell you something.' She knew it. She knew there was something wrong. She felt like her stomach had dropped to her knees.

'Okay.' Her voice came out as a whisper, so she coughed and tried again this time saying, 'okay,' much clearer.

'It's just that when I put the lead on Dusty earlier she let out a yelp of pain.' Mia looked at Alex and down at her dog, she put her mug down and began to stroke her back. It was only now she seemed to notice how lethargic she was. Mia began to take off her collar but Dusty squealed and cowered away from her. She threw Alex an anxious look waiting for him to speak.

'There's a lump on her neck Mia…' he paused, she knew he was watching her eyes fill with tears, but she didn't seem able to stop them. Her hands began to shake as she tried to take her collar off. Alex moved from the couch onto the floor. 'Let me help.' He held Mia's shaking hands and placed them onto her lap. She watched as Alex, ever so gently removed the collar.

Dusty let out a cry of pain, but Alex continued to take it off. Once he had finished he looked up at Mia. She had been silently crying, without Alex's knowledge and her heart was hurting. 'Oh Mia, don't cry.' He wiped away the tears from her face and held onto one of her hands as he continued to stroke Dusty with the other. 'It's a lump, you don't know what it is yet... and if it is something then we can deal with it.' She nodded but did not speak, for fear that she would begin to sob and lose control in front of Alex. All she thought was not my Dusty, not my beautiful, loyal dog. 'We need to get her to the vet,' he said gently, she nodded again. 'Come on Mia, I'll take you.'

'Thank you,' Mia said as she put her key in the front door and Alex followed her in. She closed the door behind them and, before she changed her mind, walked towards Alex and embraced him. She felt so sad, but luckily they had caught the tumour early enough to operate. They had spent the whole day waiting for Dusty to have her surgery and Alex had not left her side. He had even phoned Robert for her to tell her boss that she wouldn't be in that day. As Robert was a dog-lover he told her to take as much time as she needed. She was truly grateful. The vet said that there was an 85% chance of a good outcome after surgery, as long as he got the entire tumour, which he did. The vet was pretty sure that Dusty could make a full recovery; she would just need some TLC to get her back to her old self. Her eyes had been closed and her mind had wandered off. She realised that Alex had been holding her, for how long, she did not know. But she had needed to feel the warmth of his embrace and then she realised that he was resting his head on hers and stroking her hair. All of a sudden it felt strange, she felt like she had over-stepped the mark, even though they had kissed that once, which felt like a life time ago. She let go and walked towards the kitchen.

'I've just realised that I'm really hungry. Are you?' Mia said as she opened the fridge and got out a bottle of wine.

'Mia,' Alex stopped, she wondered what he was going to say as his pause was evidently for her to speak but instead they held each other's gaze until his stare grew so intense that she had to look away.

'Wine?' She surprised herself with her lack of an answer.

'Mia, are you okay?' She saw the look of confusion on his face and she knew why.

'It's just been such a long day and I thought on the way home that I haven't eaten all day. I didn't have time to have breakfast with the kids this morning and I'm starving.' Mia wasn't remotely hungry but she knew talking was better than silence or Alex asking questions, but the bumbling she appeared to be doing seemed to be flummoxing Alex enough to stop his line of questioning.

'Okay,' Alex replied.

'Shall we get a takeaway?' She began looking through her drawer for a menu.

'Sounds good.' He took the wine that she had poured for him even though he hadn't said he wanted any.

'Chinese or pizza?' Mia said holding up two menus.

An hour later, Mia thought she was going to pop and she had only eaten two slices of pizza.

'I thought you said you were starving?' Alex said, picking up his fourth slice.

'I must have thought I was,' she lied.

'Thanks again for everything today Alex,' she looked at him as he was munching away on his pizza. Once finished, he spoke.

'I'd do anything for you Mia Richards.' He said, wiping his fingers with a napkin, but still holding her gaze.

'Well, you really were my hero today and more importantly Dusty's.'

'I didn't do anything except hurt her with the lead!' he said, as he put his arm on the back of the couch and rested it on Mia's back as she smiled a weak smile.

'I've just been so caught up with helping Lucy that I lost sight of what was going on in my own life.' She paused as she picked up her glass of wine and turned to face Alex. 'Who knows how long Dusty has been in pain, I feel so bad.' Mia held her glass against her chest as she inhaled deeply.

'Hey, all that matters now is that she's okay,' he stopped as he brushed her hair behind her ear. It made her stomach flip. Then he pushed her glasses on top of her head and he leant forward and pressed his lips on hers, the warmth of his kiss made her tingle all over. He

357

pulled away and Mia felt disappointed. 'Do you think maybe that we should move this pizza that's sitting between us?' She smiled and nodded as he stood up and took the box and her glass of wine over to the breakfast bar. He lay down on the couch and gently pulled her towards him, placing her glasses on the arm of the couch as he did so. He embraced her; she was entwined in his arms and it felt so good. She put her hand on his chest and she could hear his heartbeat as she laid her head next to her hand. He stroked her hair as they lay in silence. It was not awkward, in fact she realised how easy it was and she felt a little guilty for enjoying it when Dusty had been through so much that day. Then like a bolt out of the blue, it hit her as to just how tired she was. Her whole body had finally stopped, she began to relax as the day's anguish had finally come to an end and she was so glad about it. She could feel her eyes closing and no sooner had she stopped thinking she had fallen asleep.

Mia woke and for a minute forgot where she was. She had been woken by Alex's snoring, it was pretty loud and she smiled to herself. They had been lying on the couch for over three hours; they had both lost the battle to their sheer exhaustion. She sat up ever so slightly, trying not to wake Alex. She thought about how kind he had been today and how grateful she really was to him. She looked at his rugged face. He was so handsome. She looked at his scar; she still did not know the reason behind it. Only that it was something that had bonded him and Izzy together for many years of their lives. She touched his face and ran a finger gently along his scar, careful not to wake him. She often wondered how he got it. If he had wanted to share, then she believed he would have done it by now. She thought perhaps she would never know the story behind it. She had a feeling that it would not be a pleasant story, a secret he kept maybe for more than one reason. But she knew better than anyone that sometimes secrets are best left hidden. She knew that lies destroyed things, but then so often the truth destroyed much more and sometimes, you're kept in the dark for your own safety.

Chapter 30

Ben

The waves lapped onto the sand as Ben sat taking in the sun setting on the beach. He watched as the last few surfers took in the final waves of the day. He always admired the art of surfing. He'd have loved to do it as a kid, but living in the inner city was a far cry from any beach. Instead, he had hounded his dad to buy him a skateboard, unsuccessfully of course, as all of his dad's money was always spent on booze. However, he had Alex and although his best friend wasn't spoilt, he was just lucky to have a great set of parents who actually thought it necessary to buy him presents on his birthday. Plus with Alex, he was never against sharing, they had even shared the same girl for their first kiss, Alex first and Ben about a week later. He laughed to himself at the lack of appropriateness of it all now. Rebecca Riley had been the hottest girl in the year and oh how she had known it. She had kissed most of the year group by the end of that school year and, as the years went by and they progressed through school, she was known as St Eddie's School Bike! She had not disappointed when she got pregnant at 16, she really had lived up to all expectations. He remembered seeing her with three kids at 21when he had returned home from university. How things change, he thought, although by then he was well in the throes of his alcoholism, who was he to judge. His thoughts were only broken by a gruff voice.

'Alright dude,' a surfer ran past him with his board under his arm and acknowledged Ben sitting in the sand like a lone stranger.

'Hi mate,' Ben realised that his mind had wondered on to old stories. So once again he let his thoughts return to surfing. He absolutely loved surfing and, although he wasn't great at it, he was definitely getting better, much to his surprise as he had been bad at skateboarding. Alex, however, had been one of the best at the skate park. As teenagers they visited the park every weekend for months. Alex's tricks impressed all of the older kids and Ben went along as he had nothing better to do but to cheer him on. Until one day, Alex tried this trick that he had seen Tony Hawks do and

361

landed really awkwardly, so awkwardly that he broke his arm. It took months to heal and he had to have surgery and pins in his arm, by the time that it was back to working order, the novelty had worn off with the skate boarding, much to Ben's delight. He was fed up being the observer and not being able to take part. Deep down he also thought that Alex was fearful of getting on that skateboard again and who could blame him?

'There you are! Didn't I say, Jamie, that uncle Ben would be down here?' Jane was shouting in his direction and holding her son's hand as they approached. Ben turned and saw Jamie now running towards him and watched as he launched himself on to his back. He knew this was in a bid to wrestle him, something that they had taken to doing; it was just their thing. Jane hated it, especially as it was something her husband David would never do. So Ben, of course (particularly to annoy Jane) flipped Jamie over and wrestled him right to the ground and his nephew began to giggle uncontrollably. His face was now glowing like a tomato, he looked up at Jane who he could see was trying to look cross, but was actually smiling at Jamie's fit of giggles.

'Uncle Ben,' Jamie was trying to catch his breath, 'stop please.' Ben did as he was told, not before throwing a few sneaky tickles in there. Once both were calm, Ben spoke.

'So what are you two doing down here?' Ben asked his sister and nephew, whilst inhaling deeply and moving himself back into a sitting position.

'We are being detectives, aren't we Jamie?' said Jane, who was now removing the bag she had been carrying on her shoulder. Ben had not even noticed it, but then there it was in all its glory, Jamie's beloved metal detector. He was obsessed with finding things anywhere he went. Then when Ben had bought him the metal detector at Christmas his love of finding things multiplied tenfold. Jane had been bemused by his purchase, but when she had seen her son's face the first time he had used it, she had reluctantly patted her little brother on the back. Jane was adamant that it was all a load of garbage, but both Ben and Jamie were convinced that this would one day find their fortunes!

'Uncle Ben will you take me today? It's more fun with you than Mum.' Jamie turned to look at his mum and gave her a very big sorry grin, to which she replied with a smile and a stuck out tongue.

'Of course I will squirt, let's go and explore!'

'So what treasure did you find, oh wise and great explorer?' Jane said as she threw Ben a chocolate bar.

'I can't tell you, it may bring Jamie and I our fortune, and you're not getting a bean, the doubting Thomas that you are!' Jane began to chuckle.

'So the usual then, a few shells, a can of some sort and a couple of cents?' She picked up the warm drinks she had made them both and handed one to Ben.

'Actually...' Ben paused for effect, 'we found $2 and you'd have thought Jamie had won the lottery!'

'Brilliant, I bet he was thrilled.' Jane said cupping her tea. 'Sorry I had to rush off and thanks for bringing Jamie back and putting him to bed. Sarah thought she was actually going into labour. But just Braxton Hicks.' Jane was looking at Ben and clearly taking in his confused face. 'It doesn't matter and she wasn't in labour, that's all you need to know!'

'Oh right,' Ben was thinking that whatever his sister had just said seemed to make no sense at all.

'Anyway, I can't believe that you are leaving tomorrow,' Jane said looking like a sad puppy.

'The time has come sis...' he said bowing his head in a solemn manner, 'and anyway you and David will be glad to see the back of me, I'm sure.'

'David maybe,' she winked at him, 'but not me.'

'Ah really,' and for a minute Ben naively believed her. 'Yeah, I was getting used to having the babysitter on tap!'

'And there it is, true sisterly love.' Ben threw his sister two fingers as a retaliation.

'Seriously though Ben, I will miss you.' He started to put his fingers down his throat and pretended to vomit. 'Stop it! I know we always mess about, but listen to me.' He and Jane had always shared a good relationship. They had clung to each other when they were little, he although younger had always looked after Jane, until she was old enough for university. How the pair of them had actually managed to get themselves there and break the cycle was beyond them. There she had met David who had always wanted to live in New Zealand, so they left. He felt rejected again, not that he would have ever admitted that to Jane or ever stopped her from going.

'I'm so glad you came to New Zealand Ben. I thought you would have said no after I came away and we barely ever spoke. But after these last couple of months it's been like we've never been away from each other.' Ben was staring at his knees, he assumed Jane was looking at him, but he knew what was coming next and was too embarrassed to look up. 'I'm so proud of you Ben.' He looked up and in some attempt acknowledged her love. He felt stupid when people said they were proud of him. She hadn't made the mistakes he had and she had grown up with a drunk too. He couldn't begin to find the words to thank Jane; she had help set him free from all of his demons. He would always have to fight, but with her around and especially Jamie, he had a real reason to be a sober person. 'I love you Benjamin James Webster.'

'I love you too Jane Louise Ambrose,' and with those words her eyes began to fill up. He knew that without her, his life may have turned out very differently. His big sister had opened a whole new world to him and one that he was going to start really living, right there and then.

Chapter 31

Lucy

What a mess. She looked at herself in the mirror and pulled her cheeks down towards her mouth in an attempt to pull away some of the lines. She rubbed the black bags under her eyes that seemed like soulless pits of nothingness. It only reflected how she felt inside. Lucy not only looked, but also felt, like she had aged years in the past few months and now her face seemed to enjoy telling the story. Rubbing her eyes again and feeling exhausted, she turned around and looked at the alarm clock that read 4.00am. She had found it hard to sleep from the moment Ed had left and it had become no easier as the months had slipped by. The void in her bed made her feel so alone, yet angry as she had brought it all on herself. Before she let her emotions take over yet again in the early hours of the morning, she stopped and instead chose to take in the calmness of the silence. It was a rarity that this was the noise in her house.

Nothing but stillness. She appreciated it much more now she was taking care of the children on her own. The ticking of the clock and her breathing were the only two things that she could hear. She closed her eyes and let her whole body relax. After what felt like a lifetime, she opened her eyes and slowly walked over to her bed. Lucy picked up her phone and watched as the screen lit up. There was a text that had been sent from Emma at 10.45pm.

Hey Luce, sorry been mad busy today. How you feeling? x

She would reply in the morning, when hopefully she would be feeling a little brighter. She had finally decided to confide in Emma and since then she had been in touch every day. Emma had not passed judgement on her, and she was truly grateful for this. Her friend had been a wonderful sounding board, unlike her sister, who still found it difficult, even after all of these months, to hide her annoyance towards her. However, there was no denying, that Mia had been her rock during this whole process; whenever she needed support with the children, Mia had been there.

Lucy's phone screen had returned to black. She pressed the home button once again. Nothing. Every time she looked at her phone, it was in some vain hope that there would be a message from Ed. However, the only time they had been in contact was about the kids. She had been relentless in her quest to get him to talk about 'them', but unfortunately her efforts had been futile. He either completely ignored the message or diverted the topic of conversation to Evie and Oliver.

She got into bed and pulled the duvet over her head, clutching the phone to her chest. She had always hated the covers over her head, even as a child, she felt claustrophobic, like she couldn't breathe. Recently, however, she felt like she was living her days with the covers over her head, struggling to breathe as if her energy had been zapped. However, now as she lay there, this blanket of darkness brought with it an inexplicable comfort. Under the covers there was only dark. Seeing nothing did not stop her brain from going into overdrive. Ed was gone. She had no idea for how long, or how, if possible she could win him back.

However, there was one thing that she did know, it was that her heart ached; it felt so heavy in her chest. Not just as she lay in bed thinking about what she had lost, but particularly when she saw her children's faces. Evie was a constant reminder of Ed's absence, always asking where Daddy was. Lucy had made up lies to protect her innocent little daughter but it was getting more difficult the longer he was away. Many nights, she had held her daughter in their bed as she had cried herself to sleep because she missed her daddy. The guilt of it was all but tearing her apart. She realised that she was crying. This was a new skill that she seemed to have acquired – crying and not even realising it. She only did so when she felt the wetness of the tears on her face. She rubbed them away with the back of her hand. It was then that she realised she could not recall the last time she had allowed herself to weep about the situation. She had felt alone and depressed since Ed had walked out. Yet, it was like she was too exhausted to gather the energy to really sob. Or perhaps her body had refused to produce enough tears to have a really good body-heaving cry. Lucy thought that maybe each house had a quota of tears that they were allowed to cry in a year and she knew that their household probably used their quota up some time ago. Or perhaps not, she thought, as huge howls came from Oliver's bedroom. She thought it was strange as for weeks he had been so settled throughout the night. This had been a new thing; he had always been a crier. However, it was like he knew that Mummy needed as much sleep as possible, especially because she was so unsettled through the night herself. Yet, this morning he was screaming like a banshee. Lucy knew that it was going to be a long day with Ollie; she missed her job so much. Just like that, the stillness was gone and her day was just beginning.

'But Mummy, you promised.' She looked at her daughter's face that was etched with sadness. 'You promised that Daddy would pick me up from school.'

'I know I did darling and I'm sorry.'

'And why is your eye all red?'

'It's a long story Evie, but Daddy had an emergency in work to attend to this afternoon.' The amount of lies she told her daughter was getting out of hand. She couldn't begin to explain to her four-year-old about the day that she'd had. The day had brought with it a glimmer of hope of bringing some normality back to their lives. So instead, as she had most days, she used bribery to win her daughter over. 'Shall we go and get an ice cream darling?'

'Yeah! Can I have a big flake too?'

Ollie was finally fast asleep after battling with him at bath-time. He had tried her patience more than once that evening and she was shattered. So, after reading Evie her bedtime story, she tucked the duvet around her and lay at her daughter's side for a moment. Contemplating her day, one that had been so unexpected, she looked at her daughter and leant over to kiss her goodnight. Evie murmured and turned over to face the wall, pulling her favourite teddy into her chest. Closing the door of Evie's bedroom she then descended the stairs. She headed straight to the kitchen and poured herself a glass of large red wine. She smiled to herself, a real smile, a smile of hope although she knew not to get too carried away. Sitting down at the kitchen table, she thought about how the events had unfolded that afternoon.

She had been exhausted after Ollie woke her at 4.00am. As usual, Ollie's naptime had taken place around mid-afternoon and she had so desperately wanted to curl up on the couch and join him. However, she knew since Ed had told her not to return to work, she would be damned if her job as a mother and housewife would not be done to the highest of standards. As she was in the middle of carrying out her chores that afternoon, she heard the key in the front door and assumed it was Phil. Although, it was unusual for Ed not to text to warn her when Phil was coming over to see his grandchildren. She had seen Phil, Ed's Dad more times in this last month than she had in the last three years. If Ed wanted something from the house he had always sent his dad, which had been somewhat embarrassing. Yet from the small conversations she and Phil had undertaken, she was pretty sure that he did not know what was going on, which meant neither did his judgmental mother. Lucy was keen to play it down so when Phil made polite conversation about the kids Lucy nodded and agreed. She was just so utterly grateful that the monster mother-in-law, Cynthia, had not taken it upon herself to visit too. She would have given Lucy the third degree. Lucy was pulling the washing out of the machine and shaking out the creases before she hung it on the maiden.

'Hello?' Lucy pulled the last few bits shaking them furiously to speed up the job, as she did not want to appear rude to Phil. She hadn't realised that Evie's swimming bag had been in the wash and as she shook it the toggle hit her in the eye. 'Ow!' she squealed. She walked into the kitchen with one hand covering her eye. It was throbbing. 'Sorry Phil, just had a little accident here and need to take a look.'

'Let me.' Lucy's hand had been covering her eye to the doorway making her vision blinkered. So she had been unaware that her husband was standing there. It was like the sound of his voice had stolen her breath from her body, in quite an unexpected manner. Slowly, she turned around and watched as Ed moved towards her. It had been one whole month and 3 days since she had last laid eyes upon her husband. The unexpectedness of his arrival made her lose all control of her body. She seemed unable to move or speak. So, Ed moved her hand that was covering her eye. He pulled her top and bottom lid apart. 'It's very red,' he continued to look in her eye and the closeness of him and the fact that she could feel his breath on her face was making butterflies dance in her stomach. 'What did you do?'

'I was shaking the washing and Evie's swimming bag was in there and the toggle got me in the eye.' In a normal situation, by now he would have kissed her on the forehead and pulled her in for a hug. However, this was so far removed from *their* normal. He was stood so close to her. The distance between them was inches and yet it felt like miles.

'Sit down Lucy.' He guided her towards the chair. 'I don't think it's a scratch, but leave it for a while to see if it calms down.'

'Do you want a cup of tea?' Lucy said standing up.

'I'll make it.' Ed moved towards the kettle so she let him and sat back down, grateful to him as her eye was aching.

'Don't touch it.' Ed had turned around and saw that Lucy was trying to pull at her lower eyelid.

'Sorry.' She felt like a little naughty schoolgirl. As the kettle boiled they said nothing. Lucy wanted to talk furiously for fear that if she didn't start talking, he would leave and she would never have the chance to say everything she had wanted to. It's now or never, she thought.

'I am truly sorry Ed.'

'I know,' he said as he placed the mug in front of her.

'You don't.' For the first time since he arrived they locked eyes, not because he was examining her clumsy mishap, but a real look. For the first time in a long time she felt a fleeting connection between them. 'I am sorry for so much. For not talking to you about how I felt. I'm sorry that I did what I did.' His eyes dropped from hers, she continued anyway. 'I'm sorry that I made us fall apart. I'm sorry that the kids miss you every day. I'm sorry that I made you feel this way. I'm sorry that I made you hate me.' She paused, as silent tears slipped from her eyes.

'I don't hate you.' He took a swig of his coffee. 'I did for a while, but I don't hate you anymore.' Once again she felt like her breath had been taken away. 'Everything is just a big mess Lucy.'

'I know.' It was like he had read her mind from the early hours of the morning.

'Can you ever forgive me?' she almost whispered.

'I want to.'

She felt like her heart had lifted from her feet back into its rightful position, sitting proudly in her chest like she had won a prize. 'Really?'

'Yes,' he paused, 'but I need to know everything Lucy, from the day it started and why.'

She felt like the prize had been snatched away, as if it was some kind of mistake. If he knew all of the information, she doubted whether he would still want to try again. She knew she had to be honest, as he was possibly willing to give her another chance and she would do anything for that. She took a deep breath and hoped and prayed that the next few hours and her honesty would not see her put the final nail into the coffin of their marriage.

'Then you came here today.' Lucy had finally come full circle. It had been frightening to see the rollercoaster of emotions that had taken place over the last few hours. They had both cried and got angry until the silence had brought both emotions to a grinding halt. Her anger had never before bubbled over like his because deep down she knew that she was wrong and she had made the choice to stray. It did not matter that she had never slept with Sebastian, the desire had been there, but it had been the cancer that had stopped her having him. Ed had thrown many insults her way that afternoon and he had every right to. She felt she was using words to say nothing at all as Ed did not really want to hear them, but he insisted on putting himself through all the gory details. Then when he ranted and got angry, she sat in silence and his words and her silence explained it all. Her betrayal. His pain. Her disloyalty. His anger. Her choices. His denial. But the part that hurt the most was that he said that he could never trust her again. She believed that there was no way forward for them if he could not.

'Ed, you have to...' she trailed off as she felt a lump rise in her throat. She was getting that burning sensation and she knew that she was fighting back the tears. She inhaled deeply, 'you have to start trusting me again.' It was too late; these weren't silent tears. This was the big body-heaving cry she had thought about earlier, she felt like she was losing control. She couldn't look at Ed and they both sat and waited until she had calmed down. The silence between them sat like a gaping crevasse, one that had been there all afternoon. This gorge kept them apart; she was unsure of whether he would be able to take that leap of faith back across to the side where his family were stood waiting.

'You broke my heart Lucy.'

She knew that. She had broken her own heart too. 'I'm sorry Ed, but you have to at least try, or this will never work.'

He put his elbows on the kitchen table and covered his face with his hands. 'I will try. I have to. This is our family we have worked too hard to get here.' He rubbed away the tears that were on his cheeks.

'Don't stay just for the kids Ed, they may want that now, but as they grow older they'll resent it and so will we. You need to want this for *all* of the right reasons. If it's too hard, I would understand, but we've come this far and the children have been through a rollercoaster of emotions too. I can mend their hearts now; it will be harder as they get older.'

'I wouldn't just be staying for the kids, I'd be staying to try and fix us.' She felt a new hope arise in her chest. 'But it will take time Lucy. I'm not moving back in. I need to be in charge of how fast this goes.'

'Okay.' She had no right to argue. She looked at his face, he looked exhausted and she was responsible for this, she felt so guilty. His face was red and patchy with the emotions he had exuded all afternoon.

'I think we should have a few dates, make some time for us, with and without the kids.'

'Okay,' she repeated. She would go along with anything even if there was the slightest chance their mess of a marriage could be fixed.

'I won't make any promises Lucy. I can't.' She feigned a weak smile. 'It wouldn't be fair on the kids. So for now, we just say that I'm working away still.' She nodded in agreement. He leant forward and touched her arm. The warmth of his hand made her tingle from head to toe. She remembered his touch and how she had missed it.

'Thank you for trying.' She looked up at Ed and he was staring back at her.

'No promises.' He squeezed her hand and she nodded. 'But Lucy, this is the end, of what we had. Things have changed. But what feels like the end is sometimes a chance to have a new beginning and this is ours.' Lucy smiled at Ed, at his words of wisdom. Finally, she had hope. A flicker of light had appeared at the end of the tunnel. It had been a long time coming and she was not foolish enough to think that it would be easy. This path would be a rocky one, there would be ups and downs but she was ready and eternally grateful for this second chance. She yearned so deeply for this to drive her family forward. She knew that although there was a glimmer of hope, the journey would sometimes be a lonely and painful one, but anticipated that the good times would outweigh the struggle. She just hoped that when she reached the end of the tunnel that they would be a family of four again, holding hands and smiling into the light.

Chapter 32

Jessie

'There you are.'

Jake's huge frame almost filled the doorway. He was evidently on his way to work as he stood there, in his ripped at the knee jeans and old green T-shirt. Their eyes had not yet left each other's. She wondered what was running through his head as her heart felt like it was thumping out of her chest.

'What are you doing here?' Jessie finally extinguished their gaze and dug her hands into her pockets. She realised that she sounded irate and her protective body language was screaming negativity. Wishing she could control her emotions, she dug her hands deeper into her pockets. She wasn't angry. Her heart wanted to run towards him and feel his huge arms wrapping her in his embrace, but her head would not allow it. As she felt on the back foot, she realised that she had begun to put her shutters down. Self-preservation had kept her safe this far throughout their relationship. The moment she allowed him in, confiding her darkest secret, was the moment she feared his rejection.

'What am I doing here?' he repeated her question. 'Isn't it obvious? I'm looking for you.' Jake said as he took a step towards her. Almost mirroring his actions, she consciously took a step away from him.

'Why?' She ran her fingers through her hair; it got caught in a knot halfway down the back. Only now did remember that she hadn't brushed her hair and wished that she had.

'Because we need to talk,' he said taking another step towards her.

'We have talked.' She said turning away from him and walking in to the living room. Looking for something to do, she walked towards her dirty dishes picked them up and moved swiftly into the kitchen to wash them.

'No Jessie, *you* talked and as usual *you* ran away.'

'What was there to say? We both know what I did was unforgivable. You shouldn't have bothered. There's nothing left to say. You're better off without me.'

'Isn't that my decision Jess?'

'I've made the decision so much easier for you. Just walk away Jake. I ruin everything. Now is your chance to go.'

'Just for once Jess... shut up and listen. You are not making all the decisions for me.' His tone had changed and his usual patience seemed to have evaporated. 'Get in there and sit down and listen to what *I* have to say for a change.' He pointed to the living room. His unusual authoritative tone made her do as she was told. As he marched in behind her she felt anxious about what he was going to say. Without realising it, she had walked to the furthest point in the room, huddling herself in to the corner of the couch. Jessie curled her knees to her chest in a protective manner, preparing herself for whatever was coming her way.

'I can't lie Jess. When you told me what happened, I was shocked.' She pulled her knees further towards her. 'But not for the reason you're thinking.' She took her eyes from the floor and looked at him confused. 'Jess, what happened with you and Stuart was an accident. You didn't push him in front of that car. He was chasing you...'

'And I hit him with that vase.'

'… and you hit him with that vase, but him getting knocked down – that was his own fault for not looking where he was going.' She felt her heart melt a little. She couldn't believe that he wasn't blaming her. All her life she had felt guilty that it was her fault. She had gone to the police station every day for a month and sat on the steps of the derelict building opposite. Hoping for some courage to make her go in and confess to her 'crime'. However, a female police officer had eventually made her never return to that spot on the steps again. Apparently, she had noticed Jessie every day and had grown concerned for her well-being. She thought there might have been something she needed to talk about. Jessie had grown fearful of what might happen to her if she did confess, so instead in a cowardly manner she sat at the hospital steps, waiting for news to see if Stuart was okay. It was a Friday morning that he got released, she watched a lady push him in a wheelchair to a waiting taxi.

'Jess…?' She then realised she had drifted off thinking about her past. 'Jess, are you listening? This is important.'

'Sorry.'

'As I was saying, this was not your fault. But as you always do, when you do not know how to handle a situation, you run away from it. You never give yourself or anyone else around you a chance to find out what the hell is going on.' She forced out a weak smile as she realised how well Jake actually knew her. It was incredible. 'You ran out of that pub and into that taxi so quickly that I couldn't keep up with you.' She took her knees down from her chest and crossed her legs. 'I tried calling you and texting you so many times, but of course ignoring me, as I've learnt long before now, is your coping mechanism, you love to be in denial. I didn't want to tell you what I found out about my uncle over the phone, or straight away, as I had to confirm everything and I did.' Jessie began to squirm in the chair and was very unsure where this was going. 'What he did to you Jess... he was a bastard.' She squirmed even more. She hated talking about it. 'But it wasn't just you that he was doing it to. My mum's sister Liz was married to Stuart, well if we're honest, she still is.' Jessie sat up and then realised what she was going to hear. 'He had two families, yours and my auntie Liz's. He has lived a lie all of his life and nobody ever knew it. Not until I told my mum.' Jessie put her hands on her face, thinking that she had ruined yet someone else's life. Jake moved towards her and sat next to her on the couch and removed her hand from her face. 'No, you don't understand Jess, this is a good thing.'

'How?' Jessie looked Jake in the eye.

'Because now she has a real reason for leaving the bastard.' Jessie looked more confused.

'According to Mum, she was all set to leave him, up to the point where she had packed bags for herself and the kids that weekend when he got back from working away.' He tilted his head and gave Jessie a knowing look.

'From his other family,' she interjected. 'But Mum was gone then, he was just after anything he could get.'

'You're right Jess, he is a greedy, self-centred prick. That day that he got knocked down and was in hospital for weeks, she felt tied to him, responsible for him and that was it, she couldn't leave him.'

'Shit.' Jessie said, dumbfounded. She realised that it must have been Liz pushing his wheelchair out of that hospital that day, she looked so miserable.

'He was a total bully, like he was with you. He used to knock Liz around, he never touched his girls.' Jessie must have looked bewildered. 'He has two daughters, a similar age to you, not that he actually ever liked them either. He always wanted a boy, it was like the girls never lived up to his expectations and he took that out on Liz.'

'That explains why he was so mad when Mum lost the baby, because it was a little boy.' Jessie said and Jake nodded in agreement. 'So has Liz left him?'

'Sort of. She has gone to the police about him.'

'For domestic abuse?'

'For being a bigamist!'

'Jesus!' Jessie had not even thought about that.

'Apparently he could go to prison for up to seven years. Liz wasn't sure at first. She didn't want to be responsible for him going to prison. She wasn't sure if she could send the father of her children away for such a long time. But she asked the girls and they were totally okay about it, they were so angry with all of his lies. So they actually drove her to the police station!' He smiled at this fact.

'Wowser, this is unreal. Do you think that she'll mention the violence?'

'The girls made her.' She couldn't believe this, how much of a deceitful bastard he really was.

'I've saved the best until last too Jessie,' Jake said. She looked at him, unsure if any of this information could even be deemed good, let alone 'the best'.

'Right.'

'That fucker can walk!' Jessie was actually speechless. For what felt like a lifetime, nobody actually spoke. She just looked at Jake staring at her. Finally, the only thing she could do was throw her arms around Jake's neck, as she was just so happy. He put his arms around her waist and pulled her right in towards him. After a very long embrace she pulled away and spoke.

'I just can't believe it!' she wiped away the tears of joy that had been streaming down her face. 'When? Is it a recent thing?'

'Apparently not. He has been claiming disability allowance falsely for years and years. Liz didn't even know for a long time and the girls *never* knew. If Liz ever brought it up, he used to beat her black and blue. Plus she gave up her job to look after him years ago and she knew that they would have no money if she said anything.'

'Christ, why lie about that all these years? He must have been dying to get up and walk.'

'He is the scum of the earth Jess, he really is. A benefit fraud to boot!'

'You're not wrong there Derby!' All of a sudden, things felt too comfortable, too normal. She panicked. But there was no need.

'Come home Coley... please come home.' He grabbed hold of her cheeks and kissed her hard on the lips.

'Really? After everything?'

'Jess, you did nothing wrong. You need to start believing that.' He pulled her towards him and she sat on his knee. 'This secret that you have been keeping all these years has evidently eaten away at you, and for what?' he said and she shrugged her shoulders. 'Now that it is all out in the open, look what it has actually done, you have changed people's lives for the better. Liz is like a different person and the girls are going around and seeing their Mum all of the time now because Stuart's not there. Plus I swear that my mum is going to get you an OBE or something, she is so grateful that you have set her sister free.' She rested her head against his as she listened to the words rolling off his tongue. 'And you Jess, you must feel *different*.'

She couldn't begin to explain how she felt. It was like the weight of the world had been lifted from her shoulders. Sitting on Jake's knee, she felt like she was in a dream. 'Pinch me.' She said holding out her arm to him.

'What?' he looked as confused as he sounded.

'Just do it.' She smiled at him and he did as he was told. 'So it is real?'

'Oh it is Jess.' He pulled her head around so that their foreheads were touching. 'I thought I was going to have a fight on my hands with you and you were going to push me away and that would be it.'

'I know because I'm so stubborn and run away from everything!' she looked at him and winked. He pulled her in for a long passionate kiss, she felt like she was home and my God did it feel warm and inviting. She pulled away and spoke.

'So is that a yes?' She was confused at his question. 'To coming home?

'Oh yes I'm coming home,' she said, beaming at him.

'Let's move forward now Jess. He's ruined enough lives, he ruined your past, but I'll be damned if I'm going to let him ruin our future.'

'I love you Derby,' she said, finally after all these years feeling complete.

'I love you more Coley.'

'Not possible.'

'Always got to have the last word eh?'

'Damn right!'

Chapter 33

Alex

'Make the call Simon,' Alex exhaled deeply, 'Jesus, it's worth a try.' Spinning around in his chair he faced his detective constable. The two of them had been at a loss with this case for months now. They appeared to have tried every avenue, drained every possible resource but Alex was tenacious and refused to give up. Surveillance had been carried out on the elusive drug dealer for weeks and yet they still had nothing. This pusher was a smart arse, knew every corner to cut and, Alex believed, he had friends in high places, maybe even within the four walls of the station although he was yet to prove it. He was determined to nail the scumbag. It was a last resort, but the next port of call would be to put an undercover cop in situ. The only problem would be that it would take months for an undercover to gain the trust of the dealer and he wasn't sure time was on his side.

'Nothing Sarge. Nobody even picked up.'

'Shit.' Alex stood up and opened the door to head upstairs, but before he left he spoke again. 'Try again in 10 minutes and every 10 minutes after that. I'm going for some fresh air.' He walked towards the stairwell and started taking two steps at a time until he got to the eighth floor. Walking outside he breathed in and his lungs felt illuminated. The passive smoke from everyone's cigarettes was still a comfort when he was stressed.

'Alright Alex, you're making a habit of this lately.' He saw the young DC smiling at him.

'I know Sarah, I know.' He stood as close as he could to her, without looking like a stalker, but still close enough to really inhale the last few drags of her cigarette smoke. He so wanted the cigarette between his lips.

'Right, best go. Bad guys to catch.' She handed him the last drag of her cigarette. He shook his head even though he wanted to take it. The desire to feel that initial burn in his throat and lungs that you only got when you hadn't smoked for a very long time was killing him. She threw it on the floor and he watched as the ash continued to glow. He moved towards it and actually contemplated picking it up, before stubbing it out. He realised in his own head how desperate he seemed. What would Izzy have made of it all? It had been a very long time since he had thought about his ex. But he was grateful that she had managed to get him off the smokes. The things that Izzy had actually added to his life had been few and far between, however getting him to quit smoking had been life changing as he had been totally hooked. Smoking had become his crutch after the incident, his only way of coping. That incident, that horrific night had changed both their lives and it was the night he had decided to become a policeman. Walking home from university following their final exams they were both young and care-free and talking about their future together: how many kids they'd have, what they'd be called, when they'd get married. Izzy was a different person back then. They had walked through the park; she hadn't wanted to, but of course, he had insisted on the short cut. Halfway through they were mugged by a gang of young lads, younger than them but twice as many. When they'd been told to hand over their money, Alex had refused point blank and stood in front of Izzy to protect her. However, he was young and naive, thought they would listen to reason but when you want your next fix, apparently nothing was going to stop you. He had assumed they were kids who were too frightened to take it further, but when they pulled the knives, everything changed. They had the upper hand and the weaker one in the group, who seemed to be on some kind of initiation test, swiped at Alex and scarred Alex's face and shoulder for life. While he lay on the floor two of the gang rooted through Alex's things. Then he heard Izzy screaming. It was only when the leader of the pack shouted 'no' and that they weren't there for 'that' did Izzy stop squealing. But before they ran off she yelped in pain, a bone chilling scream, they may not have touched her like one of them had wanted to, but stabbing her in the abdomen had changed her life forever. He heard her screams in his nightmares, it used to wake him for many years and Izzy would comfort him.

However, that night was the beginning of the end for their relationship, that night changed them both. Their youthful, innocent glow was snatched from them both that night. Alex became that 'fella with the scar and the lovely teeth' and Izzy became barren. The blade that had struck her had caused irreversible damage and meant that she could never have children. She hated him for it. For years she blamed him for making them walk through the park and for years he took it. He let her verbally abuse him; he let her because the guilt ate away at him for making that decision. Then as they both grew older, their bitterness towards each other only grew, but neither seemed to be able to walk away, they seemed to be inextricably linked by an invisible cord of pain. Somehow, after years of unhappiness they had managed to sever the cord and finally move on with their lives. The smoking had begun then and had got him through those first few years of harrowing pain and memories. Now when his life got too stressful, like when he couldn't crack a case, he craved his old habit more than ever.

His mind flashed to his best mate and the agony of wanting that cigarette made him empathise with Ben, at least Alex had broken his addiction. Ben had struggled for years to break his. He recollected the first time that he and Ben had shared their first drunken night together. They were 16. Quite some feat to get to that age and not have been wasted, but then that was down to Ben and his alcoholic father. At 16, the party invites had come flying at them thick and fast, but this one in particular they just couldn't not attend. The hottest chick in school was hosting it. She was 2 years older than them, and they were the only fifth years to be invited. However, as soon as they had arrived they realised that it was a decision between taking drugs or drinking. Neither of them had ever really spoken about drugs up until that point, so instead that night they both got obliterated. They had drunk before but not to this extent. He knew that Ben's addiction had begun that night, and he felt partly responsible. But at last after many chances, he seemed to have finally found the right path. Ben loved his life down under and it appeared to be agreeing with him. Alex didn't have any siblings, so Ben had become part of his family. That surrogate brother he had always wanted. Alex's wonderful parents had taken Ben under their wing. The boy of damaged parents, they had tried to help and were so kind to him and Jane, he knew that Ben would always be grateful. It had broken his heart when he had to order Ben back to rehab, but Alex had been his one constant to keep him sober. He felt that he had let Ben down somehow, not seeing the inevitable train crash. He'd derailed in the most horrific way and there was nothing that he could to fix the situation, except hold Mia together. Without him living away and Mia's forgiveness he knew that he would have had to take him to the station. It had all gone against his moral code, but he let Mia make that choice and because she had given him a second chance then he felt there was hope. His phone beeped in his pocket and there was a picture of his best mate with his nephew both splashing about in the sea. He smiled to himself at how far Ben had come. Proud of his sobriety, it still didn't stop him from missing him every day.

It had been a long day and he felt exhausted, he knew that if he went for a run around the park he would feel so much better. He sat and listened as the news barked out the latest doom and gloom. He turned his engine off when the traffic woman had begun to rabbit on; he had no need for it that evening as his car sat stationary and would remain that way for the rest of the night. Sitting in the darkness he took in the stillness of the evening, he let the madness of the day slip away. He closed his eyes just for a minute, acknowledging the peace. Right, he thought, it's time to get out of this car.

Just as he was about to open the door, he saw Mia and Dusty run past. Her tiny frame holding onto her beloved dog's lead. He was so relieved that Dusty had made a full recovery, not just because he knew how much Mia loved that dog, but because he too had grown pretty fond of her. He watched as she fumbled to get her keys from her jacket pocket. Quickly, he got out of the car fearful that he'd miss her.

'Mia!' he shouted from his car as he began to walk over to them.

'Hello,' she replied. Dusty had begun to bounce around at the sight of him. Mia let her go, as it was safe for her to run towards him in the resident's car park. He bent down and he allowed her to nuzzle into his face.

'Good run?' He had grabbed Dusty's lead and was now walking over to Mia, who nodded.

'All set for the half-marathon?' he said, smiling at her.

'I think so. I've got it down to just over 2 hours.'

'That's great! Will you give the full marathon a go after this?'

'I might just!' she said, sounding excited.

'You going to head out for a run?' She took Dusty's lead and their hands brushed and their eyes flickered at each other.

'I know I should, but I'm still undecided.'

'Just go! You'll feel better if you do, you know you will!' She smiled at him and started to lead Dusty to her front door. 'See you later Alex.'

As Alex ran around the park, he was still thinking about work but now Mia was flashing into his thoughts edging work out into the cold. The last time he had been around was the night that they had kissed and fallen asleep on each other. Nothing had happened since then, although he was fully aware that due to his night shifts he had been off radar. Those late night shifts had given him food for thought. He felt that now was the right time, Mia seemed to be in a good place, she had just released her next book and it was flying off the shelves. He couldn't have been prouder. She was a little dynamite. He had been dodging pedestrians who seemed to be strolling so slowly around the park or maybe he was sprinting as he was now on his second lap. He thought he had spotted his friends earlier.

'Hey Jess, Jake,' Alex said as he came to an abrupt halt at the loved up duo sitting on the wall. Jessie bounced up from where she was sat.

'Alex! I'd give you a kiss, but you're all sweaty!' so she patted him on the arm.

'Hi mate.' Jake also stood and shook Alex's hand.

'How are you two? I haven't seen you for ages.' Alex couldn't help but stare at Jessie, she seemed different. He couldn't explain it; there was a glow on her face and a certain light to her eyes.

'We're good,' she beamed up at Jake and he reflected her smile. 'And how are you Alex?'

'I'm sorry, I've got to go!' He realised how rude he seemed, but he needed to do something. Something that just couldn't wait any longer. It was like he had slipped into a different gear, he felt the wind on his face and realised that he couldn't get there quickly enough.

Banging on Mia's door, he felt like he had been there for ages. He could hear her unlocking all of her bolts.

'Are you okay Alex?' she was looking at him rather anxiously. He realised that he must have looked frantic having sprinted from the park and he could feel the sweat trickling down the side of his head.

'Yes.' He was trying to catch his breath.

'Sit down; I'll get you some water.'

'No Mia, please.' He gently pulled her back towards him. 'I need to say this now.'

'Say what?'

'You are the kindest person I have ever met Richard Aims.' Her confusion was broken by a big grin spreading across her face. 'I mean Mia Richards.' He moved his hands down her arms until they were both holding hands. 'You are beautiful,' he watched as her eyes darted to the floor. 'Modest, generous, intelligent... you are the most wonderful woman I've ever met.'

'And you're over-egging the adjectives! What's gotten into you? I thought...'

'Let me finish Mia,' he cut her off. 'I have to get this out. From the moment I saw you in the restaurant, I couldn't stop thinking about you. Then when you walked into Ben's party, it was like fate was bringing us together.' Mia had started to giggle. 'I know I sound like a new age hippie but—' before he could finish she grabbed his face and began kissing him, he was startled

403

but delighted. He lifted her tiny frame onto the breakfast bar and they kissed like teenagers for what felt like forever.

'God Mia, I thought we'd never get here.'

'Me neither,' she said, as she held onto his face.

'I love you, Mia.'

'I love you too, Alex.'

'Where are we going?' he said.

'To get you clean!' she said as she led him towards the bathroom. Loyal as ever, Dusty followed Mia and Alex. .

'Thanks Dust, but I think I've got this one covered.' Mia said as she knelt down and kissed her dog on the top of her head. 'What are you waiting for?' Mia said, standing up and turning to face Alex.

'Eh?'

'Get in there and get your kit off. Like we said, it's been a long time coming and I can't bloody wait a minute longer!

Acknowledgements

Thank you to everyone who has supported me on this journey. To my gorgeous girls – my biggest cheerleaders - who always asked about my writing and kindly, read my book way back in the beginning when it was in its rawest form. To my hilarious Nan who asked about every character that I created and wanted to know exactly what was going to happen to them, sometimes before I even knew myself! To my family who were always there when I needed them. A special thanks to my parents for their unconditional love, encouragement and belief in me. To my wonderful friend, Liv Walsh, who has helped me every single step along the way – you'll never know how truly grateful I am. Finally a huge thank you to anyone who bought my book.

About the Author

Hi everyone. I absolutely adore writing and so decided to undertake the venture of writing my first novel – which you have just finished! Thank you so much for reading 'Would You Share Your Secret?' and I really hope you enjoyed it. I would really appreciate your time to write a review – it doesn't have to be long.

If you would like to find out more about me and my second novel then click on the website link below:

www.johook.com

Made in the USA
Charleston, SC
22 July 2016